SPIN

SPIN

A NOVEL

BASED ON A (MOSTLY) TRUE STORY

PETER ZHEUTLIN

PEGASUS BOOKS
NEW YORK LONDON

SPIN

Pegasus Books, Ltd.
148 West 37th Street, 13th Floor
New York, NY 10018

First Pegasus Books edition June 2021

Interior design by Maria Fernandez

Library of Congress Cataloging-in-Publication Data is available.

ISBN: 978-1-64313-752-0

10 9 8 7 6 5 4 3 2 1

Printed in the United States of America
Distributed by Simon & Schuster
www.pegasusbooks.com

For Judy, Danny, and Noah and the dogs, past and present,
that have graced our lives: Albie, Salina, Jamba, and Tot . . .

. . . and for Mary Levy Goldiner, Annie's granddaughter,
who, when we first met by telephone more than fifteen years ago,
introduced herself by saying, "Peter, this is your long lost cousin, Mary."

Written for Mary,
October 6–November 6, 1947,
New York, New York

Do not open before August 31, 1961 (your 30th birthday).

—scrawled on a large manila envelope
found shortly after the writer's death
from a stroke on November 11, 1947

One

Dearest Mary,

I'm an old woman now. Exactly how old depends on which of the many stories I've told over the years you choose to believe, for I have not always been the most reliable witness to the events of my own life.

I was born in Boston on Christmas Day of 1876. Or perhaps Boston in 1873. Or maybe it was Pennsylvania that same year. Or Poland in 1871. Or Russia in 1869. The official records of my life—the various birth certificates of my children (your mother, aunts, and uncle), my marriage registration, census records, and the like—could be used to prove any of these. But I will tell you this: my parents, your great-grandparents, came to this country from a village near Riga, Latvia, then part of the Russian Empire, in 1875, and I came with them. I was five years old.

When I was a young woman, I did some wild things and they had disturbing consequences for our family, but we'll come to that. I had four siblings, including a twin brother Jacob, but he was born five years after me. Jake, as we called him, died on Boston Common on May 12, 1894, after an argument with our father Levi. He flew out of the house, got drunk, fell asleep, and froze to death . . . in mid-May. But my father died in 1887, seven years earlier, as did my mother, just two months after my father. Be patient. I will explain.

When you were a little girl I told you bedtime stories about a bicycle trip I made as a young woman, and, as children do, you had a million questions and always wanted to know more. Rooted in a real experience, those stories became more and more outlandish as we added new adventures and new characters over the years. We traveled together in our imaginations to far-off, mysterious lands and met all kinds of colorful and sometimes dangerous characters. We created a world known to just the two of us, and what fun we had in that private world! As you became a teenager, story time became more of a conversation between two women, one grown old and another on the cusp of adulthood. With less imagination and more memory, you learned over the years the outline of the journey I had made as a young woman, but I left much unsaid that I want to say to you now. But some of what I am about to tell you would be hard for a young girl of sixteen to understand, which is why I hope your mother, to whom I plan to deliver this for safekeeping, has honored my request that it not be given to you until your thirtieth birthday or, if she doesn't live to that day, that you have honored my request that it not be opened until then.

When my parents died in early 1887, it fell to my older brother, your great-uncle Bennett, then twenty-one, and me, barely seventeen, to care for our younger brother Jake, age ten, and our baby sister Rosa, who was just eight years of age. The eldest sibling, my sister Sarah, had married and moved to Maine. Jacob was not my twin, and he obviously didn't freeze to death in the month of May after fighting with our father, but it was a story I told often, even to you, to test the credulity of people. I'm sorry you never met your great-uncle Jacob; he had an innate gentleness about him.

The next year, 1888, almost a year to the day after my mother passed away, I married your grandfather, Simon "Max" Kopchovsky, a simple peddler, who, at twenty-six years of age, was several years my senior. I was still a young woman, just in my late teens, but it was not uncommon for girls to marry at that age back then. My parents arranged the marriage, my father having met Grandpa at shul.

Our first child, Bertha Malkie, was born in December of that year. We called her Mollie, but we never told you about her, and unless your mother has shared the secret, her existence will be news to you when you read this. She died when she was just twenty-three. Well, she was dead to me anyway.

Your aunt Libbie, our second child, was born in March 1891. And your uncle Simon, named for his father, unusual in a Jewish family, was born in May 1892. Barely out of my teens, I had three children of my own to take care of, and my younger brother and younger sister, too. Your mother Frieda, born in 1897, was our youngest.

In the early 1890s, we were living in a tiny third-floor apartment in one of the tenements that lined Spring Street in Boston's West End. The West End in those days was a community of many tongues: Hebrew, German, Polish, Italian, Yiddish, Portuguese, and several others. It was a veritable Tower of Babel. There were even many Negro families in the neighborhood, and Irish, too.

Running errands, if the weather was warm and the tenement windows thrown open to catch the sea breeze, I could smell the pasta sauces, the boiled cabbage and the corned beef, the chicken broth and the pierogis. In every apartment were people who had come to

America from all corners of the world, and who crowded into its cities and slums with their undiminished optimism about life in America.

About a third of Boston's Jews lived in the neighborhood; most, like Grandpa, were devout and Orthodox. Grandpa spent most of his life in shul, while I tended to the children as most Jewish mothers did. We Jews prized family and education above all, and it was expected that I, as a Jewish mother, would attend to nothing else.

But it wasn't enough for me. I wasn't put on the earth to spend my life cooking and cleaning and changing diapers. It seemed like every year I had another baby under my apron. Life was full of drudgery.

The sounds and smells of the neighborhood tempted me. There was a big, wide world beyond the banks of the Charles River, and I wanted to see it and smell it and taste it.

One day, about a week after Valentine's Day 1894, I'd been shopping for Shabbat dinner—a brisket of beef, some potatoes, and, a miracle for February, even a sad-looking cabbage. The streets were icy, and the wind stiff off the ocean. A perfectly miserable day in what was always a perfectly miserable month in Boston. Just as I approached the front door of our building I slipped on the icy cobblestones, and the groceries went skidding halfway across the street. I wasn't hurt—well, maybe my pride a little—and I gathered the groceries, whisked myself inside, and sat on the first-floor landing to collect myself. I was exhausted, physically and emotionally.

Unlike almost every other woman I knew, I had a job, part-time, outside the house. It was scandalous in a small way, and though no one had the nerve to say it to my face, all our Jewish neighbors thought my working was a dereliction of duty and inappropriate. You'd have thought I was running a charnel house out of our apartment. But three days a week, for eight hours a day, I went door-to-door to businesses in downtown Boston selling advertising space in several of the Boston newspapers. My brother Bennett was a newspaperman, and though he was dubious about it, I pressured him into helping me get the job. Truth be told, we needed the money. Grandpa had a little cart from which he peddled sundries, but really his full-time job was prayer. If nothing changed, the life that lay ahead would be spent in housework and borderline poverty. And things were hard in 1894. President Cleveland was presiding over what came to be called the Panic of 1893, an economic depression that would last until 1897. Grandpa wasn't much of a breadwinner, and I wanted to work. I liked to work. But it was also a necessity. Still, I believed I was destined for bigger and better things.

By the way, early in his first term as president, in the late 1880s, Cleveland's sister, Rose Elizabeth, served as unofficial First Lady of the United States, for the president was then a bachelor. There were whispers even then that Miss Cleveland, who went by "Libby," preferred the intimate company of women. The chatter intensified when she was seen regularly with a Massachusetts woman, Evangeline Simpson. (When Evangeline died in 1930, she requested to be buried in Italy next to Libby.) It all had a whiff of scandal about it, but ever since I was a young girl of about fifteen, I admired Libby. I would read about her performing her duties as First Lady in the newspapers. Over the years, when rumors about her sexuality would surface, I took a quiet satisfaction in it. Why shouldn't a woman be free to love another woman? In my experience, men are no bargain. It's not a coincidence that I named my second daughter, born in 1891, Libbie, though we spelled it a little differently.

As I sat on the first-floor landing on that frigid February day, the question rattling around inside me, though it was not yet fully formed and I could not have stated it with the clarity I am able to now, was whether my life's story as a woman already had been largely written for me. Was it already written, too, for the two young girls to whom I was now struggling to be a mother? Could a woman step from the line? Could she control her own life and body? Could she dance while others sat up straight and proper? This is why women like Nellie Bly, Susan B. Anthony, and Annie Oakley were so fascinating to me and millions of women of the time. They got us thinking about what was possible. I was particularly taken with Nellie Bly, and as I sat there in the cold hallway of the apartment building, my mind landed, as it so often did, on a story I had followed as a young woman with bated breath as it unfolded regularly in the pages of the *New York World* newspaper.

The *World* was the most sensational and widely read newspaper of the day, copies of which would usually arrive in Boston a day late. The *World* reported the serious news, but there were also stories of the bizarre rituals of African tribes, two-headed children, miracle cures, and other curiosities. Those sections of the paper were like the freak show at the circus. And were they ever *delicious*!

The *World* was the crown jewel in the newspaper empire of the great Joseph Pulitzer, and they were the first to have a celebrity woman writer, a woman of considerable gumption and daring who would go to great lengths for a story. Once, she even had herself committed to a mental hospital so she could write about it from the inside. That was Nellie Bly—at least that's what she called herself. She was born was Elizabeth Cochran.

When I was in my late teens, in 1889, Bly undertook the most amazing stunt of her career, and it made her very, very famous. She set out to travel all the way around the world and get back to where she started, Jersey City, in fewer than eighty days. Some years before, the author Jules Verne had published a series of articles that would become his famous book *Around the World in Eighty Days*, in which a man named Phileas Fogg sets out, on a bet, to prove that a traveler could, by ordinary conveyance, circumnavigate the globe in eighty days.

Well, Nellie Bly's brainstorm was that she could make a faster circuit of the earth than the venerable Mr. Fogg and that the attempt could be a lucrative publicity stunt for Mr. Pulitzer, who would fund the mission and publish her accounts in serial form in his newspaper. And so it was that I, like nearly every other American who could read, followed her adventures with barely contained excitement, wishing desperately that I, then of tender years, could be like her. After all, since arriving in Boston as a little girl, I had rarely been beyond the city limits.

Bly's around-the-world trip made her an international star. When she had finished her record journey, not only did she publish a book about it, but McLoughlin Brothers turned her adventure into a popular board game, Round the World with Nellie Bly, a game that became one of my most prized possessions.

With my groceries still in my lap, I was abruptly jolted back to the present when the letter carrier came in the front door to leave the day's mail. The children were upstairs, in the apartment below ours, being watched by my sister-in-law Baila, Bennett's wife, who had two small children of her own. She often watched your little aunts and uncle when I was at work or at the markets, and Jake and Rosa were at school or attending to their studies. Thank God.

Anyway, I collected myself and trudged up another flight of stairs to gather the children, and then another to begin getting dinner ready. I was most unhappy with my life, and a wave of melancholy washed over me. Such moods were becoming increasingly common and unnervingly severe, and there were times when I feared they might overwhelm me completely, that I might drown under their weight. There were even times when I felt such drowning would be a welcome relief. My friend Susie, to whom I will introduce you shortly, was my only escape and all that stood between me and a fall into the darkness.

Unbeknownst to me, at around the same time I was enduring yet another day of domestic "bliss," a group of men, distinguished gentlemen of wealth and industry, were gathered around a large fireplace inside the Algonquin Club on Commonwealth Avenue in the city's Back Bay neighborhood. No Jews allowed, of course. All the city's movers and shakers belonged to the exclusive, cigar-smoke-filled club, which occupied a large brownstone building appointed with thick leather chairs, dark mahogany walls, and butlers who would glide silently about the place catering to the whims of the members.

Colonel Albert Pope was one of the club's best-known members. Pope had been a manufacturer of sewing and other small machines but in more recent years had turned his sights to a vastly more lucrative market: bicycles.

The bicycle craze had started in Europe, mainly in France and England, and spread to the States. But it caught on in a big way with the invention in the 1880s of the "safety" bicycle. Unlike its predecessor, known as the "penny-farthing" in Britain and the "ordinary" in the States, the safety had wheels of identical size and a chain drive that made the bicycle much safer and easier to ride than those machines with the huge front wheel and the tiny back wheel, a contraption so awkward it was difficult just to mount, let alone ride without killing yourself. There were few women athletes in those days, and a handful of them raced those ungainly machines, but as a recreational tool, the bicycle, for many reasons, was off-limits to women. It was considered unladylike for a woman to be seen in public exerting herself on a bicycle or, God forbid, exposing her ankles in the process. The moralists, often backed up by the testimony of medical men, argued that riding a bicycle, which brought a woman's private parts—oh, let's call them what they are, you're a grown woman now—genitals in contact with the saddle, would be sexually stimulating to women, and lead to all kinds of moral decay. It may be hard to believe today, in 1947, but some clever fellow even invented what they called a "hygienic" saddle with a space cut out so a woman's genitals would hover above open space rather than touch the saddle. You'd have thought that women on bicycles was the end of femininity and a harbinger of the decline of Western civilization itself! Such folly.

For the most part, women didn't listen, and they were purchasing bicycles in droves. And before you knew it, the bicycle had become a symbol of women's emancipation. In 1895, Frances Willard, who founded the largest women's organization in history, the Woman's Christian Temperance Union, learned, at the advanced age of fifty-three, to ride a bicycle, and she wrote a little book about it in which she explained why, amid the boom in bicycling among men and women, she took up riding: "I wanted to help women to a wider world from pure natural love of adventure—a love long hampered and impeded, and from a love of acquiring this new implement of power and literally putting it underfoot." I like to think I inspired Willard to make that statement, but, again, I'm getting ahead of myself.

I loved that little book, and it's been in the top drawer of my dresser for years. I must have read it a hundred times, and I told your mother that when I die I want you to have it. That little book meant so much to me. When you finish reading this I think you will know why.

At that gathering inside the Algonquin Club, the conversation turned to one of the great debates of the day: the status of women. For years, women had been organizing around the right to vote and were trying to assert themselves in new ways in society. Long under the domination of men, women were yearning for greater autonomy and to be treated as equals. The press even coined a new term for these women: a woman who pushed the boundaries was deemed "a New Woman" or, collectively, "*the* New Woman."

In his zeal for profits, Colonel Pope was extensively marketing his "wheels," as they were often called back then, to women. Though he may not have realized it, he was helping to undermine the very social order so prized by his fellow clubmen. While many of these men saw the push for women's equality as an amusement, and a trifling one at that, underneath their smugness and contempt lurked a real fear that the world as they knew it might well be thrown off-kilter if this women's movement got out of hand.

As I later learned, someone in the gaggle of men chatting with Colonel Pope remarked on the journey of one Thomas Stevens, who left San Francisco on a high-wheel in 1884 and arrived back almost three years later to claim the distinction of being the first person to go around the globe on a bicycle.

"Surely no woman could match such a feat!" someone declared, and the issue was joined. As the debate raged, Colonel Pope immediately saw the possibilities. The entire argument over the rights of women, over women's equality—and it was a debate that was sweeping the nation—could be used to sell countless bicycles to women eager to claim their independence.

Pope was a quick thinker. He listened quietly as the men, engulfed in a cigar-smoke fog, appeared to come to a consensus that no woman could do what Stevens had done. Pope cleared his throat, and all eyes turned to him, for he was the biggest fish in this stuffy little pond.

"Is there one among you brave and opinionated souls willing to put your money where your mouth is?" he asked. Nervous glances were exchanged. "I will wager twenty thousand dollars to ten that it can be done, and I will find the woman to do it!" declared Pope.

Now, you may be wondering how I know all this since I obviously wasn't there. It was recounted to me weeks later by someone close to Colonel Pope, a man who worked in his bicycle store on Washington Street.

After a moment's silence, John Dowe, his fortune made in the sugar trade, raised a hand. "I'll take that wager, Colonel." And with that, one of the butlers was dispatched to bring pen and paper. For the next hour the terms of the wager were argued over and agreed to. Pope could select any woman he wanted for the task, and she would be obliged to meet several conditions in order for the colonel to claim victory. First, she would begin her journey penniless, earn her way around the world, and send home no less than five thousand dollars above her expenses, an enormous sum in those days and a considerable one even today. She was not to accept anything of value without performing some task in exchange. Not just a mere test of a woman's physical strength and endurance, this would be a test of a woman's resourcefulness and her ability to fend for herself in the world. Second, the trip had to be completed within fifteen months. This was a clever suggestion by Pope. It added yet another dramatic twist to what would already be quite a bit of theater: a race against time, as it were, just as Phileas Fogg's and Nellie Bly's adventures were paced against the clock. Third, to prove she had been around the world, the woman would collect the signatures of American consuls in various cities identified in advance. Finally, she would be required to ride at least ten thousand miles and would receive prize money, a breathtaking ten thousand dollars, put up by Colonel Pope, if she succeeded. One newspaper called it "one of the most novel wagers ever made." Indeed, the wager would be irresistibly alluring to the papers, always on the lookout for stories that could grab a reader's attention and hold it.

Dr. Albert Reeder, a local physician and an Algonquin member trusted by both Dowe and Pope, agreed to hold the money wagered in escrow until the outcome was determined. All that was left to do was to find the woman bold enough, maybe even just crazy enough to accept the challenge.

Let's be honest. I wasn't a good mother, and I have tried, as a kind of restitution, I suppose, to be a good grandmother to you, my only grandchild. I mean, what kind of mother leaves three young children and a husband behind to go gallivanting around the world on a bicycle? I was supposed to love my babies, but I felt, to be frank, detached from them. All the women around me spoke of the "maternal instinct," but I didn't have a nurturing bone in my body. I didn't neglect them—well, not until I got on that bicycle—and they were always well fed and had clean clothes to wear. I have my regrets now, but that's water over the dam. I've never been given much to introspection or looking back, and I still think psychiatry is a bunch of hooey. But it's a fair question you might have: Why was I so distant from my own children? How could I leave them behind for a lark around the world on a wheel? Why didn't I have the maternal instinct almost all the women around me did?

Who can really say? Why do some people prefer vanilla and others chocolate? Why do some prefer egg whites and others egg yolks? Why are some shy and introverted, and others outgoing and extroverted? It's just the way we are, gifted at birth with traits we might be able to suppress but never entirely erase, and some do a better job of conforming than others, though not, I should say, necessarily to their benefit. I can't tell you *why* I am the way I am any more than I can tell you which came first, the chicken or the egg.

But, you might ask, why are some people capable of coloring outside the lines and others not? I was hardly the only child living in America who had been abruptly uprooted at a tender age and brought to a strange country where we didn't even understand the language. I wasn't the only teenage girl in the West End whose marriage to an older man she didn't know had been arranged by her parents. And I certainly wasn't the only young mother overwhelmed by the responsibilities of being a wife, mother, and homemaker. But I was the only one who broke free to pedal around the world. A restless, spirited, contrarian nature plus opportunity equals rebellion.

So how was I, a Jewish mother with three small children (your mother was not yet born), who had never even ridden a bicycle before, chosen to settle Colonel Pope's wager? Can you imagine a less likely candidate for such a thing? I was only about five feet three inches tall then (I've lost an inch or two in my old age) and weighed about a hundred and ten pounds. The only muscles I had I earned from lugging groceries and babies around.

It was mid-March, a few weeks after that day I slipped outside the apartment and scattered the groceries, the day I was, for the umpteenth time, wondering if this was all there was to be in my life. For about a year, I had been calling each week at Colonel Pope's bicycle store on Washington Street, the largest of his many shops that sold Columbia bicycles, Pope's brand, to take their adverts for the various newspapers I served as an ad agent. I made my money by commission, and they were a reliable customer, advertising almost daily, such was the interest in bicycles in those days. There, I would sit in the small, cluttered office of the store manager, a kindly man named Alonzo

Peck, and discuss their advertising needs for the coming week. Peck was a likable, well-meaning fellow, with a well-groomed handlebar moustache and a head nearly devoid of hair (which had the effect of making his ears seem especially large), and was always well dressed, a loyal foot soldier to the domineering Colonel Pope.

On that day in mid-March when I called on him, I chanced to see a familiar figure looking over the new 1894 models that had recently arrived in the showroom, a young, light-skinned Negro woman about my age, perhaps a little younger. I'd never met her and did not know her name, but I must have seen her dozens of times, always fleetingly, sometimes in our West End neighborhood, sometimes downtown, sometimes in the Public Garden or the Common, and always speeding by on a wheel. She was ubiquitous on her bike, a familiar sight in the city, but no one really seemed to know who she was.

That day, as I sat down with Alonzo Peck, he seemed unusually excited and eager to share some news.

"Mrs. Kopchovsky! As always I have been looking forward to your visit, and today I have good news to share!"

"And what is that?" I asked.

He fairly burst with pride as he told me he'd been made a captain.

"A captain in what?" I asked. "Have you joined the navy?" He was too old to be joining the navy, but I asked anyway. He laughed heartily.

"Oh, Mrs. Kopchovsky," he chortled. "That's a good one! Of course not. A captain in the League of American Wheelmen."

The L.A.W., as it was called, was an organization well known to Bostonians and beyond. It was organized by Colonel Pope to advocate for the betterment of roads for cyclists, who often had to contend with roadways covered in deep sand, or so badly rutted as to be virtually impassable, especially in wet weather when they turned to mud. Few roads were paved in those days, and those that were mostly were made of cobblestone, hardly conducive to riding a wheel. The whole effort became known as the Good Roads Movement. As usual, though, Colonel Pope was thinking ahead. The first gasoline-powered automobiles had started to appear in Europe, and he foresaw the day when he would, with both feet and a lot of capital, jump from bicycles into the automobile trade. The Good Roads Movement was designed to serve the needs of cyclists, but it was also a stalking horse for the coming age of the automobile. The L.A.W. was rigidly structured, and Alonzo was proud of having been made a captain in the organization's hierarchy.

"You know, Mrs. Kopchovksy," he said, "I don't meet many women with a sense of humor, or at least not willing to use it so easily in the company of men. You've a lot of pluck."

"Aye, aye, Captain," I replied, giving him a mock salute, which set off another round of hearty laughter on his part.

When he regained his composure, he looked at me as if a light had gone on in his head.

"You might be just the person," he said, almost to himself, his fingers stroking his impressive moustache.

"Excuse me? Person for what?" I replied.

Alonzo continued stroking his moustache, an affectation common among hirsute men.

"A week ago, the colonel summoned me to his office, and told me he wanted me to be on the lookout among our customers for a young woman with spark and determination, someone who might be fearless enough to take an extraordinary journey," Alonzo answered. He leaned forward and spoke in a near whisper.

"Please keep this between us for now," he continued, and he then proceeded to tell me the story I've told you about the wager Colonel Pope had entered into with John Dowe.

"Alonzo," I said. It would have been unseemly in public but in private I often called him by his first name. We had become well acquainted in our weekly meetings, chatting about family, business, the weather, and life; the usual things. "You know I have a husband and three small children to care for. It would be impossible." In fact, it seemed utterly preposterous. Until he said this:

"You could become the next Nellie Bly!"

I shook my head and smiled. I was flattered. I was intrigued. That *would* be a dream come true. But I knew in my heart it was completely out of the question. Besides, I'd never ridden a bicycle in my life!

"Well, I would love that," I said. Nellie Bly was everything I wanted to be: independent, wealthy, a globe-trotting celebrity, a woman unbound by convention and tradition, a woman who called her own shots. "But the children . . . "

"I know," Alonzo said sympathetically. "It's just a thought. You're clever and cheeky enough, though. The woman the colonel chooses has to be possessed of more than strong muscles. She will have to be resourceful, daring, and, of course, good at making a spectacle of herself. This is, after all, going to be one of the greatest publicity stunts of all time, and you're already in the advert business. It'll put Barnum and Bailey to shame."

"I'm sure you'll find the right woman," I parried. "There doesn't seem to be a woman in Boston these days who isn't riding a wheel. There'll be one plucky enough for this. As a matter of fact, maybe there's one here in the store right now."

"What do you mean, Mrs. Kopchovksy?" he asked as I gathered my things and we walked out into the showroom.

"Over there. The Negro woman admiring that new wheel." I moved my chin in the direction of the woman across the showroom who was running her hand along the frame of a beautiful new Columbia. "Do you know her? I see her all over the city in all seasons going here and going there on her wheel. She seems to be everywhere, but nowhere for very long, as she is constantly on the move."

"Ah, yes, of course," said Alonzo. "Kittie Knox. She's making quite a name for herself in the cycling world, and running into some strong headwinds, too. Some don't welcome her presence in the L.A.W. or at the racetracks, seeing as how she is a mulatto woman."

"Interesting," I said. Such prejudice was not at all surprising. "But she would seem to be the answer to your search, would she not? Young, athletic, and experienced on the wheel? Have you proposed the colonel's scheme to her?"

"It's quite out of the question, Mrs. Kopchovksy," he said, "for obvious reasons."

"Well, it's not obvious to me, Alonzo," I said, though it was perfectly obvious what he was suggesting. I just didn't like it, and I wanted Alonzo to acknowledge it explicitly, for I simply believed that if women should be the equals of men, that applied to people of the Negro race, as well. Alonzo shifted uncomfortably. He was an open-minded man; the colonel not so much.

"I did raise her name with the colonel," Alonzo replied sheepishly. "You are quite right. She would be an ideal candidate. Experienced on the wheel, young, adventurous, and audacious, too. Everything you have said. But the colonel wants a woman all women will identify with, and a Negro woman will not do. He is firm about that. And the obstacles she would face in the going because of her race would make her success nearly impossible. The decision was not mine, Mrs. Kopchovsky, as I'm sure you understand."

The last he said as an apology. I think he knew that while the colonel had a point about the obstacles, he only had a point because Negroes, like women, were second-class citizens and a Negro woman even less than that. He was eager to change the subject.

"Just think about it," he said, as he helped me on with my coat. "You might really be just the woman to do this."

I smiled politely and thought to myself, *I think you might just be right.*

"Good day, Captain!" I said, and again lifted my hand to my forehead in a salute.

"Good day, Mrs. K," he answered, straightening his back and returning my salute. He held the door for me, always a gentleman, and I stepped out into the late winter sunshine on Washington Street.

Two

That night, as usual, Grandpa ate in virtual silence as the children fussed about. Grandpa had arrived in Boston as a young man from Ukraine. He spoke English with a heavy accent. When he wasn't in shul he was often bent over a prayer book he kept on a small table next to the one comfortable chair in our living room. He was a kind and gentle man, but an inward-looking one. It's why I enjoyed my job so much. Talking to Alonzo and other customers was often the only conversation I would have for days on end, though Bennett and Baila lived just one floor down and I had a warm relationship with them. We often talked, of family matters mostly, world events, politics, and the like. Grandpa wasn't much for conversation, and he was also a passive man, a counterpoint to my flintiness.

By the time I'd gotten the children settled down for the night in the small room that was our second bedroom, and finished the dishes, Grandpa was asleep in his chair, as usual, his prayer book open and resting upside down on his chest. I flopped onto a kitchen chair, weary from a day of work selling adverts (I often walked several miles) followed by several more hours of domestic labor that started as soon as I walked through the door and retrieved the children from Bennett and Baila's. As our household grew, Jake and Rosa, now in their teens, took to sleeping regularly at Bennett and Baila's, for their apartment had a small den ours lacked that could be used as a makeshift bedroom. Both were quiet and studious and occasionally helped out watching the children, sometimes ours and sometimes Bennett and Baila's.

It was just before midnight when I washed my face and brushed my teeth to get ready for bed. How many nights had Grandpa slept in that chair, snoring heavily, slumbering too deeply to come to the bedroom? Countless. I slid under the covers and looked through the window. I could see a few stars twinkling brightly in the clear night sky. Maybe, just maybe, my own stars were starting to align, too.

Albert Augustus Pope, the colonel, was a Civil War veteran, a man of about fifty when I first saw him in his store, though we had never formally met. He was a man of great distinction and regal bearing, with a full white beard and moustache and a full head of silver hair. He'd fought at Antietam when he was just nineteen, a brutal day that saw the deaths of nearly eighty men from his unit. He would live to fight another day at Fredericksburg, Vicksburg, and Knoxville, facts I would learn later in my life when I became more curious about his, given the impact he had on me. Everything Pope touched seemed to turn to profit. By 1894, he had been in the bicycle trade for nearly two decades.

A week after Alonzo Peck first told me of Pope's plan to find a woman for his great publicity stunt, I saw Alonzo again while making my usual rounds. Though I mentioned it to no one, not even

Grandpa, *especially* not Grandpa, I had become obsessed with the proposition. I could think of little else. I was looking for an escape. Maybe it would be by bicycle.

"Good morning, Mrs. Kopchovksy," Alonzo said when I found him buried in his ledger books in his cramped and cluttered office.

"Good morning, Captain." I stood up straight and gave him another mock salute. It was becoming a ritual we both enjoyed.

We chatted about the weather; a touch of early spring was in the air. The snow that lined the sides of Washington Street was draining into puddles in the roadway. I was looking for an opening to raise the subject of the publicity stunt without seeming overeager, in case a candidate had already been found.

"I've been thinking about that bicycle trip you mentioned," I said, understating the level of my interest, which had grown steadily by the day. "Have you found a candidate?"

"The colonel has met with a few, but none have sufficiently impressed him," Alonzo replied. "Why? Are you considering the prospect? The colonel might find it unseemly for a young mother with children to undertake such a venture. You told me it was impossible yourself."

"Yes, I know," I said, lowering my gaze and staring into my lap. Then I lifted my head and looked Alonzo right in the eye. "Can you schedule an appointment for me with the colonel?"

"He's leaving presently for Hartford to attend to business, but he will return in two days' time. I'll have a word with him. If he wants to meet, I'll send for you. I will give you my highest recommendation."

A few days passed before one of the shop boys from the store came by Spring Street with a note for me. I was home, washing the children's clothes in the bathtub, when I heard a knock on the door. The *knock-knock* didn't even register with Grandpa, who was deep into his Torah studies in the living room. I swear, that man could focus even with three screaming children bouncing off the walls of the apartment. Inside the envelope was a note from Alonzo: "Colonel Pope would like to see you in his office at the store tomorrow at 10 A.M. sharp. Good luck!"

Nothing had been decided, but I was beginning to feel as if this was somehow my destiny, that my moment had come. That night, I slept fitfully. I breathed a word to no one.

It was about a thirty minute walk from Spring Street to the store on Washington. It wasn't one of my usual workdays, so Grandpa wondered why I was dressed in my formal work attire. I had arranged the night before for the children to be with Baila for part of the day, telling her I had a date to have tea with a friend. I told Grandpa the same.

"It's rather early for tea," he said in his heavily accented English.

"Yes, I know, but Susie is feeling down and asked if I might come early to cheer her up," I replied. My friend of many years, Susie Wyzanski, lived not far, on the periphery of Beacon Hill. "I'm taking the children downstairs for a few hours. I should be back around noon."

Grandpa nodded. He was perpetually circumspect. It was always hard to know what he was thinking.

It was an unusually pleasant day for late March, clear and mild, with a slight southerly breeze. I even spotted little clusters of crocuses in the tiny gardens in front of the brownstones on Charles Street.

I expected to be nervous. Not only was I growing more and more attached to the idea of the undertaking, but Colonel Pope had a reputation for being imperious. A man of his station did not suffer fools gladly. But my confidence was up, perhaps because I knew that was the impression I had to make: that I was a woman undaunted, that I was self-possessed, unafraid, and even cheeky. With each step I felt as though I were walking into a new, uncharted future, one I would embrace without fear. I would impress the great Colonel Pope as one of those "New Women" the newspapers were always writing about, ready to take on the world and make it my own.

I knew I was getting ahead of myself, but it also crossed my mind that if I were the colonel's "chosen one," I might in the process just lift up a few other women who, like myself, were already world-weary at a young age. Mostly I wanted to change my own life, but I glimpsed the possibility that a journey such as this might inspire a few others, just as Nellie Bly's had inspired me. And maybe, though I could not be the mother the children needed, I could be one of those women they, especially the girls, needed, to show that you can, with enough audacity, map your own path in this world.

Well, at least that's what I have told myself over the years to rationalize a harsh and selfish decision. But there is some truth to it, and this is certainly the truth: if I couldn't provide emotionally for my family, at least I could provide materially, and I stood to profit handsomely if I could persuade the colonel that I was his girl.

When I arrived at the store a few minutes before ten, Alonzo was waiting for me in the showroom.

"Are you ready, Mrs. Kopchovksy?" he asked. "The colonel is waiting. Be forewarned, he can be gruff and demanding. It's how he's become so successful."

"Aye, aye, Captain," I said with a grin. Alonzo smiled. He was rooting for me.

He walked me up the stairs to the colonel's office and knocked lightly on the door.

"Come in!" The voice was deep and resonant. Alonzo opened the door and announced my arrival.

The colonel stood up behind his desk and nodded to Alonzo, who left and shut the door behind him. I glanced around quickly at the rich furnishings. The office was suited to the man.

"Good day to you, Mrs. Kopchovsky," said the colonel, as he walked around the desk and extended a large hand.

I returned his firm handshake with one of my own. Most ladies of the day would have extended a limp hand to be gently placed in the palm of a gentleman.

"That's quite a grip you have, Mrs. Kopchovsky," said the colonel. His tone was serious.

"As is yours, Colonel," I replied. He arched his eyebrows. I'd taken him a bit by surprise. No man, let alone one of his station in life, expected to be spoken to as an equal in those days, especially a man of advancing years by a woman in her early twenties.

"Please. Have a seat," said the colonel, gesturing to a leather chair in front of his desk. "Would you like a glass of water?"

"I suppose it's too early for whiskey, so yes, thank you," I replied.

Colonel Pope seemed startled momentarily; then a small grudging smile gradually worked its way across his face.

"You are a woman of some humor, I see."

"And you are a man who seems to enjoy a woman with a sense of humor," I answered without missing a beat.

"Indeed, but it is rare, is it not, for a woman to be so forward?"

"Women rarely feel they have permission to engage in humorous conversation. It is rare only in that sense," I replied. "Among ourselves we often display great wit."

"I see," said the colonel. His smile had dissipated. He poured me a glass of water.

"Mrs. Kopchovsky, Mr. Peck has highly recommended you for the proposition, the details of which he has already informed you. But I will come straight to the point. Despite the hard times we are in, people continue to buy bicycles at a rapid rate. The market among women, for whom the wheel is still relatively new, has great potential. I want someone in whom every woman can see herself, for the purpose of the proposition is to sell bicycles. The women of this country are restless, but advancing their agitation for the right to vote, for equality, is not my interest. I am in the bicycle business, not the women's rights business."

"I do understand, Colonel," I said.

"You certainly have enough cheek," the colonel continued. "That you have already made clear. But you are a Jewess, are you not?"

"I am, Colonel."

"And you have young children, or so Mr. Peck has informed me."

"Yes, Colonel. Three."

"And they are how old?" asked the colonel.

"Five, three, and two," I answered.

"I will not pry into the reasons why you are prepared to abandon them for a time, but it is most unseemly, is it not?"

"It would seem that way, yes. But I can make arrangements for them, and my husband will be here."

"And your husband? What does he think of this?"

"I don't honestly know, Colonel. I haven't spoken of it to him. There's been no reason. But I assure you I would not undertake such an adventure without his permission."

I knew this last bit to be false, but it was the only answer to give a man. Grandpa might be unhappy, but he would put up faint opposition if I made clear what I was about to do. He suffered his disappointments in silence.

"Colonel," I continued, "we are not a family of means. As Mr. Peck surely told you, I am a working woman. I solicit adverts from your business every week. This opportunity, should you see fit to give it to me, is a chance for me to provide for my family. I would be very determined to succeed and claim the prize money. It is enough to fix us for life."

The colonel nodded. I sensed he was impressed with my motivation, at least the part of it I described to him. I said nothing of my yearning to break free of the bondage of domestic life.

"Kopchovksy. That is your married name, is it not?" asked the colonel.

"It is."

"And your given name?"

"Anna Cohen," I replied.

The colonel sighed. "It is even more of a Jewish name than Kopchovksy."

I nodded.

"Tell me, Mrs. Kopchovksy, what experience do you have riding a wheel?"

"I have never in my life ridden a wheel," I said with a directness that startled even me. It seemed this would, in baseball parlance, be the third strike. "But I could learn it in a week."

"You have a healthy reservoir of self-confidence, haven't you?" asked the colonel.

"Indeed I do, and it is well warranted, I assure you," I replied firmly. If I had any hope of earning the colonel's favor it lay in convincing him that I possessed the qualities most needed to succeed in an endeavor sure to be dangerous and grueling. I was quite sure the colonel had never heard a woman speak as I spoke to him that day.

"Well," said the colonel, as he started to stand up, signaling to me that our meeting was over. "You certainly have pluck, Mrs. Kopchovksy. You are most unconventional. I will need a few days to think it over. Mr. Peck will be in touch with you."

I rose from my chair.

"May I have that glass of whiskey now?" I asked. My grin and my eyes conveyed that I was joking. At least I think they did, for the colonel made no move to pour me a glass of whiskey and he didn't smile.

"If nothing else, Mrs. Kopchovksy, you have made an impression," the colonel said, though his meaning was ambiguous. "Thank you for an interesting conversation. Now, head home, I'm sure your children are waiting."

As the door shut behind me I took a deep breath and exhaled. There was no telling what impression I'd made, but I was relieved. I'd given it my best shot. What the colonel wanted was a heroine of the wheel, a woman hungry for fame and fortune, who would inspire women who had yet to be infected by the bicycle craze to flock to his stores. I doubt the colonel was even aware of it, but I knew to a certainty that what he was looking for was a woman in form and biology, but one with just enough of the masculine characteristics men of his station so prized in other men, but disdained in women—audacity, ingenuity, resourcefulness, fortitude, toughness, determination, combativeness, cunning, and even ruthlessness. If a woman were to have a plausible chance of accomplishing the formidable mission he had in mind, she would have to be all of those things. I'm not proud to say it now, but a woman willing to abandon her children for many months for a purpose such as this had to be ruthless in some measure. And a Jewish woman in a world rife with anti-Semitism willing to undertake such a journey had to be especially tough. Maybe those strikes against me would turn in my favor as the colonel weighed his decision.

As I walked over Beacon Hill toward home and the husband and three children who demanded my never-ending attention, the gold dome of the statehouse glistened in the early spring sunshine. In that moment I knew I wanted this more than anything I'd ever wanted in my life.

Three

In the weeks that followed my meeting with the colonel, I heard not a word. Even when I made my regular weekly calls at Pope's store on Washington Street and chatted with Alonzo, he said nothing and I didn't want to ask. As long as there wasn't a no, my hopes could remain alive. With each passing day my longing increased. Life at home was such drudgery; my only respite were the hours that I worked selling adverts. Grandpa wasn't a bother, but he wasn't much of a presence, either. I was only twenty-three. I wanted more. I needed more. The more I thought about escaping, the more desperate I was to escape. The desire fed on itself.

I told no one of my meeting with Colonel Pope, not Grandpa certainly, and not even Susie, my beloved Susie, my calm in any storm, my confidante and, I will say it now, my lover. Does that surprise you? Such intimacy between women was far more common, even in those days, than people believe. On some of the days when I was out of the house working, I would meet her at her lovely town house near Beacon Hill for late-morning tea and talk. The intimacy that often followed was the only time in my days of almost nonstop work, selling for the papers or at home, that I felt truly alive. I hope this isn't uncomfortable for you, but Susie was the only person with whom I had been intimate at that point in my life apart from Grandpa, which is to say it was practically my *only* experience. It was mostly unspoken, but many women of the time could find true understanding only in other women. Our lives were circumscribed in the same ways, our options similarly limited, our innermost thoughts and desires expected to remain unspoken and unrealized. That is why more women than anyone knew or suspected sought and treasured intimacy with each other. We joined with each other on even ground, something we rarely if ever experienced with men.

Though many women were swept up in the suffrage movement, and the movement for women's equality, it was mostly something for women of means with the time to attend meetings and conferences, write letters and polemics, and devote themselves fully to the cause. Though I was not at all active in this movement, I believed deeply in a woman's right to self-determination and autonomy, and I wanted to fulfill my own destiny, not the one society had in mind for me. In time, I would don the mantle of the women's movement, even become a symbol of it, but my reasons were more practical than political. I wanted to change my life, and the chance to win a considerable sum in the process, one that would secure the family's financial future, also lured me. On the journey I did not yet know I was about to take, publicity would be the fuel that drove me. And what better way to focus the public eye than to be at the center of a high-stakes wager to settle one of the burning issues of the day—whether a woman could equal a man. But again, I am getting ahead of myself.

Nearly six weeks had passed since my meeting with the colonel, and I had called several times on Alonzo to collect his advertising orders for the week ahead. In late April we were about to wrap up our usual meeting when he asked me a question that caught me off guard.

"Would you be willing to change your name, Mrs. Kopchovksy?"

"Pardon? Change my name? Whatever for?"

"And would you be willing to say as little as possible about your personal life, and perhaps, for certain purposes, become an unattached woman without a husband or children?"

Then it struck me. These were questions Alonzo was putting to me on the colonel's behalf. In the weeks since we'd met, my hopes had soared and then come back to earth. I wasn't sure what to think now. I was uncharacteristically silent. Alonzo allowed himself a wry smile.

"Here is the colonel's proposition," he said. "You impressed him with your wit and your cheek, but this is, after all, about business. The potential market for women's bicycles is still largely untapped. He wants to make a big splash with this scheme. He is prepared to extend the opportunity to you, but with conditions. The first is that he would, for present purposes at least, insist that you adopt a name—forgive me for saying so—that does not sound Jewish. The colonel is adamant that the majority of women would never embrace a Jewess as a role model. You are free to suggest a name of your choosing, which the colonel would have to approve."

The suggestion did not offend me, even if it saddened me a bit. Kittie Knox was dismissed out of hand for her race, something that could not be hidden. Hiding one's Jewishness, while difficult for some, was a more feasible proposition. Such was the reality of things. I didn't have time to dwell on it—I was still trying to absorb the shock that the fantasy I had indulged in recent weeks was inching toward reality. I started to speak.

"Alonzo," I said, but he interrupted me.

"There is a second condition you must consider," he added. "It would be scandalous for a woman to abandon her husband and children for such an undertaking. The colonel understands it would be impossible to keep such a secret here in Boston where you are known to many people, especially since you are engaged in the newspaper business. But once you are some distance from home you can be whomever you wish to be. Your real identity would be easy to obscure and a new one easy to create. The less said about your husband and your children, the better."

In the weeks that I had fantasized about escaping Boston by bicycle it had never occurred to me that I might choose to become someone else entirely. A new name. A new past. A whole new life. *A new woman*. I could reinvent myself from top to bottom. It thrilled me from the moment the words escaped Alonzo's lips. I didn't need to think it over, and I didn't need to discuss it with Grandpa. He would know that once I had put my mind to the task he would have little choice but to acquiesce. More difficult would be appealing to Bennett, for I would need him and Baila to agree to help Grandpa care for the children. My mind was racing, my heart, too, but I didn't want to appear overeager. I'm not sure how long the silence lingered between us as my mind conjured images of far-off places, of the great steamships I would have to take across the oceans, and of the exotic people who would stare in disbelief as a woman wheeled by on a bicycle.

I leveled my gaze and looked directly into Alonzo's eyes.

"When do I start?"

Alonzo smiled broadly.

"Shouldn't you discuss this with your husband first? His permission is not assured, I would assume."

"His permission is not needed," I replied. Alonzo looked quite startled. "His forgiveness, perhaps, but not his permission."

"Mrs. Kopchovksy," he said, "you are a bold woman. I have no doubt you will make a big success of this. The colonel thinks the first days of summer are a propitious time to start. That will give you time to get your affairs in order and attend to the logistics, of which there will be many. For starters, the colonel will pay for you to take riding lessons at the cycling academy on Tremont Street. You are, I believe, unacquainted with the wheel."

"True, but I should master it before long."

"I am sure of that, Mrs. Kopchovksy," Alonzo replied. "I am quite sure of that."

"There will be time to discuss the details further," he continued, rising from his chair. "For now I suggest you attend to your affairs at home and prepare your family. I do admire your grit, Mrs. Kopchovksy, but I have to say, I am glad you are not my wife." He smiled.

"As am I," I said, returning his smile. "As am I."

Of all the countless tasks I would now have to attend to in order to prepare for my departure, telling Grandpa, Bennett, and, of course, my dear Susie would be the most difficult. It was the conversation to come with Susie I dreaded most. Not because she wouldn't understand; no one in my life understood me and my deepest desires as well as Susie. I knew she would find our separation painful, as would I, but I also knew she would become my biggest booster. She wanted nothing more in life than my happiness, and I hers.

As I walked home that evening after a full day of work, I pondered when would be the opportune time to have these difficult conversations with Grandpa and my brother, and I started to go over in my mind what I would say to each. The children were too young to understand. My departure from their life would be both sudden and inexplicable. Only Mollie, at five, would be able to grasp it at all, and to her I would only be able to say that Mother needs to be away for a while but Papa and Uncle and Auntie will be here to take care of you. It is with great guilt that I say this now, but the idea of being separated from the children caused me only minor discomfort. I cared about them, wanted the best for them, but the maternal love we expect to wash over us after the birth of a child never materialized for me. I have few regrets in life, but this is one, that I was unable to provide the maternal love every child deserves.

I decided to tell Susie first, perhaps because I knew she would support me and bolster me if any self-doubt started to materialize. She would also, I was sure, offer good counsel on how I should address the news with Grandpa and Bennett. Susie was just a few years older than me, but unmarried, unusual for a woman of the time approaching her late twenties. There were rumors about that maybe Susie preferred the company of women, but we were extraordinarily discreet, and no one, to my knowledge, suspected the love between us.

When we weren't in each other's company, Susie and I communicated mostly by letter or note, either sent by messenger (many neighborhood children would run notes to and fro for a penny apiece) or dropped in person at each other's door as we went about our daily chores. Only the wealthy and prominent had telephones—Colonel Pope had one in his office—and since few had phones, there were few people one could call. The next morning I would send a note to Susie proposing we meet for tea the next Thursday, two days hence, one of my regular workdays. Until then, I would keep the adventure on which I was about to embark close to the vest.

At home that night, the familiar routine unfolded: I fed Grandpa and the children and put the little ones to bed as Grandpa snoozed in his armchair, his prayer book open and upside down on his chest yet again.

Susie's return note said she would, as always, be waiting eagerly for my visit. She would expect me Thursday at eleven o'clock. It was a rendezvous I was looking forward to—I *always* looked forward to being with Susie—but I was also dreading telling her we would soon be separated.

We first met in school as teenagers. Not all young girls went to school, but we both came from Jewish families that revered education above all else. I was about thirteen then, she about sixteen. Our flirtation began shortly thereafter, but it remained no more than that until shortly after Grandpa and I were married. Susie feared the marriage would be the end of our friendship, that I would have no time for friends, especially when I told her, just two months after our marriage, that I was pregnant. But the opposite happened. I felt trapped by circumstances immediately and sought comfort in Susie's company and then her arms. Only in her arms did I feel understood. Only she seemed to grasp that there was more to being a woman than housework and child-rearing and tending to an emotionally distant husband. If anyone would understand the extreme nature of the rebellion I was now planning, it was Susie.

It was now the second week of May, May 10 to be exact. I remember it well. Springtime in Boston, though it often seemed grudging, was always my favorite season of year. After months of bitter winds and snow that often made trudging even short distances an ordeal, May always brought nature forth in all its glory. The trees began dressing themselves in green, the forsythia exploded in a sea of yellow, and the daffodils and tulips made their most dramatic stand. The Boston Public Garden was the first botanical garden in the country and nearly sixty years old in 1894, and there was no place more magnificent to be on a mild day in May than there.

When I arrived at Susie's that morning she had, as usual, prepared tea and scones, but I implored her to walk with me to the Garden.

"There may not be a lovelier day for it!" I said.

"But I've made tea," she replied, her eyes asking me to sit down.

"I know. Let it sit. Come. I have something to discuss with you."

"Annie Kopchovksy. You are nothing if not persistent," said Susie. "Resistance is futile. Let me get an umbrella. The sun is strong."

You could not have distinguished us from the many hundreds of women who had chosen this morning to exhale after the long winter by walking along the graceful paths that curved around the lagoon and under the massive oaks and willows that adorned the Garden. We all dressed alike: long skirts down to our ankles, black shoes laced to where they met the hem of our skirts, white blouses with leg-o'-mutton billowy sleeves tapered at the elbow and buttoned at the collar (we called them shirtwaists then) and worn under waistcoats and jackets (we called them bodices) tailored narrow through the midsection. Oh, and a proper brimmed hat, too, adorned with a ribbon or feather of some sort. Like much else, women's fashion, too, was changing in the 1890s. Gone were the restrictive corsets and fussy ornaments and bustles that made our rumps look absurdly large. I didn't know it then, but in the months ahead my own style of dress would undergo even more radical changes as I sought a costume more conducive to life on a bicycle, changes that were emblematic of the larger transformation that was afoot in women's lives, changes of which I was but dimly aware. But on this morning I gave my clothes not a second thought. I wore the same uniform whenever I was about in public, and it was no different than that of anyone else. Conformity in all things was expected of women.

Susie and I had walked these paths many times before. It was not uncommon for women to walk arm in arm while enjoying a stroll, and on this morning that's what we did.

"Susie," I said, "I think you are going to be deeply disappointed with what I have to say. It hurts me to tell you what I have to tell you."

She looked concerned but not alarmed. And then I told her the story pretty much as I have told it to you thus far, about Alonzo and Colonel Pope and my decision to leave a few weeks hence to go 'round the world by wheel. By the time I had finished we had walked to the far corner of the Garden, near Boylston Street. A few people strolled by in the distance, but we had some privacy under the blooming willows. Susie turned and faced me and took both my hands in hers.

"Annie," she said with sympathy, "you know I adore you and I will miss you terribly. But this is your destiny! You will make a great success of it!" And then she did something we never dared do in public: she pulled me toward her and kissed me firmly on the mouth. For a few moments we stood there and embraced. As she released me she looked me directly in the eyes and asked, "Have you told Max yet? This will not go down well, I suspect."

"I haven't," I answered, glancing at the tops of my shoes. "But truthfully I am more concerned about telling Bennett. He and Baila will have to bear the burden of the children, and I know he will think it is all madness. Sheer madness. I will tell him first and then Max. I just have to find the right time, though there won't be a right time."

"You will have to be ready for many slings and arrows," Susie said, shifting the conversation a bit. "This is a radical thing for a woman to do, especially one with young children."

"I know," I said, nodding gently. "But I will endure it. What I cannot endure are more years of this tiresome routine. It is not the life I was meant to live."

Susie knew me and understood me better than anyone and may have been the only person in the world who could have talked me out of my plan. Far from doing so, she was my biggest champion, and she never wavered, not in her desire for my happiness nor her confidence that I would make a success of the journey ahead.

As we walked back toward Beacon Hill, Susie peppered me with questions, about my direction of travel, how I would learn to ride a bicycle, my plans for earning money en route—countless questions that I hadn't even asked myself, let alone begun to answer.

By the time we had returned to Susie's door there was no time for tea. We'd been walking for close to three hours.

"I have to hurry," I pleaded. "I have to shop for dinner and get home to Max and the children. But let's do this again next week. Your questions are helpful to me. There is so much to think about and so much to be done."

Susie's eyes darted left and right, and when she was sure it was safe to do so, she kissed me once again on the mouth, took my hands, and looked directly into my eyes.

"I do love you so, Annie. There is surely no woman in the world quite like you."

"I will miss you dearly," I replied, thinking ahead. "But I promise to come back. I do hope you will be waiting for me."

"Of that there is no doubt, my dear. Go on. I will be all right." A tear ran down Susie's cheek. I knew I was breaking her heart, and it pained me, but sometimes for a woman to be who she is meant to be hearts must be broken.

Two days after my walk with Susie, tragedy befell our family. My brother Jake, "my twin," just seventeen years old, died of pneumonia. Though later in life I often said he was my twin—I even told my own adult children that—he was not, as I have told you. We were born five years apart. Nor did he get drunk and freeze to death after arguing with our father, as I also said. Father died in 1887, when Jake was only ten. And who freezes to death in mid-May? I can't tell you why I told those stories except that I always had an aversion to the ordinary if I could conjure the extraordinary. What can I say? I took a certain mischievous pleasure in spinning tall tales. It was just my nature.

A couple of weeks after we buried dear Jacob, still grieving, I decided I would speak with my brother first and then Grandpa. Even Jake's untimely death could not stop me from going. I had been handed a once-in-a-lifetime opportunity, and I was not about to let it slip away. My younger sister Rosa took Jake's death the hardest, for they were close in age and were each other's best friend and constant companion. Rosa, already battling the obesity and melancholy that continued to the day she died in 1945, would take my leaving doubly hard, just one more responsibility I was about to dump into my brother Bennett's lap.

I knew Bennett would be angry, but I also knew he and Baila would, when push came to shove, take care of the children. They would feel they had no choice. They would do their best in abnormal circumstances to provide normalcy in the children's lives. Grandpa would be stoic; if he ever felt anger, he never showed it. He was a man for whom the disappointments and setbacks in life were expected and accepted with unnerving quietude. Though he could not have predicted the form my rebellion would take, I knew he would not be surprised that I was prepared to upend our lives in dramatic fashion. I suspect his only question was not whether such upheaval was in the offing, but when.

My brother, like many young professional men on the rise, was a serious fellow. He wore pince-nez spectacles and sported a handlebar moustache that was very much the fashion in those days. Our older sister Sarah was in Maine, and so Bennett, especially after the death of our parents, had become the paternal figure in our family, and he felt a deep sense of responsibility to me and Jake and Rosa. His wife Baila was a kind and gentle woman who loved my children as her own. Indeed, given the hours she cared for them during my working days, I can say that she was a far more maternal presence in their lives than I was, but that is not saying much. Not that I was as aware of it then as I am now, but given my detachment from them I was able to convince myself that my extended absence would do the children no harm and might even do them some good, for Bennett and Baila were far better with children than Grandpa and me.

My brother Bennett.

Bennett worked on the business side for the *Boston Herald Traveler* newspaper, overseeing revenues from subscriptions and advertising, and often arrived home to the apartment below ours after the dinner hour. He worked too hard, I thought, but he was determined to escape the limited circumstances we faced as a family of immigrants who had arrived in Boston in 1875. Our father Levi worked as a real estate agent until he became infirm in his early sixties. Our mother Basha took in piecework, but money was always tight.

About a week after my walk with Susie, I slid a sealed envelope with a note for Bennett under the door of their apartment: "Dearest Brother," it read, "I have something of import to discuss with you that requires privacy. Have you an hour to spare on the weekend? Perhaps we can walk together by the river. Anna."

At first Bennett seemed absolutely stunned as we walked along the banks of the Charles. I could see it in his eyes and the way his body stiffened when I told him of my plans, which included foisting much responsibility for the children onto him and Baila. For a good five minutes the silence between us seemed to portend a volcanic eruption from my brother, who stared intently at the ground as we walked. When it came, the eruption was as controlled as the man himself. He spoke firmly and with authority, but he never raised his voice.

"Anna, the stain on the honor of this family, which is sure to come from this if you follow through, will be deep and dark," he said, choosing his words with care. "But it pales in comparison to the pain you will be inflicting on your own children and on Rosa. With Jacob gone, she needs you more than ever. How could you? What are you thinking? This ill-conceived lark will cause terrible damage to all those closest to you."

I could hardly tell him that the person closest to me in the world, Susie, had already blessed this "lark."

"I know you too well to think the forbidding of it would be of any consequence," Bennett continued. "But I implore you to consider the harm to be caused by this selfish, self-destructive, outlandish plan of yours. It is shameful."

"Dear Brother, I mean no offense when I tell you that I do not expect you to understand what has led me to this decision," I said, trying to sound as gentle as possible. "We are, all of us, living lives that have been scripted for us by the expectations of others, of our larger society. You can see for yourself the general state of agitation among women who are pushing for greater autonomy and equality. But I am not interested in politics. I am not marching or protesting or gathering petitions. I am not trying to prove a point. But I need to take control of my own life and take my destiny into my own hands. I can no longer live as I have and expect that happiness will find me. I have to take the reins, or the handlebars, and steer myself into the future, not be steered by the expectations of others. And I stand to return with a substantial sum in my pocket, enough to provide for the family for years to come."

I am sure Bennett could hardly believe his ears, for such talk was barely comprehensible to a man of the 1890s.

"And Max?" asked Bennett. "He doesn't know yet, does he? He would have said something to me, I am sure. How can you do this to him? He has been a good husband to you. He will be bereft."

"I will tell him soon," I replied. Bennett looked at me as if he were a stern father.

"You will be abandoning your husband and children, but Baila and I will not abandon them, as I suspect you know."

"I do. And I know the burden I am placing on you and Baila. You've every right to be angry. But please know I am grateful." Bennett smirked.

"Right now your gratitude is hard to accept, Sister. What I'd be grateful for is your coming to your senses."

"There is little chance of that, Brother," I answered, hoping to elicit at least a smile if not a small laugh. Bennett's demeanor didn't change. "Besides, you and Baila are far better equipped than I to give the children the love they deserve. I see it in the way you love your own children and mine. It may seem selfish, but I may be doing the children a favor."

"And what do you know of bicycle riding?" Bennett asked. "I've never seen you with a bicycle."

"I commence riding lessons next week. It doesn't look terribly difficult. Millions of people are doing it."

"You may be back sooner than you think," Bennett said. "After two or three days, you may find the comforts of home are superior to the rigors of the road. And you'll have made a fool of yourself in the process."

"Then you have little to worry about," I answered. My tone turned slightly defiant. Until now I was deferential to my older brother, because I knew the magnitude of what I was asking of him. But the suggestion that I might not finish what I started hit a tender spot. No one, not even my dear brother, should question my determination to make a success of this highly unusual venture. Nothing quite got my back up like someone telling me I couldn't do something.

"Please, Brother, one favor," I continued. "I need to be the one to tell Max. I know you will talk with Baila, but give me a few days, please."

"It is not for me to tell a man that his wife is about to abandon him and their three small children," answered Bennett, driving home once more how appalling he found the entire business.

We walked home in silence. I knew Bennett was already resigning himself to whatever the weeks and months ahead would bring. Stubborn could have been my middle name.

Two nights later I decided I could wait no longer to talk with Grandpa. I was dreading it, not because I knew I was in for an argument or a fight, but precisely because I knew I wasn't. The man, rest his soul, was terribly passive. Not even passive-aggressive, just passive. His lack of passion for anything but his beloved Torah, his complete lack of risibility, made for a very boring marriage. Here I was, full of vinegar, and he couldn't muster a pinch of salt. I knew he would be terribly distressed and unhappy, maybe somewhere deep inside quite angry, but it would barely register. And when I spoke to him late that evening, after the children had been put to bed, he didn't disappoint. The shock, once he realized I was serious, registered in his eyes but not in his voice. All he said, really, was, "You are meshuga, but we will survive." And then he walked away and into the bedroom, reinforcing, unintentionally, of course, precisely what was wrong with our marriage from my point of view. I wanted excitement, spark, an occasional battle of wills . . . *a pulse*!

There was, I knew, no way to explain this to the children. Libbie was but three and Simon just two. Even Mollie, at five, would be utterly confused and unable to grasp any explanation I could conjure except to say that Mother would be going away for a while and would come back as soon as she could. So inadequate. Though it barely registered then—I was, quite honestly, too selfish and self-absorbed—I have felt in the years since occasional pangs of guilt over a departure that would be as sudden as it was inexplicable to the children. They paid a high price for my freedom, especially Mollie, but we'll come to that.

The next week I presented myself at the academy for the cycling lessons Alonzo had arranged at Colonel Pope's direction. The instructor was a young man of about twenty, a handsome fellow named Michael who had about a half-dozen assistants out on the flat wooden floor where men and women of various ages were struggling to master the art of the wheel. They looked like small children trying to ice-skate for the first time.

"It takes eight or ten lessons before most people are ready to go out on their own," Michael explained. "It's not as easy as it looks when you see people riding through the park."

"I shall conquer it in two," I said, looking Michael in the eye. "Look at that." I gazed out over the assembled students going every which way, falling, stumbling, occasionally gliding a few feet or so, their faces frozen in terror. "Far too much fussing about."

"They're not so much afraid of losing their balance as their dignity," I added. "If you don't worry about your dignity, the task looks quite simple."

Two lessons later I pronounced myself ready to Michael.

"I have to hand it to you, Mrs. Kopchovksy," Michael said with a smile. "You're a fast learner. Only a handful of students have shown the knack you have for the wheel. I think you are ready for the park."

Michael knew nothing of my plan, so my response meant nothing to him.

"The park cannot contain me," I replied. "I'm ready for the world!"

It was now early June. Alonzo and I continued to meet during my regular visits to the store, where, in addition to collecting that week's adverts, we worked out the details of my departure. We chose, with the colonel's approval, Monday, June 25 as the big day and the steps in front of the statehouse on Beacon Hill as the place for a grand send-off. There was still much to be done.

I'd purchased a steamer trunk in which I would pack extra clothing and the personal effects I would need to refresh from time to time, with enough room for souvenirs I might collect along the way. My plan was to ship the trunk, by rail or steamer, to be held for me at various points along the way.

As the purpose of the journey, as far as Colonel Pope was concerned, was to serve as a roving advertisement for his bicycles, Alonzo arranged for a brand-new women's drop frame Columbia to be delivered fresh from the factory a few days before my departure. The plan was for Alonzo to wheel it up to me as I stood on the statehouse steps.

The drop frame was a modification to bicycles necessitated by their growing popularity among women. Women were still expected to wear long billowy skirts while astride a bicycle, and not a patch of skin above the ankle was to be exposed. Mounting a bicycle with a top tube running from the seat post to the front stem, the part to which the handlebars are attached, was highly impractical in long skirts: one had to gather nearly the entire skirt and lift it over the top tube as one leg was lifted over as well. It was preposterous and made riding difficult, and so the drop frame was introduced, allowing the woman rider to simply step through the frame.

The bicycle Alonzo had selected weighed forty-two pounds and had a simple spoon brake, a terribly inefficient device that consisted of a piece of metal shaped like a spoon and attached to a plunger, which was attached, in turn, to the front stem. To slow the machine the rider pushed down on the plunger, and the spoon, slightly curved to match, more or less, the width of the front wheel, would create friction. As a practical matter this brake was a farce. The real braking came from the rider resisting the forward spin of the pedals by applying back pressure. What became known as the "freewheel mechanism" was still a few years in the future, which meant that whenever the bicycle wheels were turning, the pedals were turning as well. On flat surfaces the rider could, with relative ease, bring the bicycle to a stop this way, especially because the casual rider was typically traveling at a leisurely eight miles an hour or so. But when going downhill it was nearly impossible to resist the spinning pedals, which continued to gather momentum the farther one descended. Often the rider had no choice but to move her feet to the side, let the pedals spin wildly, and hope for the best. For a woman in long skirts, this was especially difficult; many women had their skirts caught in the spinning pedals and were either stripped practically naked in the process or found themselves bloody and bruised and seated on the ground next to their ruined bicycles. Prudent riders often walked their machines down long or steep hills. These were skills one could not learn on the flat wooden floor of a cycling academy; I would have to learn, by trial and error, as I went.

I still had to attend to an important detail the colonel had insisted upon. I needed another name, an alter ego, so that the colonel's marketing plans would not be marred by having as their central figure a Jew. It would have been easy enough to make up a name, but I had a better idea, and it came to me as I made my work rounds in early June. One of my customers, with a branch office in Boston, was a spring water company with headquarters in Nashua, New Hampshire. The spring itself was in the nearby town of Londonderry, and the water had naturally occurring traces of lithium, an element used since the early 1800s to treat gout, but which by the later part of the century was known to have mood stabilizing properties. It was called the Londonderry Lithia Spring Water Company. The product was distributed and widely advertised throughout many parts of the country, as far away as Denver.

I was aware that some of the more famous bicycle racers of the time, men such as William Sanger, made extra money by endorsing products such as bicycle tires. I was required by the terms of the wager to earn five thousand dollars and to meet my expenses, and I hit upon the idea of turning myself into a mobile billboard. I had been selling adverts for the newspapers for several years; why not sell adverts and adorn my bicycle and myself with them? What a spectacle I would be! It was, if I say so myself, a stroke of genius and would, as you will see, become my principal source of income in the months ahead.

Londonderry's Boston sales representative was Benjamin White, a genial man of middle age, who was easily charmed. Being one of the few female advertising solicitors in Boston gave me an advantage my male competitors lacked. Rare was the man who was resistant to a young woman's flattery, especially if she was attractive (no false modesty here; I was a comely young woman) and a little flirtatious.

Three weeks before my scheduled departure I called on White. I told him I was taking leave of my job and that this would be our last meeting for a while. He seemed disappointed and asked the reason for my leave. When I told him of my plan he was as aghast as he was delighted.

"Oh my, Mrs. Kopchovsky! I can scarcely believe it," he said. "Whoever heard of such a thing! A woman going alone? Around the world? On a bicycle no less?"

I assured him I was not pulling the wool over his eyes.

"I have a proposition," I said with dead seriousness. "Your company stands to profit from this venture, as well as Colonel Pope's." I had, through Alonzo, secured the colonel's permission for this part of my scheme.

"How so, Mrs. Kopchovsky? How so?" I had piqued his curiosity.

"The Londonderry brand is quite famous, is it not?"

"I suppose it is. Recognized in many parts."

"I am required on this journey to earn my way, and plan to put my experience as an advertising woman to work during the enterprise," I explained. "I propose to fix a placard with the Londonderry name to my bicycle for the duration of my journey in exchange for one hundred dollars." I sounded as if I fully expected White to agree on the spot. What I really expected was for him to tell me he would need to check with his superiors in Nashua.

"That's a large sum, Mrs. Kopchovksy." He sounded skeptical.

"There's more," I answered. "I propose to go as 'Annie Londonderry.' It rings like a bell, does it not?" White smiled.

"You are an ingenuous woman, Mrs. Kopchovksy. You seem possessed of a limitless supply of outlandish ideas." He meant it as a compliment.

"Let me see what I can do. Stop by early next week and I will have an answer for you."

The deal was struck and in the weeks and months ahead, Anna Cohen Kopchovksy, the daughter of Latvian immigrants, the wife of a simple peddler, and the mother of three young children, would gradually disappear, and a new woman would be born: the daring woman on a wheel, the globetrotter extraordinaire, Annie Londonderry.

Four

June 25, 1894, was a mild, slightly overcast day. I barely slept the night before. As self-assured as I was, the butterflies in my stomach were active all night long. What had seemed in my imagination a lovely flight to freedom suddenly seemed a daunting physical, logistical, and emotional challenge.

I had, two days before, shipped my trunk by rail to New York, my first destination, to the home of friends on the Lower East Side where I would stay while in the city. I would carry little with me, for all I had was a small leather carrying case secured to the seat post. In that small case I packed a change of undergarments and two "road books" published by the Massachusetts and New York chapters of the L.A.W. These were bound booklets with detailed directions for cyclists, maps, and, down to the finest details, descriptions of road conditions for virtually every mile. One could use the New York book as a guide all the way from New York to Chicago, and my plan was to ride for Chicago after I'd reached New York. In the back were the names of hotels that welcomed cyclists and offered discounts to members of the L.A.W., a membership I had secured. Paved roads were few and far between outside of cities back then, so the descriptions of road conditions were extremely helpful. As I would learn almost immediately, some roads in Rhode Island were nothing but soft sand and impossible to ride; the cyclist would have to dismount and push the bicycle, sometimes for several exhausting miles, before finding a surface firm enough to support the weight of a cyclist and her machine. As you can surmise, long-distance cycling was already a popular pastime, principally for men. But for most, long-distance didn't mean going 'round the world, and for most of my odyssey I would not have the luxury of the L.A.W. booklets to guide me.

There was one other personal effect in my saddlebag. It was my idea to bring it, even though I had no idea how to use it, and I purchased it in Boston just a few days before leaving. I never loaded it, though no one knew that but me; it was really just for show. After all, Annie Londonderry was about to put on a 'round-the-world spectacle the likes of which had never been seen. The journey was full of inherent danger, of course, but I never missed an opportunity to throw an extra measure of theatrics into it. Many reporters I would meet along the way were quick to mention it, and I always made a show of brandishing it: with my underwear and my roadbooks I packed a brand-new Smith & Wesson revolver with a beautiful pearl handle. That pistol seemed the perfect emblem for the journey, hinting, as it did, at the danger and excitement ahead, and for the alter ego that would grow with every mile. I wish I had a dollar for every man who said of me along the way, "She's a pistol, all right!"

Thanks to Colonel Pope's connections with all the newspapers, and my own affiliations, news of my impending departure had spread throughout Boston, and by late morning a crowd of more than five hundred had gathered at the statehouse to see me off. The colonel had arranged a horse-drawn carriage to take me and a small delegation of women, including Mrs. J. O. Tubbs, head of the local chapter of the Woman's Christian Temperance Union, Frances Willard's organization, from the store on Washington Street up to the statehouse.

Susie and another friend of ours, Pear Stone, were waiting at the statehouse, as was my rather forlorn-looking brother Bennett. He barely nodded at me when I looked his way, and he never even came up to say goodbye. I suspect he thought the farce would last a few days at most. The governor of the Commonwealth, Frederic Greenhalge, was supposed to be there but, much to my disappointment, never showed. Needless to say, perhaps, Grandpa and the children did not come. Earlier that morning I kissed each of them, muttered a word of apology to Grandpa, told them I would be back, and left for the walk to Washington Street. There was no time to linger in a sad farewell, nor did I wish to.

You can see from the photograph I am enclosing with this letter what I wore that day: a long dark skirt, a dark tailored jacket with billowing sleeves, a white shirtwaist with a striped collar and a neat bow tie, dark gloves, and a flat-topped hat. My hair was tied up in a bun under the hat. And that little white ribbon on my lapel? The symbol of Frances Willard's WCTU. I think I looked rather stylish, don't you?

Alonzo stood off to the side holding the Columbia bicycle I was to ride. He was dressed in his formal bicycle riding attire: close-fitting pants and a neat jacket adorned with epaulets bearing the abbreviation MASS. to indicate his rank as a captain in the Massachusetts chapter of the L.A.W.

The crowd quieted as Mrs. Tubbs stepped to the podium that had been set up.

"May she set a noble example wherever she goes!" she exclaimed. "We wish her to spread good tidings among the Bedouins and the nations of the earth!" As she introduced me, I kissed Pear and Susie each on the cheek, asked them if my hat was on straight, and addressed the assembly.

"I am to go around the earth in fifteen months, returning with five thousand dollars, and starting only with the clothes on my back," I said, speaking as loudly as I could so those far back in the crowd, which had blocked Beacon Street, could hear. "I cannot accept anything gratuitously from anyone." For dramatic effect I then turned the pockets of my jacket inside out to show they were empty.

As we had planned on the carriage ride, Mrs. Tubbs stepped forward and offered me a copper coin.

"A penny for luck!" she said.

"I can't take it," I replied. "I must earn it."

"Take it as pay in return for speaking for the white ribbon, then," Mrs. Tubbs responded. Then she pinned that little white ribbon on my right lapel, and the crowd applauded.

There was more staged theater to come. Next, Mr. White of the Londonderry Lithia Spring Water Company stepped forward and held up a one-hundred-dollar bill, a very substantial sum in those days. He handed it to me and then, using picture wire, affixed a small placard that simply read "Londonderry" to the skirt guard, a screen mesh that fit over the rear wheel and kept a woman's skirts from getting caught in the spokes. As agreed, I would carry the Londonderry banner to publicize the brand and would, as I traveled, call myself "Annie Londonderry."

"Anyone else make a bid for space on the wheel?" I asked the crowd. That day no one did, but in the days ahead I would be nearly covered head to toe in small patches, ribbons, and banners advertising all manner of things, from milk to perfume.

"There being none, I will now say farewell!"

Alonzo wheeled the bike forward, and we made our way to Beacon Street, the crowd parting to permit us through. Alonzo held the wheel as I stepped through the frame. I tried to catch Bennett's eye, but he was looking down at his feet in despair. I waved to the crowd and with a gentle push from Alonzo I sailed away like a kite down Beacon Street as a huge cheer rose up from the throngs behind me.

I did not go far before turning into an alley near Susie's house. Up on Beacon Hill the crowd began to disperse.

This was my official start, but I didn't actually leave Boston for another two days. As we had arranged, Susie arrived in the alley about twenty minutes later and we moved the bike into the basement of her building. Other than lie with Susie for the next two days, early on the morning of the twenty-sixth, before sunrise, I rode the wheel to the Towne Portrait Studio, where I had arranged to have formal photographs taken, the one I have enclosed among them. I had several hundred made and shipped to New York, where I would add them to my trunk. As I became better known, I figured people I met would gladly pay for a photograph and an autograph and I could earn some of my money that way. I would not be disappointed.

As you can imagine, the next two days with Susie were bittersweet. She never wavered in her support of my venture, but as the hours till my actual departure ticked down, the sense of longing and sadness grew deeper and deeper. Men, especially of that time, understood so little of women, and rare was the man who even conceived that a woman might have a rich inner life, thoughts worth weighing, and feelings that needed tending. That, as I have said, is why many, many more of us than anyone understood sought comfort and communion with each other.

Again before dawn, so as to minimize the risk of being seen, on the morning of June 27 I left at last, after spending the night wrapped in Susie's arms. We went to the basement together to retrieve the wheel, and as we stood at the basement door, gripped each other with such intensity I thought we might pass right through each other. We didn't speak. We didn't have to. We had said all we needed to say in the previous thirty-six hours.

I wheeled the Columbia onto Charles Street, gave Susie one last kiss, mounted the wheel, and bumped along the cobblestones toward the Fens, near where Fenway Park stands today. Many streets in Boston were paved with macadam, and for the first few miles as I pedaled from downtown through Jamaica Plain, Forest Hills, and West Roxbury, the riding was smooth.

My destination that first night was Providence, about forty-five miles south, ambitious considering I had only taken a few short rides on the streets outside the cycling academy where I'd learned to balance myself on two wheels. At first I was encouraged, for the weather was mild, the smooth roads made riding a breeze, and I was able to cover the first eight miles or so in about an hour, relying on my road book for directions. At Dedham the macadam ran out, and I was soon traveling on packed gravel, a bit harder riding, but still quite passable. These gravel roads took me through Norwood, Walpole, and Wrentham. Susie had given me two apples and a piece of cheese, which I ate at midday. Between Attleboro and Providence the roads were again paved with macadam, and nine hours after leaving Boston I arrived in the Rhode Island capital.

The one hundred dollars I had earned from the water company I had left with Dr. Reeder, who had come to the statehouse, for I had arranged to send my earnings, less what I was spending, back to him periodically. He would be responsible for tallying those earnings to ensure I met the requirement that I earn five thousand dollars above my expenses en route. It was also agreed that once accounted for he would periodically deliver the money to Grandpa, for I was the primary breadwinner in our household and he would need it.

Thus, when I arrived at the Providence Hotel late that afternoon, I had no money to pay for my lodging. So I bartered with the hotel manager to allow me to earn my stay by working the candy counter at the hotel store for several hours and to give a short lecture in the lobby on what we called then "physical culture" (exercise and physical fitness) to a few curious guests who saw me standing there with my wheel. I would often have to improvise such arrangements, but a woman's charm went a long way with men in those days. I told the hotel manager I had studied medicine for two years, hence my expertise on physical culture. It wasn't true, of course, and it would not be the last time on my journey I would claim medical expertise.

By late evening I was exhausted. I'd been up since before dawn, ridden more than forty miles, and fulfilled the promises I'd made in exchange for my night's lodging. I was asleep within minutes of getting into bed. But I awoke in the middle of the night in excruciating pain. The muscles in my thighs and calves were cramping so badly I thought I might pass out. It was nearly an hour before they released themselves. I paid dearly that night for my lack of physical preparation. So much for my expertise in physical culture!

When my muscles had finally relaxed, I fell back into a deep sleep until morning.

The roads leading south out of Providence were an unwelcome change from the good roads the day before. Gravel gradually gave way to sand, sometimes several inches deep, for miles, which made wheeling impossible. I had no choice but to push that forty-two-pound machine through the sand until, at last, it yielded to packed dirt firm enough for riding.

In southwest Rhode Island there were many modest hills, and the glide on the downhills was positively exhilarating! It felt as though I was defying gravity itself. I was untethered and free, and with each passing mile the burdens of marriage, motherhood, and work seemed to recede. I was on a freedom ride on a bicycle built for one!

Over the next three days I made my away along the coast of Connecticut from Stonington to Darien, sleeping one night in an inn and two in fields under the stars with only my clothing to cover me. The weather was fair, luckily, and I was able to average about forty miles each day. Though my clothes had begun to smell, and I had no bath, the occasional stream allowed me to wash my hands and face and refill the small flask I carried for water.

At Darien I picked up the Boston Post Road, the old historic mail route that linked Boston and New York in Revolutionary days. From Greenwich I crossed the Byram River Bridge into Port Chester, New York, and on July 2 I reached New York City, and none too soon, for the weather had turned hot and humid that day and riding in my formal attire was a misery. I knew then that this uniform was not at all suited to long-distance riding and that while in New York I would have to adjust my costume and make it suitable for distance wheeling.

It was my first time in New York since passing through as a young child when we arrived in this country, and I had only a few hazy memories of the place. Boston, compact and provincial, seemed tiny by comparison. The roadways were clogged with carts, carriages, horses, and electrified trolley cars. Newsboys in knickers and caps on every corner hawked their wares, wearing aprons adorned with the name of the newspaper they were selling. The city was alive with incessant activity, and tall buildings cast shadows across the streets.

The tallest in the city, indeed the world, was the New York World Building, also called the Pulitzer Building, the home of Pulitzer's famous newspaper. Some eighteen stories, it dominated Park Row, home to nearly all of the city's many newspapers, just as the *World* dominated its competition. Completed just a few years earlier, Joseph Pulitzer, then nearly blind, had spent two million dollars of his own money to have the elegant building constructed. It was topped with a gold dome that reflected sunlight so that the glow could be seen, some said, forty miles out to sea.

Publicity was very important if I were to succeed in this endeavor; it would be a kind of fuel I would need if I were to earn the large sum of five thousand dollars, and Colonel Pope certainly expected me to make as big a splash as I could wherever I went. I thus early got into the habit of sending telegrams or telegraph messages whenever I could to newspapers in cities and towns in which I expected to arrive and to the many bicycle clubs that had formed all over the United States in the two decades that cycling had grown into a popular pastime. News of my venture, and of my departure from Boston, had made it into newspapers not just in Boston but even in Washington, D.C., Chicago, Pittsburgh, and other places, too, for news in those days could travel rapidly by telegraph. I was a novelty to be sure, but I knew I would have to find ways to make myself a good story along the way, for with fame would, I hoped, come fortune.

I had sent wires to all the big New York City newspapers from New Haven—the *Herald*, the *Times*, and, of course, the biggest of them all, Joseph Pulitzer's *World*.

My first day in New York, I rode directly to the offices of the *World* and presented myself at the front desk. As I stood in the high vaulted lobby, I looked up to see four bronze female torchbearers adorning the space, representing literature, science, art, and invention. I imagined that when my journey was over a fifth might be added to represent equality.

Sketch from the *New York World*.

A young reporter came to the lobby from the newsroom many stories up to talk with me. To my surprise he had already done some digging into my story, for he knew my real name and that I was married with children. I was delighted to see the story in the paper the next morning with the headline WHEELING 'ROUND THE WORLD: MISS LONDONDERRY MUST EARN $5,000 BEFORE BOSTON SEES HER AGAIN. But I was less thrilled that he felt it fit to mention that "her maiden name was Annie Cohen and she is married to a man named Kapchowsky," which he misspelled. I did not want my cover blown, and it was, thankfully, one of the last times anyone dug deep enough to discover what I had hoped to conceal. I don't know how he learned I also had three children, something else I was eager not to discuss, for it would not reflect well on me and would raise all kinds of questions about my character, but I have to admit he was clever in writing about it. "It was suggested to mademoiselle that she might carry her children on a bicycle built for four," he wrote, "but she answered that she had enough troubles of her own."

I also realized that I would have to get used to nearly every reporter, all men of course, commenting on my physical appearance, often in flattering tones, but too often in unflattering ones. "The bicyclist's features are of the Slav cast, but her face is lit up by beautiful brown eyes," reported the *World*.

That first day I also called at the offices of the *Herald* and gave an interview to a reporter there. I early fell into the habit of impulsively making up bits that I thought would be noteworthy even if there was nothing to them but hot air. I told the *Herald* man that I would be riding in a few days to Washington, D.C., hoping for an audience with President Cleveland, and would then be bound for Honolulu and China.

I had no intention of wheeling to Washington—I was heading for Chicago—but it made for an interesting story! To quiet the skeptics I also avowed no doubt of my ultimate success.

"In her opinion there is no reason in the world she should not go around the world in fifteen months, support herself and bring back $5,000 besides," wrote the *Herald*. And to make sure everyone knew I was a tough cookie not to be trifled with, when asked if I was afraid of being accosted by tramps I replied, "No, but I carry a revolver to protect myself," and displayed the pistol. Bit by bit I was building the edifice of my new persona—this worldly, audacious woman on wheels.

In New York I stayed with friends, the Swids, at 208 East Broadway. You never met them, but they had moved to New York from Boston around the time your aunt Libbie was born. Now, you might think that with only fifteen months to make the circuit I would be eager to get back on the road as soon as possible, but I remained in the city for more than three weeks. I loved New York and the pulsating energy of the place.

For several days I worked on devising my new riding costume, experimenting with different combinations and deciding finally on a short skirt (well, shorter than the one I left Boston in, but one that still reached nearly to my shoe tops) and a pair of bloomers underneath so that I could, when needed, lift my skirts up out of the way of the spinning pedals and still be dressed in something other than my underwear!

I also decided to return to the offices of the *World* to see if they might provide me with a letter credentialing me as a correspondent of the paper. It took several days but I was finally able to arrange a meeting with the Sunday editor, a famous newspaperman named Morrill Goddard, one of Pulitzer's top lieutenants.

Morrill Goddard was about thirty years old in 1894. He had a full, bushy beard, dark hair parted in the middle, and sported pince-nez with a silver chain from which he could hang them around his neck when he removed them, which he often did when he spoke to you, the better to stare you straight in the eye, which he also often did. As editor of the *Sunday World* he was something of a cross between a serious newsman and a sideshow carnival barker, presiding as he did over a special section packed each week with sensational, often unbelievable stories intended not to inform but to titillate or entertain. People loved it.

To get to Goddard's office on the twelfth floor I rode, for the first time in my life, an elevator, a rarity since few buildings at the time needed them. The sensation of being whisked upward quickly in such a fashion was thrilling! As I entered Goddard's office he stood to greet me. He was brusque and businesslike but not unkind. He knew who I was from the reporting in his own newspaper. I told him a letter of credentials would greatly ease my passage in far-off parts of the world, and that in return I would, at the end of my journey, write an exclusive first-person account for him to publish in his Sunday pages, which, as you will see, I eventually did.

"I admire your confidence, Mrs. Kopchovksy," he said before I interjected.

"I am Londonderry now, Mr. Goddard."

"Yes, yes, Miss Londonderry, then," he said, a little irritated. "But I have doubts that you will ever finish the task you have set for yourself."

"Then you have nothing to lose," I proffered. "Only the cost of a sheet of stationery. But if I should succeed, you will have quite an exclusive."

"Come back tomorrow. I will have my secretary type a letter for you. It will be at the front desk. In an envelope for"—and then he leaned forward and said with emphasis and a note of sarcasm—"*Miss Lon-don-derry.*"

There was another reason I lingered so long in New York even as the wager clock was ticking. A couple of days after I arrived I started to receive letters addressed to me in care of the Swids from my brother Bennett, from Grandpa, and even one in her child's awkward hand from Mollie. Bennett and Grandpa urged me to reconsider. They thought I had taken the joke far enough already. It was folly. It was farce. It was a betrayal of my marriage and my children. Mollie's note simply said, "Please come home, Mama. I miss you."

As emotionally distant as I could be, only the hardest heart could fail to be touched by such pleas. For a few days I was torn. Surrender to the pleas of my family or steel myself and forge ahead? It would have been embarrassing to say the least, especially having made such a spectacle in Boston, and having wrangled credentials from the *World*, to give up the venture having ridden only to New York. Colonel Pope would no doubt be furious that I had embarrassed him, too, and it would surely be a source of much laughter among the chauvinists and dismay among the women seeking a more equal footing with men. As much as I was hurting the family, I simply could not imagine retreating into my old life after only a paltry effort to separate myself from it.

Still, I dithered, uncharacteristically for me, troubled by the price I was asking others to pay. What ultimately tipped the balance was a letter I received a few days later, in mid-July, from Susie. I saved it and have it still.

> Dearest Annie,
>
> I hope this letter reaches you before you depart from New York. It's taken me a few days to sort out my feelings of the past few weeks, and the early days of your absence, which have been lonely and filled with longing for your physical presence. But my heart is full knowing we belong to each other and I want you to make a big success of your adventure, to fulfill yourself, and, by and by, to send a message to the world that women should take their rightful place alongside men, not as their inferiors but as their equals. In my conversations of recent days, many of which have revolved around your extraordinary undertaking, it has become clear to me that you carry with you not just your change of underwear and your pistol (what a hoot!), but the hopes and expectations of our sex. As word of your exploits grows and spreads across the country and the world, women by the thousands will be cheering you on in the hope that you will strike a blow for the greater

cause. Go, Annie, and go as though we were riding a tandem together for I am with you, if not in body, then fully in spirit.

Love,

Susie

Whatever second thoughts had clouded my thinking were dispelled by Susie's letter. I wrote letters home to Grandpa and Bennett and enclosed in Grandpa's a short note for Mollie, on which I had made a little sketch of a woman on a bicycle. The essence was that I understood their pain, that I missed them, but that having begun, I could not turn back so easily. Perhaps there were obstacles ahead, obstacles unforeseen, that would force a premature conclusion to the effort, but for now I would press forward. I told Bennett and Grandpa that I would, as much as possible, wire them about my intended itinerary and would welcome letters or wires with news of home, but that I wished they would henceforth refrain from writing anything intended to induce me to feel guilty. I was learning in these early days that the physical demands of the journey would be one test, but that mental fortitude would be equally important. I could not allow myself to be burdened with doubt and that required that I wear a coat of armor around my emotions, never that close to the surface anyway. I would not wallow in homesickness, or second thoughts about leaving Grandpa and the children. It sounds ruthless and it was. I can't say I am proud of it, but it had to be done.

Committing myself to continue on was one thing; a relatively easy thing. The actual going, as I was about to learn, well, that was another story.

Five

My advanced planning was sadly lacking. In the weeks before I left I was focused solely on the leaving and not the actual going. I had no route of travel plotted other than a general conception that I would ride first to New York, where, I thought, I could secure more publicity, and then west. No other city within a few days' travel, indeed no city in the world, offered the opportunities for self-promotion as New York did, and as you have seen, I took advantage of that. Leaving as I did in late June, I calculated that I could, if I averaged forty miles a day across the country, reach the West Coast before winter gripped the plains and mountain west. Because the L.A.W. road book for New York included detailed directions to Chicago and the route was well traveled by cyclists, I decided Chicago would be my next destination.

I alerted the New York newspapers that I would be leaving the city on July 28 promptly at noon from the entrance to City Hall.

July had been miserably hot in New York, and July 28 turned out to be the hottest day the city had seen in thirteen years. By midday the temperature had reached ninety-five degrees and the humidity was suffocating. Yet several hundred people assembled at City Hall to see me off, still in my long blue skirt, slightly shortened, but with the bloomers underneath to allow me to lift the skirts when needed without exposing myself. Just before I left, I quietly took the revolver from my saddle kit and tucked it into the waist of my skirt.

As I glided away I heard a huge roar go up from the crowd, and without turning around to look I lifted my right hand, waved the pistol, and headed up and through Central Park. From Yonkers I went north toward West Point and encountered the largest hills I had yet experienced. Trying to propel a forty-two-pound bicycle up those hills wearing a skirt and long-sleeved blouse in the scorching heat tested both my muscles and my fortitude, and I often had to dismount and push the machine up the inclines. But what a thrill it was on the way down! With safety pins I tacked my skirts up and out of the way of the spinning pedals and careered down the hills hoping for the best. I am proud to say that while I came close to losing control several times, not once did I fall. Because of the hills, though, progress was slow, and it took me nearly a week to make my way to Albany.

Now surely you are thinking, "What an indirect route you were taking!" After all, Albany is just a hundred and fifty miles west of Boston, a distance I could have covered in a few days had I ridden there directly at the outset. Instead of reaching Albany in early August, taking nearly six weeks in the process, I could have been there in early July. With only fifteen months to make a circuit of the earth, I'd taken a whole month just going from Boston to Albany! As I said, planning was not my forte; improvising was, and I was, in every sense, making it up as I went along.

The reason the well-worn cycling route from New York to Chicago took riders north to Albany instead of across New Jersey and Pennsylvania is easy to understand when you consider the terrain. Instead of hundreds of miles of hills, the cyclist could, all across New York State, ride the Erie Canal towpaths that paralleled the canal and along which teams of horses and mules would, in those days, pull barges along the canal. Sometimes cyclists startled the animals, to the chagrin of the teamsters. But the riding was easy, it was impossible to get lost, and one could find camaraderie with other cyclists.

In the cities, such as Utica and Syracuse, I bargained a few hours of labor, making beds, folding linens, and such, for hotel lodging. But several nights I chose simply to sleep outdoors, under bridges or in barns, sometimes with permission, sometimes without.

One morning, outside of Syracuse, a farmer nearly tripped over me on his way into his barn to milk his cows. I thought he would yell and run me off, but he was so startled by the sight of a woman and a bicycle in his barn, he was rendered speechless. I apologized and explained myself and spent the first part of the morning collecting eggs from the hens and carrying milk cans in exchange for my breakfast. Remember, I was obliged not to accept any gratuity, though, as a practical matter, who would ever know? The farmer, a man named Reilly, and his wife mostly looked at me as if I had landed from outer space, but I kept up a constant banter, regaling them with tales of my adventure thus far, most of which I made up on the spot—of nearly drowning in the canal when a team of runaway mules forced me off the path, of highwaymen who robbed me of my coins near Canajoharie, and of hanging from a railway bridge with one arm, my other clutching my bike, as a freight rolled by. They stared at me with utter astonishment, but it was, for me, a way of testing out stories for future audiences, especially reporters whose thirst for the sensational never waned.

What did start to wane between Syracuse and Rochester were my spirits. Late-afternoon thunderstorms, typical in summer in western New York, often left me drenched to the bone. It was hard enough slogging mile after mile when my clothes and the path were dry; when they were both wet it was a misery. My clothes took on extra pounds and chafed against my skin, slowing my progress considerably. By the time I reached Buffalo I had been gone two months and ridden not quite five hundred miles. Simple math will tell you that I had used up more than 10 percent of my allotted time, traveled less than 5 percent of the miles required under the terms of the colonel's wager, and was not even halfway between Boston and Chicago. The prospects for my success seemed to dim by the day.

In the little town of Westfield I spotted the small office of the local newspaper, stepped inside, and spoke to a young reporter there about my venture. When he asked of my life in Boston I told him I was a student at Harvard. Why Harvard, aside from the fact that everyone knew the name Harvard?

Four months before I left Boston, a Harvard student named E. C. Pfeiffer, using the assumed name Paul Jones, left Boston on a bicycle to go around the world without so much as a change of clothes, ostensibly to settle a wager of five thousand dollars, earning money as he went. Two weeks into his effort he admitted it was all a fake; that he was just out to get some notoriety and earn a little money. The story fascinated me, especially because a credulous press had given Pfeiffer, or Jones, so much attention merely for proclaiming his intention to make the journey. Not to be snakebitten again, some of the Boston papers, reporting on my impending journey, referred to me as a "female Paul Jones," suggesting that I, too, might not be legitimate. But when that reporter asked me about my life in Boston, I thought of Jones and "Harvard" popped into my head and right out of my mouth. I often operated that way, dear. I was always impulsive.

The roads along the Lake Erie shore from Pennsylvania into Ohio were pleasant and flat, often crossing over farmland and through towns such as Ashtabula, whose streets were lined with large trees and handsome homes. But I was road weary and exhausted, and my progress was slow. By the time I had crossed Ohio and Indiana and arrived at last in Chicago on September 24, I had been on the road three months. I had vastly underestimated the rigors of the journey and vastly overestimated my physical abilities. And my arrival in Chicago just as summer turned to fall laid waste to my plan to get across the continent before winter would take hold in the plains and the mountain West.

Once eager for publicity, I realized with some consternation that several of the Chicago newspapers had learned of my arrival in the city, meaning whatever I decided to do was sure to bring some notice, and honestly, I wasn't sure if I could go on. In that case, the limelight would be nothing but an embarrassment.

The *Inter Ocean*, one of the major papers, described me as being "in prime condition" for continuing the journey, but in truth I was plain exhausted and would have been happy to never again place my rump in a bicycle saddle. I'd lost nearly twenty pounds since leaving Boston, a large amount for a small woman, and I was a mere one thousand miles from where I'd started. I had now used up 20 percent of my time to cover but 10 percent of the required miles. Being exposed as lacking the fortitude and strength to continue the journey would be humiliating to say the least. In Chicago, Annie Londonderry and I had some big decisions to make.

Six

By latching on to the debate over women's equality in my quest to make a name for myself, I had, in a sense, laid myself a trap. Though I was far from a big celebrity at this point, some of the most widely read newspapers in New York and Chicago, the two biggest cities in the country, had reported on my venture, and many smaller papers in between had run their stories, too. And the letter Susie sent me in New York was a reminder that there were stakes larger than my own personal success or failure. Failure would surely be used as a bludgeon by the forces of chauvinism to beat down the idea that a woman was in any way the equal of a man. Maybe I would fail in the larger effort, but surely I had to make a better showing than merely managing to pull myself into Chicago after three months on the road.

My first inclination, when asked about the road ahead by the reporter from the *Inter Ocean,* was to say that I would from Chicago head south to warmer climes and make my way to the Pacific coast across the Southwest. Such a route was, in fact, the only plausible alternative without risking being caught in the northern plains or western mountains in winter. Snow falls in the Rockies even in summer; by late fall and early winter, passage would be impossible, especially given the lack of anything resembling decent roads in the 1890s. Thomas Stevens, less than a decade before, had pushed his wheel up and over mountain passes, along foot trails and railroad tracks in the American West in winter, and his trip around the world had taken nearly three years. I now had but one in order to claim victory and the prize money. It seemed an impossibility. To save face I told several reporters I now had a different objective in mind—to set the speed record for a woman riding from Chicago to New York. But, really, I wasn't at all sure where I was going or when or how.

I rented a small room by the day in a boardinghouse just off Michigan Avenue near downtown. With my bicycle in the room, there was barely enough space to turn around. There was a communal bathroom down the hall. I needed a few days to decide on my next move.

Over the past two years I had read much about Chicago because of the World's Columbian Exposition that opened there in May 1893 and drew visitors and exhibitors from all corners of the globe. Photographs of the "Great White City," the exhibition halls, pavilions, and other structures built on the lakefront to house the fair, were everywhere and it must have been quite a magical sight, all whitewashed and illuminated at night. The fair closed in October of that year, and early in 1894 a terrible fire destroyed the White City. I had missed seeing it by just a few months.

For several days I simply walked the noisy, crowded streets of Chicago. They teemed with activity. People poured into the city every day on trains from all parts of the country, some seeking jobs, some on business, some just drawn by the great metropolis by the lake. It was a city with a throbbing pulse, like New York.

I found the city exhilarating, even in a way that New York was not. New York was, for all its tumult and dynamism, an establishment sort of town, a global center of finance, the arts, and industry, a place where strangers came to assimilate and were swallowed up by Gotham. By contrast, Chicago felt like a place that was still in the process of becoming, of inventing itself, with each new arrival ready to make his mark on the city rather than the other way around. If New York was the middle-aged parent, Chicago felt like a rambunctious teenager. Even the ever-present stench that wafted over the city from the stockyards just south of downtown didn't dim the effervescent mood of the place. If the Midwest was America's breadbasket, Chicago was its meat locker. It seemed that hardly a head of cattle raised on the Great Plains or the farms of the Midwest didn't find its way by rail to the Chicago stockyards to be slaughtered and packaged for sale.

As I wandered around the city I became aware of a growing conflict inside myself. I had adopted a new persona, but I had not yet *become* the new woman I aspired to be, and so as both Annie Kopchovksy and Annie Londonderry wrestled with the decision of what to do next, I was torn. Annie Kopchovsky was worn out and deflated and suffered nagging bouts of guilt about the family she'd left behind. Annie Londonderry, on the other hand, was determined not to surrender to the hardships of the moment and desperately wanted to avoid the humiliation of giving up, disappointing Colonel Pope, losing the prize money, and letting down her sex. This argument raged inside my head for days. I slept fitfully and spent my waking hours distracted by the inner voices pulling me in different directions. I'm not, as you know, someone given to belief in the supernatural, but with no reconciliation in sight, I started hoping for a sign, some fortuitous event, that might nudge me one way or the other, and it came, perhaps not surprisingly, in a bicycle shop.

About a week after my arrival in Chicago I chanced to pass a bicycle shop selling the Sterling brand, well known as a high-quality machine and widely advertised with the motto "Built Like a Watch." I went in just to have a look and to compare the Sterling models to the Columbia that had carried me from Boston. A nattily attired gentleman approached.

"Are you interested in a wheel, madam?" he asked. "All the women are riding them, you know."

"Thank you, no. I am just looking," I replied. "I have a wheel already. In fact, I have ridden it here from Boston."

I expected to be laughed at in disbelief, but to the contrary, the gentleman looked at me intently.

"You aren't Miss Londonderry, are you?" he asked.

"I am indeed."

"Well, this is a pleasure and an honor," he said, extending his hand. "I have been reading of your adventure in the *Inter Ocean*." He seemed excited to be in the presence of a celebrity. "I read you were in the city, but I never expected to meet you in person." He bowed politely.

"The pleasure is mine, Mister . . . I don't believe you have told me your name, yet you already know mine."

"Higgins," he answered, "Jeremiah Higgins, but you may call me Jerry. All my friends do, and as you are a woman of the wheel, I consider you a friend."

"And you may call me Annie," I countered. "The pleasure is mine."

"Tell me, Miss Londonderry . . . I mean Annie . . . how has your Columbia served you so far? It is a quality machine, I believe." He explained that he had read I was on a Columbia.

"It is a rugged machine and I have had no failures since leaving Boston, not even a flat tire," I answered. "Of the quality I have no complaints. But it is quite a heavy thing to be pedaling over great distances."

"Let me show you something, Miss Londonderry." Jerry simply couldn't get comfortable calling me Annie. He was a little starstruck. He led me across the showroom to behold a new arrival, a beautiful cream-colored wheel with a handsome leather saddle, wooden rims lacquered to a shine, cork handlebar grips, and chain rings that looked as though they had indeed been fabricated by a Swiss watchmaker. It was a work of art.

"Perhaps you should be wheeling around the world on this," said Jerry. "It is the lightest wheel we have ever made. Just twenty-one pounds. Probably half the weight of the beast you are riding now."

I ran my hand along the frame, admiring the simple beauty of the thing.

"Perhaps I should!" I replied. "But this is a wheel built for a man."

"So it is. But what of it? I have never understood why we expect women to ride a wheel in long skirts. It's wildly impractical, is it not?"

"I have a thousand miles behind me that says it is so," I answered.

"You are surely familiar with the divided skirt," said Jerry.

"Bloomers, you mean? Of course. But I am far too modest for such radical attire." I was wearing bloomers underneath my long skirts, but had never worn them alone as outerwear.

"Nonsense. A woman willing to take on the world by wheel cannot be modest. In bloomers you could easily ride a man's wheel. And imagine the freedom of movement it would bring!"

"It is a novel idea, but I haven't the means to purchase a new bicycle. Besides, as you have probably read, I am promoting the Columbia wheel on this journey."

While Colonel Pope surely expected I would make the journey on his brand, in fact I had no obligation under the terms of the wager to remain on a Columbia. Perhaps it was an oversight, but that was not among the conditions. The idea of riding a wheel half as light, in clothing far better suited to distance riding, had great appeal. There was little chance at this point that I would win the colonel's wager anyway, having frittered away three of the fifteen months just getting from Boston to Chicago. But any chance I had would depend on my making better time, and a lighter bicycle would be of great help.

"Miss Londonderry, I don't just sell the Sterling wheel, I have a high position with the Sterling Cycle Works," Jerry said eagerly. "I am the company treasurer. I am sure I can convince my colleagues that putting you on a Sterling would be good for business. And we could advertise with your image on our wheel and pay you something for your endorsement. Have you seen our ads featuring Miss Oakley?"

From his pocket he withdrew a thick card with a photograph of Annie Oakley, the famed marksman, or markswoman, I should say, sitting sidesaddle on a Sterling while aiming her rifle. "Annie Oakley Rides a Sterling," it read. I had not seen it before, but it was a clever way to advertise, attaching your brand to a famous personality, a lesson not lost on me. After all, I had carried the Londonderry brand on my wheel since leaving Boston.

"Think it over and come back in two days' time," Jerry said. He was very self-assured and persuasive. "I will secure the necessary permissions by then, and if you agree, we will send you off from this city on this beautiful wheel, albeit one better sized to your small frame."

"Thank you, Mr. Higgins. Jerry. I will do that." I extended my hand. "You have given me much to think about. Thank you. Until Thursday, then."

"Until Thursday, Miss Londonderry. Until Thursday."

It didn't really take much thought. The colonel would likely be furious if I switched mounts, but it would give me perhaps my only chance at winning the wager for him and the prize money for myself. And, as I said, nothing required me to make the circuit on a Columbia. I figured he would rather have me win the wager on a Sterling than lose it on a Columbia, though I might well lose it either way. And so I resolved to make the decision on my own without communicating with Alonzo. A Sterling it would be the rest of the way, however long that proved to be.

Seven

You are probably wondering what was happening at home in Boston at this point. I'd been gone three months. For my part, I wondered little. The occasional letter from Bennett or Grandpa reached me, for every so often I wired Bennett telling him where I expected to be two weeks or so hence; many letters no doubt missed me, arriving at the local post office after my presence in a given town was already a memory. The letters I did read, and I confess I reached a point where I often never opened them or tossed them away unread, were filled with familiar mundane details of daily life that were of little interest. The fact is, I was trying to shed an old skin and grow a new one, and being tethered, even faintly, to home didn't serve that purpose. This isn't to say I was completely oblivious to the burdens, emotional and physical, I imposed on those I'd left behind, and going through my boxes in recent weeks I came upon several letters I did save, though why I chose these particular ones I cannot say for sure half a century later. I suppose they struck a chord at the time. There was one exception, however. Every letter from Susie that reached me I saved.

I don't mind sharing some of the letters from home with you now, for they will help you complete the picture of the forces that shaped the life of the family into which you were born. I have numbered them so you can read them more or less in the order I received them on the road. Here I will share two. The first is from Bennett, received in Chicago while pondering how to proceed now that it was apparent that riding west was out the question. It bore the shocking news that my sister, Rosa, just sixteen, was about to marry, and I knew in my gut my leaving her had something to do with it. She was bereft, Jake was gone, and now I was gone. I am sure she hoped marriage would bring solace, though solace eluded her all her life. The second is from Susie, also received about the same time in Chicago. It is intimate, but you are now thirty years old and, I presume, wise to the world.

> September 30, 1894
>
> Dear Sister,
>
> Your occasional wires reach me, and while I am gratified to have some idea of your whereabouts, they contain little that helps me understand how and why you persist in this unorthodox quest of yours. You ask me to be sure to convey your love to the children, but by virtue of their tender years it would really pass over their heads. And I am struck that you ask no questions about their welfare other than to express the wish that they are faring well. They have, not surprisingly, grown very attached to Baila, with whom they spend most of every day. I suppose from their point of view (and would they be wrong?) Baila is their mother now. Libbie and Simon are too young, of

course, to understand this at all. Mollie is full of questions about where you are and why you have gone and when you are coming back, questions for which neither Baila nor I nor their father has anything close to a satisfactory explanation.

Caring for five young children takes a toll; Baila looks to have aged several years in three short months, and yet, as exhausted as she is, she is uncomplaining. Her love for your children is as the love for her own. I hope you can appreciate the magnitude of the burden you have placed on her. I say this not to make you feel guilty, I suspect you may be beyond that, but because you should know.

Sister Rosa has grown quite solemn since your departure. Since the deaths of Mother and Father and Jacob, she grew to depend quite deeply on you. I think this explains why she has decided to marry in a few days' time a young man named Simon Newman. She is just sixteen, still a child, but she desperately needs someone to look after her. I have counseled against it, she is too young and immature, but her mind is made up. She looks up to you and I hope you will spare a few minutes from time to time to pen letters to her. I think it would lift her spirits to hear from you.

As for Max, it is hard to tell. He has never been a man of many words, and whatever he suffers, he suffers in silence. When he retrieves the children in the evening, or after he has joined us for dinner, which he does often, he seems weary, and Baila goes upstairs with them to help with the bedtime routine while I attend to little Harry and Bessie. Having their three young cousins about every day is fun for them, but five children not yet of school age in the apartment makes for long days.

I am long past thinking anything I can say will alter your trajectory at all, but I will close by asking you to again consider the costs your adventure are imposing on your husband, your children, and on Baila and me.

Your loving brother,

Bennett

October 1, 1894

Dearest Annie,

I do hope you are well! I confess to being disappointed that I have had only one letter from you these past three months; I hope you have been receiving mine. I have written you at least twice a week since you left in June. Perhaps it is hard to find the time to write when you must be exerting all your energies on the wheel. But I also suspect that it is easier for you to exist in the new world you have entered and to inhabit whatever new persona you have adopted for the journey without too many reminders of the world you left behind. I did receive your telegram with your address in Chicago and I trust you are still there as it sounded as if you might lay over for some days.

When my eyes open in the morning—that is the hardest time of day for me for it is only when I am sleeping that I am not missing you, your company, your lively mind and crackling wit, and, not least, your touch. Ours has always been an impossible situation in so many ways; you, married, and a mother three times over. Even if you were not so engaged, we would still be hiding behind the curtains. I sometimes imagine the day when people could simply be free to be who they are, to come out of hiding and live as they were meant to live. I am well aware of the whispers that follow me wherever I go—my neighbors, the catty ladies of Beacon Hill, even my own family. Why, they ask, is she not yet married? Surely she needs a husband and at her age the opportunities are dwindling. But I don't want to live a lie. I am perfectly prepared to be a spinster. You, Annie, are the love of my life, and though I am under no illusions about the future, I am also prepared to accept all the limitations that accompany our love for each other. It is enough for me.

Please do write more often. I am missing you so.

Love,

Susie

Eight

A few days before my departure from Chicago I collected my new bicycle from Jerry Higgins at the Sterling shop, and as I no longer had any use for the Columbia, I left it with him to do as he saw fit. He said he would try to sell it and wire the proceeds to me, but I never did receive anything for it. The Sterling people, eager to capitalize on the fact that the now modestly famous Annie Londonderry would henceforth be astride a Sterling, arranged for a professional drawing to be made of me, now attired in bloomers, sitting on the wheel, a drawing that appeared in advertisements in various cycling magazines. I found a copy while looking through my scrapbooks a few days ago and am enclosing it here. Don't I look fine?

Jerry Higgins also gave me a list of Sterling dealers in the United States and France and assured me all would be notified of my journey, that I was promoting the Sterling brand, and that they should extend to me any courtesy I might require, and I did on several occasions avail myself of their hospitality as you will see.

I took a few days to acquaint myself with the Sterling. It lacked a brake, but the spoon brake on the Columbia had proved virtually useless anyway, so I would still be relying on back pressure on the pedals to slow the machine. But the most important difference, other than the fact that it was a bicycle built for a man, was its weight. As I rode through the streets and parks in Chicago I felt as though I were gliding on a slipstream. Moving half the weight I was used to, not to mention the pounds I had dropped during the journey thus far, I felt as though I could ride forever. The discouraged state I was in on my arrival in Chicago disappeared. The combination of the lighter-weight bicycle and my new attire, which gave me complete freedom of movement, contributed to my confidence. Perhaps I had declared defeat too soon when I had announced that the 'round-the-world quest was over in favor of a speed record between Chicago and New York. But there was another factor that led me to change my mind yet again and to declare that I would, after all, girdle the globe if I possibly could.

Throughout my stay in Chicago I had many women callers and met countless others during my rides through the streets and parks. It seemed all knew who I was and my purpose; they had been following the stories in the papers. It had, until now, only partially dawned on me that I was not just riding for myself, but for my sex; that my success would be theirs and my failure would be theirs, too. To a woman, they implored me not to give up the quest, no matter how unrealistic it was now that less than one year remained on the wager clock. "If it takes two years, so be it," said one. "Better you should fail in the wager but succeed in the larger purpose and prove that a woman can do what any man can do!"

At night these entreaties tumbled around in my head. A new bike, a new riding outfit, and all these "New Women" got my gumption up, and I resolved not to throw in the towel so easily. Annie Londonderry got the better of Annie Kopchovsky. I would fight on, for myself, for the prize money, for my sex, and for my pride.

The only question was whether to continue west or reverse course, ride back to New York, and from there sail for France. To go to the West Coast at this time of the year would, as I said, require that I take a long route south, perhaps to New Orleans, and then across the southwest to avoid the coming winter weather. If I made haste, I could reach New York in about two weeks' time, but that would mean the entire ride from Boston to Chicago would be for naught and that I had wasted four precious months of the fifteen stipulated in the colonel's wager. If I chose the latter route, to make a complete circuit of the earth I would now need to return to Chicago, not Boston, and do so in just eleven months. Either way, the prospect of winning the colonel's wager was slim indeed, if not impossible.

So how did I decide which way to go? Simple. I flipped a coin, and on October 14, 1894, at precisely 10 A.M., having alerted the local press, I stood with my Sterling at the Drake Fountain in front of Chicago's city hall and began retracing my steps to New York.

The send-off from Chicago was a huge lift to my spirits. Dozens of members of a local ladies' cycling club joined me for the ride down Michigan Avenue and all the way to Pullman on the city's South Side, where the pungent aroma of the city's slaughterhouses was especially strong. As the procession made its way, more and more cyclists joined the parade until we numbered in the hundreds. But by the time I reached the Indiana line, only a few riders remained, and then they, too, gave up the chase and turned back for the city.

There was an important lesson for me here. Publicity was like oxygen. People had started to pay attention, especially women. Their spirits lifted mine, and frankly, I loved being at the center of a spectacle. Were it not for the ink the newspapers gave me in Chicago I probably would have pedaled out of the city alone. I might not win the colonel's wager, and the prize money, but celebrity, and the rewards that come with it, was still within my grasp. I resolved on the way back to New York to redouble my efforts to draw the interest of the newspapermen, and that meant making as big a spectacle of myself as I could, even if I had to stretch the truth from time to time or, as you will see, invent it from whole cloth. The goal was to create a larger-than-life character, a bold and daring woman on a wheel, impervious to danger, who would overcome every obstacle in her path through sheer force of will. With the country mired in a depression, people thirsted for inspirational stories, for heroes, and I was determined to give them one. The newspapers were only too happy to oblige and were always filled with sensational stories whose truth or falsity was beside the point. It's different now, but in those days newspapers were entertainment, not just news, and the competition for the sensational and the outlandish was quite keen. I saw the chance to slake the thirst of newspapers and their readers for just that.

But there were private sensations, too. As you now know, I was very much in love with Susie and I missed her terribly. But there was no oath of fidelity between us, and after four months on the road I longed for the intimate company of a woman and found it for a few short but thrilling days in Indiana. I do hope I am not embarrassing you, dear. I wonder what you will think of your dear old grandma when you read this!

After spending the first night out of Chicago in Michigan City, I arrived in South Bend in the state of Indiana. There, an admirer, a lady cyclist who also rode a Sterling, called on me at my hotel in the city. Her name was Jessie Padman, and the attraction was immediate. She was a woman of about my age, lithe and fine featured, with long auburn hair. And, like me, married. We had much to talk about and fell into easy conversation for much of the afternoon and into the evening. Her husband, she said, was away on business to St. Louis and Memphis, and as she had no children she had no obligation to be home. By morning we resolved to ride together until we reached the outskirts of Toledo nearly one hundred and fifty miles away, a distance that would take us four days. The companionship was most welcome, as was the intimacy we shared, for on our wheels we were truly kindred spirits.

Calling on newspaper offices in every town through which we passed, we found a receptive if sometimes skeptical audience. The *Elkhart Daily Truth* called me "unusually vivacious," but the *Goshen Daily News* was skeptical of my claim to be circling the world, speculating, not without reason, that I was really scheming with Sterling to advertise its wheel.

As we crossed Indiana, the list of Sterling dealers given me by Jerry Higgins in Chicago began to pay dividends. In Ligonier the local Sterling agent, Edward Sisterhen, hosted us for dinner, and later that evening we found lodging in Kendallville with the town pharmacist and Sterling agent Paul Klinkenberg and his lovely family who reveled in the stories of my adventure thus far.

The next day, Mr. Klinkenberg arranged for an interview with the local newspaper. Given the whirlwind romance of the past few days, I could not help but be amused when the newspaperman asked me if there was any danger of my falling in love with a handsome cyclist and abandoning my venture, to which I replied, "I am too intent on gaining the distinction of being the only lady rider who has ever encircled the earth to entertain any marriage propositions!"

It would hardly be the first time I would be asked questions like these, and I bristled at the condescension implicit in them. It was as if men thought that every woman's goal in life was to find a man to serve! But I tried to be good humored about it, for I didn't want to jeopardize any opportunity I had to get my name in print. These questions also revealed something else about where we women stood in those days. It was simply unimaginable to most, male or female, that any woman, least of all a married woman, would undertake such a journey, for what husband would permit it? I may have had serious shortcomings as a mother, but it crossed my mind that maybe the day would come when the two little girls I'd left behind wouldn't be asked such questions, and if it did, it might be because of the combined weight of small acts of rebellion like mine.

Near the Ohio line, in the town of Butler, Indiana, I said goodbye to Jessie Padman. It had been an exciting whirlwind of a few days, but we both knew from the outset that ours would be but a fleeting infatuation, a little oasis of desire that would dissipate as quickly as it had appeared, like a dust devil in summer.

Though it was well into October as I crossed northern Ohio toward Cleveland, the weather was mild and, save for a few rain showers, mostly dry. I reached Cleveland on October 25 and again relied on the hospitality of the local Sterling agent, Grover Wright. With his help I arranged to make appearances and give short talks about my trip to the local clubs, where I tried out another of the moneymaking schemes I employed to support myself on the road and, hopefully, realize a little extra I could send back to Dr. Reeder by postal money order. I got in the habit of buying up little souvenir pins of places I'd been for a few cents apiece and reselling them for a quarter to people charmed by my little talks who wanted a remembrance of our meeting. But profits were small, and I knew I would need more ambitious business plans in the weeks to come.

Being joined for parts of the ride by other cyclists, either singly or in groups, also soon became part of my regular routine. There was no shortage of riders, mostly men, eager to be part of the journey and, no doubt, to spend some time with an attractive woman they assumed to be available. One such companion was a man named Thomas Bliss, a Cleveland wheelman who attended one of my evening talks in the city. We spoke afterward, and he inquired if I would welcome his company for the two hundred miles to Buffalo. He seemed affable enough, a bit shy even, and I told him I would be happy for his company. It was always safer to travel in a pair and to have help in the event of a mechanical failure or flat tire. Though many would try, Mr. Bliss not among them, with varying degrees of assertiveness, I rebuffed all their romantic advances save one, a man I would meet in California many months hence, but we will come to that. I was quite capable of handling myself in these situations, and I never feared for my safety in the company of any of the men who, eager for the distinction of having shared in Miss Londonderry's 'round-the-world adventure, passed some of the miles with me.

By now I was finding the riding—arduous and exhausting on my way *to* Chicago—pleasurable and liberating as I rode *away from* Chicago. It wasn't just the lighter weight of both my bicycle and myself. I had, willy-nilly, ridden myself into strong physical condition over those early months. I was more muscular and more capable of sustained exertion. My confidence, at a low ebb when I reached the city, now soared, and I felt as though I could, literally and figuratively, conquer the world.

Though I had earned a modest amount of attention from the newspapers since I'd left Boston, it was going to require a more determined effort on my part to turn myself into the sensation I hoped to be if I was to succeed in earning the daunting sum of five thousand dollars. I would not only have to be more systematic and regular in heralding my arrival in every town, large or small, through which I would pass, but I needed to ensure that there was drama, real or imagined, that would make irresistible copy for reporters hungry for a good scoop. The more outlandish I appeared, and the more sensational the stories I had to tell, the more ink that would be spilled about me, and I took to the challenge with gusto.

In Buffalo I used my skills as an advertising solicitor to sell space on my bicycle and my body to local businesses and turn myself into what the *Buffalo Morning Express* would call "a riding advertising agency." Just as I had earned my first one hundred dollars by carrying the Londonderry placard on the Columbia, I could earn substantially more by renting space on my person and riding through the city streets adorned with adverts for local merchants. Covered in ribbons and patches and banners of all sizes for all sorts of goods—dairy, hardware, clothing concerns, bicycle shops, you name it—everyone stared at the woman in bloomers covered head to toe in advertisements. It was not a hard sell; merchants immediately saw the potential in this novel approach.

"She wears ribbons advertising various goods and will receive $400 for one firm's ad that graces her left breast," wrote the *Morning Express*. "On her right bloomer leg she carries $100 worth of advertisements and she has just closed a contract to cover her left arm. She says her back is for rent and she hopes to get $300 for it." Thus did I spend a few days in Buffalo earning a substantial sum in a short time.

That was just part of the spectacle. The other lay in spinning tall tales, and I often surprised myself with what came out of my mouth without any forethought at all. In time, the tales would become taller and taller, but for now they began somewhat modestly when I met with the man from the *Morning Express* in his cramped office.

Photo from the *Buffalo Morning Express*.

"I arrived in Ashtabula dead broke," I told him, "and had to spend the night sleeping in a cemetery." I also told him I had completed three years of study at Harvard Medical School and would finish my degree when I returned to Boston, though I knew, and one could have easily checked, that admission to Harvard Medical School was not permitted for women and would not be for decades yet to come. I claimed to be of German descent and to speak German and Swedish, though this was nonsense. When asked about the dangers of the road, I drew my revolver from the pocket of my bloomers and waved it in the air. Newspapermen can be so easily gulled, and I would exploit their credulity often. Perhaps you will think your dear grandmother to be a liar, but I prefer to think of myself as the writer of a play in which I was the star, a production that would unfold in stages, and often *on* stages, across many continents!

It was in Buffalo that I really felt I had ceased to be Annie Kopchovsky, the Boston housewife and mother, and emerged as if from a chrysalis as the daring heroine of the wheel, the globe-trotter Annie Londonderry. I had shed one skin and put on another, and I was intoxicated by the freedom of it all. And that, I think, is why I now felt no qualms about inventing a new, ever-changing history about myself, one limited only by the bounds of my imagination, to go along with my new persona.

Thus liberated, I began speaking in ever more dramatic terms about myself and my journey, seeking as I went to top myself, to see how far I could go in testing the gullibility of people and the press.

I persuaded a man from another Buffalo newspaper that mine was "one of the most perilous and remarkable trips ever undertaken by a woman," as he put it down. When asked if I wasn't "taking a big risk in traversing portions of savage lands," I laid it on thick. "Well, $10,000 is a large amount, and I know that I am taking a big risk, and may never again see my native land, but the grim shadow of death is ever at one's elbow." Oh, it makes me smile even now to think what cheek I had in those days.

In Buffalo I made yet another modification to my riding costume, one of many in the evolution of my attire, which had me wearing long skirts at the outset and by the end a man's riding suit. (Did that ever cause a stir, as you will see!) Bloomers had been a big improvement, but their billowy legs often caught the wind, so I purchased a pair of trim pants, cut several inches off the legs and secured the bottoms, knickerbocker style, with elastics. I wore black stockings below, and a tweed coat, vest, and blue yachting cap, all purchased in Buffalo. The outfit was rather outlandish—I was dressed as a man—but that was the whole point!

My lodgings in Buffalo were provided by the Ramblers Bicycle Club; there were now wheel clubs in almost every city and town of any size in America, and some, such as the Ramblers, were large enough, and flush enough, to have their own clubhouse with meeting rooms and even accommodations for cyclists passing through. I attended their Halloween ball on a rainy night, hoping for better weather the next day when I was to say farewell to Mr. Bliss and leave for Rochester.

The skies did clear overnight, and as I rode east out of Buffalo the temperatures were in the mid-fifties, quite comfortable for cycling, but the previous day's rains had made a muddy mess of the unpaved roadways outside the city. As incredible as it may seem, when roads were impassable, cyclists often sought out railroad beds for riding as they were typically elevated a few feet above grade so the rainwater would run off. Such riding was hard on the wheel and bone-shaking as you had to move the wheel over the endless stretches of railroad ties, but at least it was passable. The two-day slog to Rochester was an ordeal and, even on the railroad beds, a messy affair.

I was splattered with mud when I arrived in Rochester, my new, manly riding outfit still adorned with the advertisements I had collected in Buffalo. I was quite a sight, which is why I went directly to the offices of the *Post Express* before finding a place where I could wash and clean my clothes. I wanted to present myself in all my glory.

When asked there about my unconventional appearance, I replied, "I am going around the world and with that object in view cannot afford to let conventionalities impede my progress. I have grown accustomed to this costume and do not mind the stares of people." Indeed, the stares of people were exactly what I wanted. Asked what I expected to do when the trip was over I answered, "Why, I'll marry some good man and settle down in life." Fortunately, Grandpa didn't read the papers from Rochester!

At receptions for me hosted by the Century Cycling Club and the Lake View Wheelman's Club, an escort was arranged for the ninety-mile ride to Syracuse. On the morning of the fourth of November, three gentlemen riders and I departed with the ambitious goal of making the trip in one day, which would mean covering about twice the distance I normally rode. But the weather had turned cold and windy, and we fell fifteen miles short of our goal, spending the night in the small town of Jordan. It was about nine thirty the next morning when we arrived at the Globe Hotel in Syracuse.

Thanks to my telegrams, the newspapers had been writing of my impending arrival for several days. My efforts to ramp up the press I was getting were beginning to bear fruit.

I reached Utica a couple of days later where the *Sunday Journal* announced the arrival of "a dead broke girl," a reference to H. H. "Dead Broke" Wylie, who the year before had set the record for cycling from Chicago to New York (on a Sterling), a distance he covered in just over ten days. As he traveled without money on what was popularly known as the "dead broke plan," he was bestowed with his unusual nickname.

By now I was being portrayed as a representative of my sex, something I welcomed wholeheartedly for it would do nothing but add to public interest in my endeavor, as wherever one stood on the question of women's equality, pro or con, my success or failure would provide ammunition for the debate. The *Sunday Journal* put it this way:

> The latest phase of women's development and women's enterprise along a unique line struck this city at 3:45 P.M. yesterday in the form of a charming and striking young lady attired in men's bicycling costume and "treading" a twenty-pound Sterling wheel in gallant style in very ungallant weather. Miss Annie Londonderry is the name of the daring young woman who is undertaking a bicycle trip around the world. She believes she can do it, and with the grit and enterprise of modern femininity has determined to do it, or die in the attempt.
>
> (*Utica Sunday Journal*, November 11, 1894)

I was glad for their choice of words—"grit and enterprise"—for I was growing weary of being referred to, as most papers did, as "plucky," a word that was only applied to a woman in an effort to feminize traits otherwise seen as masculine. "Plucky" seemed to soften the edges of a bold and brazen woman somehow.

Keeping up with my determination to make as big a sensation of myself as possible, in Utica I had some new stories to tell, including one of a tramp who tossed a railroad tie on the tracks that upended my bicycle and dumped me into ashes piled along the railroad bed. Such white lies were never challenged; I found more resistance in my bicycle pedals than in the minds of eager newspapermen, though later in the trip that started to change. But for now my ability to project myself with great confidence and to spin entertaining if fanciful tales were enough to distract from careful scrutiny of the details of my travels.

As the weather had been wet and cold for several days, with some of the money I had earned I allowed myself the luxury of taking the train to Albany on the evening of the eleventh of November. I had a little less than two weeks to reach New York, where I had booked passage to Le Havre aboard the French liner *La Touraine* on the 24th, ample time to cover the modest mileage from Albany to New York City.

In Albany it crossed my mind to send a telegram to Grandpa and to arrange for him to bring the children for a reunion in New York. But it was a fleeting impulse. I had, mile by mile, day by day, morphed into a new woman, growing into my new persona, and finding new resolve to make a success of the entire venture. I was concerned that a brief reunion might only be confusing for the children and open new wounds. But I was equally concerned that such a reunion might weaken my resolve, tug at me to return home where nearly everyone thought I belonged, and puncture the inflated character I had become. To succeed, to overcome the challenges that lay ahead, especially in far-off lands, I could no longer in any measure be Annie Kopchovksy, Boston housewife and mother; I had to fully inhabit the character of Annie Londonderry, the daring, indefatigable globe-trotter with a pistol in her pocket and quicksilver in her shoes. There was no room to be both; Annie Kopchovsky had to be put aside.

Nine

What a glorious sight she was. *La Touraine* was more than five hundred feet long, handsome, and imposing. She could carry more than a thousand passengers and had a staff of expertly trained French chefs who worked in a world-class kitchen. The French Line boasted that she was "a piece of France itself." The crossing to the north coast of France would take but nine days.

The date was now November 24, 1894. I had arrived in the city a few days before and again stayed with the Swids, and it was they who came to the docks along the Hudson River to see me off that morning.

As I rolled the Sterling up the gangplank I was exhilarated about beginning this new stage of the journey. When I had last passed through New York Harbor by boat, I was just a little girl of five, arriving in this strange new land with my parents and my brother and sister. I recall only the long lines at Ellis Island as we were processed by the immigration authorities, and little else. In the years since, the Statue of Liberty had taken her place at the entrance to the harbor, and she was a majestic thing to see as *La Touraine* slipped through the Verrazano Narrows and out into the Atlantic.

I have never been, especially as a younger woman, given to sentimentality. You know that. But as we passed the great statue I couldn't help but feel a surge of pride and gratitude for the country that had been our home for the past not-quite-twenty years. We were not rich by any means, not materially, but our opportunities, if we cared to seize them, were virtually limitless. I was living proof of that.

Though it was now late November, the air was unseasonably mild as I stood at the ship's railing breathing in the salt air. I knew not what lay ahead, but my spirits were high. As Manhattan slipped over the horizon, it was time to start putting into action the plan for the Atlantic crossing I had conjured in the two weeks before sailing. For the next nine days I would have a captive audience of a thousand passengers, many of them people of means and distinction from all corners of the globe, and hundreds of crew, and I was determined to leave an impression on every last one of them. When they disembarked in Le Havre, whether they were on the Grand Tour, returning home to wherever they came from, or on a brief holiday from the States, they would know of Annie Londonderry, the cheeky woman going 'round the world on a wheel. Rarely would I have in one place an audience of this size who would spread word of my mission to friends and family and business associates, thus amplifying my fame, my press, and my means of making money as I went, for word of mouth, as anyone in the advertising business knows, is the most effective publicity of all. And while on board, people would be hungry for diversion and entertainment. In the middle of the ocean there is little to pass the time but books, meals, games, conversation, and gazing at the vast horizon.

Getting attention could not have been easier, dressed as I was in a man's riding attire and coasting slowly along the ship's massive decks on a handsome cream-and-gold-colored Sterling. From my first little spin around *La Touraine*'s top deck to the last—and I made probably hundreds of such circuits—people gathered in twos and threes and then by the tens and twenties to admire my wheel, gawk at my costume, and question me about my purpose and my background. About the former I was direct; about the latter I had great fun. I was, again, a student of medicine at Harvard, where I earned extra money dissecting cadavers, having left my job as a stenographer, where I invented a new form of stenography. I had been orphaned at a young age but was left a large fortune that allowed me to pursue whatever whims and adventures struck my fancy. I was the cousin of a United States congressman and the niece of a United States senator. Each of these I stated with such conviction that not once was I challenged by anyone about any of it!

The ship's captain, Captain Frangeul, quickly learned that he had a celebrity on board and invited me on several occasions to take my dinner at his table in the ship's ornate dining room. By the way, you will be interested to know that nearly two decades later, on April 12, 1912, *La Touraine* was in contact with the *Titanic* and messaged the doomed ship about the presence of icebergs in the shipping lanes of the North Atlantic. The crew of the *Titanic* messaged back its thanks. Less than forty-eight hours later the *Titanic* hit an iceberg on its maiden voyage and sank, with terrible loss of life.

It was clear that Captain Frangeul was smitten with me and charmed by my effortless and animated conversation, but he was a very proper gentleman and limited himself to compliments that, delivered in his heavily French-accented English, drifted around me like softly falling snow. So taken with me and by my story, the captain proposed that I give a series of lectures during the passage about my journey thus far from Boston to Chicago and back to New York and my intended route once we reached Le Havre. To this, of course, I readily agreed, for it was an opportunity to be sure no one left that ship without knowing who I was. Eager for diversion, hundreds of passengers showed up at a time in the dining room, whose seats had been rearranged theater-style to listen to me hold forth on the perilous journey thus far, one filled with near-death escapes, mean-spirited tramps, and violent weather. I had refined a story about crossing a railway bridge in New York State in which I found myself face-to-face with an oncoming train and insufficient time to turn and outrun it. Facing certain death, I had no choice but to dismount, take the wheel in one hand, and dangle from the edge of the bridge by the other as the train, just inches away, sped across the trestle. To fend off tramps and highwaymen I often had to fire my pistol, surprising them with the accuracy of my warning shots that whizzed just inches from their heads. Dodging mighty bolts of lightning as if thrown by Zeus from the heavens also featured prominently in my stories. Whether people took every word literally was irrelevant; what mattered was the entertainment and leaving an unforgettable impression.

There was no shortage of important personages aboard who, courtesy of the captain, were given front-row seats to these improvised lectures during which I would perform small tricks on the wheel in an area that had been cleared of seats, tricks that I had practiced, such as coasting on the machine backward or balancing astride the wheel without moving, tricks that delighted everyone. Among the dignitaries was Dr. Chancellor, the U.S. consul at Le Havre, whose signature, coincidentally, was one of those I was required to collect to prove my passage around the world. Also aboard were the Baron and Baroness de Sellieres of Burgundy, the Prince and Princess Ruspoli di Poggio Suasa of Italy, and an attractive middle-aged couple, Mr. and Mrs. Potter Palmer, socialites from Chicago who told me they had read of my visit to their city a few weeks before.

On the last night of the transatlantic crossing I left my quarters well belowdecks where those of the lower classes could afford passage and went up to stroll along the main deck. It was a cold night, but clear, and it seemed a billion stars twinkled above the inky black ocean. I had two blankets from my bed wrapped around me for warmth. As it was frigid, I didn't expect to find anyone else outside in the freezing air, especially not at such a late hour, for it was approaching midnight. But near the bow I saw a lone figure staring out across the water. I couldn't tell in the darkness—only the lights from bridge dimly lit the scene—if it was a man or a woman, but in any event I decided to pass quietly behind them so as not to disturb what seemed to be a deep contemplation. As I walked past as discreetly as I could, a woman's voice, a refined, tempered voice, broke the silence.

"Miss Londonderry, is that you?"

I turned and recognized the face beneath the scarf as that of Mrs. Palmer, whom I had met several times over the past week in the ship's dining room, once taking dinner with her and her husband at the captain's table.

"It is, Mrs. Palmer. It is. And why are you out here on this frigid night? Are you unable to sleep?"

"I'm just thinking, Miss Londonderry, just thinking. By the way, you have made quite an impression on everyone aboard this ship in the past week, and certainly a profound one on me."

"How so, Mrs. Palmer?" She was a handsome woman of about forty, tall, with a fine, feminine figure, and sharp but elegant features. Her clothes were of the finest quality. Everything about her spoke of great wealth; she and her husband had procured a two-bedroom suite for the passage, no doubt at a princely sum.

"What do you see when you look at me, Miss Londonderry?" Her tone suggested this was a rhetorical question, so I did not answer. She did not mince words and came quickly to her point.

"You probably see a woman who appears to have everything, and indeed, there is hardly a thing in the world, not a luxury or a bauble, that I could not purchase. Mr. Palmer and I spend more than half of every year traveling the world like this and we spare no expense. We have a beautiful home on the lakefront in Chicago with a full-time staff of six, including a French-trained chef. Mr. Palmer sees to it that I want for nothing, and yet I want for everything."

"But it seems," I ventured, "that you do have everything, Mrs. Palmer." She looked down at her shoes, then lifted her head and fixed her gaze on me.

"Listening to you these past few days, it has occurred to me that I have virtually nothing of real value, Miss Londonderry. Oh yes, I have many things, too many things, but those that I lack cannot be purchased. Our life is filled with elegant parties. The people we socialize with are men of industry and great means and their dutiful and glamorous wives, worn much as man puts on his shoes and his vest. Conversation is predictable and dull, the social calendar repetitive, and the roles we all play well understood and adhered to as if a religion. My every word is spoken as if written by a playwright and my every move made as if determined by a director. And marriage?

It is like a precisely choreographed minuet right down to the passionless sex."

Realizing that she had let slip words unintended, Mrs. Palmer suddenly looked mortified, shocked that the words had even passed her lips. I looked at her, uncharacteristically without words of my own for a moment. It seemed an eternity, but it was probably just a few seconds before she regained her composure.

"Oh my, Miss Londonderry, please do forgive me. I should never have said such things or put you in such an awkward position. I am terribly sorry for being so indiscreet."

"It is quite all right, Mrs. Palmer," I said. "Sometimes we can only keep our feelings bottled up for so long. I suppose that is why I am sailing on this ship with a bicycle." But I said no more. Mrs. Palmer knew nothing of my real story, of Grandpa and the children and the endless toil of my life back in Boston, only the yarns I had been spinning into a quilt all week.

Mrs. Palmer allowed a small smile and nodded.

"You see, Miss Londonderry, as I have watched and listened to you these past several days, I have wished to *be* you. You are free as a bird it seems. Your life is an adventure and an unscripted one at that. I am terribly envious. I would like nothing more than to trade these clothes for a riding costume and this ocean liner for a bicycle and join you and leave my world behind for the one you are about to discover."

It was clear that she was not seriously proposing this but just expressing a flight of fancy (in two senses of the phrase), so I did not feel the need to tell her I preferred to go alone.

"Miss Londonderry, would you do me a great kindness? Please, as you go, write me a letter from time to time. I will give you our address in Chicago. It would mean the world to me to have some personal word from you, to sustain in a small way this connection we have made this week. I shall be looking for news of your adventure in the press but would be so grateful for your letters. Would you do that?"

I knew I would not, and Mrs. Palmer would not be the last to make such a request or feel a strong kinship with me that was unrequited, but I assured her I would. I took Mrs. Palmer's attachment to me as a good sign that my venture was speaking to some great, unmet need of women in the civilized world. I was about to ride away from Mrs. Palmer forever, but for now, I was a salve for her needs and yearnings and disappointments.

Mrs. Palmer took my hands in hers and thanked me profusely, then said Mr. Palmer would be getting worried as she'd been out on the deck for longer than she'd expected.

"I will see you in the morning, then, Miss Londonderry, before we reach port, so I can say goodbye."

"Yes, Mrs. Palmer," I replied. "Until the morning."

She turned and walked back, one gloved hand gliding along the railing, toward a gilded life from which she felt there was no escape. It was hard not to feel sorry for her, a woman who had everything but what mattered most.

Ten

I never did see Mrs. Palmer the next morning. In all the commotion, as the hordes prepared to disembark in Le Havre, our paths did not cross and she never did pass me a slip of paper with her address on it. Just as well.

Captain Franguel had sent word to my cabin early that morning that he wanted me to have the honor of being the first to disembark. In a brief note he expressed his gratitude for my having made the crossing one of the most lively of his tenure as a captain with the French Line. I was happy to be so honored, for it would help make my arrival in France a moment for all who witnessed it to remember.

As I wheeled my Sterling through the throngs assembled on the deck to the top of the gangplank, the captain, in his dress whites, awaited me. Only those close to the scene could hear his remarks, but up and down the deck people jostled to get a good view as he shook my hand. In his deep baritone he declared that on behalf of all who had had the pleasure of meeting me on the voyage I should go in good health and create good will among all the peoples of the earth I would encounter in the months ahead. He signaled to the bridge, and the ship's horns let out a deafening sound. Then I turned and waved in every direction, one hand on the Sterling, and made my way onto French soil as the crowd roared its approval.

The captain had seen to it that one of the ship's crew would be waiting with my steamer trunk on a dolly and would escort me through customs.

It was the third day of December, and I took a minute to think of your aunt Mollie, for it was her sixth birthday. I was sure Baila and Bennett would make it as happy a day for her as they could, but I briefly felt a pang of guilt that I was not there on what is, for a child, the most important day of the year. But there was little time to linger on the thought as I was immediately caught up in a dispute with the customs men.

Though I often claimed to be fluent in French (and several other languages I did not know!) when I was not *in* France, in truth I knew but how to say "thank you" and a few other phrases I had collected during the voyage. To cover for my ignorance of the French language, I often said that the terms of my wager prohibited me from speaking French. Thus was the encounter at customs a tangled, confusing affair that even the French-speaking crew member assisting me with my trunk was unable to untangle. Apparently, unable to immediately ascertain the value of my Sterling for the purpose of calculating the import duty, the customs men insisted that it be impounded until such time as the value was determined and the duty paid. The spirited argument between the customs agents and the poor man assigned to assist me involved much gesticulating and raised voices and crosstalk, all to no avail.

As the argument progressed I looked at the crowd now flooding the customs area and searched for Dr. Chancellor, the U.S. consul in Le Havre. Luckily, he passed right by me and did his best to intervene, but again, it was no use. He gave me instructions on how to reach him from Paris and assured me he would see to it that the duty, once figured, was paid and the bicycle safely packaged for shipment to Paris. This was very reassuring. And I asked him, for I had been remiss on board, to sign his name in a little notebook I carried to prove, as I was required to do, that I had indeed passed through Le Havre.

With the battle over the Sterling lost for the moment, I thanked my helper for trying: "Merci! Merci!" We secured a receipt for the bicycle and assurances that once the value was ascertained and the duty paid the bicycle would be released to Dr. Chancellor for shipment to the bicycle shop of Mr. and Mrs. Victor Sloan, the Sterling agent with whom I had made arrangements to stay while in Paris.

La Havre was a bustling port city with great ocean liners coming and going nearly every day. The train station was not far, and there I purchased a ticket to Paris and sent a telegram to the Sloans telling them I would be arriving at the central train station early that evening with my steamer trunk, but not my wheel, in tow.

On the train I dozed off and on, tired but excited to have this new leg of the journey, the first outside of the United States, under way. But most of my excitement was focused on Paris, one of the world's greatest and most glamorous capitals. I could not wait to see Eiffel's tower, built just six years before, but already famous as the city's most recognizable structure.

The Sloans were waiting at the platform holding a sign that read BIENVENUE MLLE. LONDONDERRY! so that I would recognize them immediately. They were an ordinary-looking couple of middle age, he (Victor) rather tall and thin with a moustache like my brother Bennett's; she (Catherine) a bit stout, but with a warm smile and a twinkle in her eyes. They spoke some English but were not nearly fluent, and of course, I spoke hardly a word of French. But they seemed excited to see me and to serve as my hosts for what would turn into a stay of more than three weeks, in part because the Sterling didn't arrive until two days before Christmas and in part because Paris was positively intoxicating.

Sometimes alone, sometimes with Catherine, I walked for hours on end, sipping coffee in any number of magnificent cafés alive with conversation that I strained to decipher, Catherine serving patiently as my French tutor so that I might leave Paris with a few more phrases in my French arsenal.

Paris was quite unlike New York and Chicago. Where the energy of those American cities was raw, rambunctious, and brittle, both cities of hard edges, Paris was infused with a different kind of energy, a refined intellectual and understated energy. Life seemed more graceful, more contemplative, more sophisticated. Elegant would be the one word, above all, to describe the City of Lights. This was the Paris of Camille Pissarro, Louis Pasteur, a young Marcel Proust, and Henri de Toulouse-Lautrec, who could be found most nights where I once caught a glimpse of his eminence, at Le Moulin Rouge, the world's most famous cabaret, making sketches of the poets and painters, professors and writers who gathered there to smoke, dance, carouse, and debate the great political and philosophical issues of the day. During the day these conversations shifted to the city's countless cafés, or the homes of its leading lights, a phenomenon that came to be known as "the salon." Sophisticated and cosmopolitan, two million Frenchmen called Paris home.

By the mid-1890s, Paris had been a magnet for decades for countless Americans drawn by its culture, intellectualism, and charm. The famed sculptor Augustus Saint-Gaudens, painters such as the great John Singer Sargent and Mary Cassatt, and writers of renown such as Harriet Beecher Stowe, author of *Uncle Tom's Cabin*; James Fenimore Cooper, who wrote *The Last of the Mohicans*, spent years in Paris, as did Samuel F. B. Morse, the painter and inventor of an electric telegraph and the Morse code. All found either inspiration or consolation in Paris. Saint-Gaudens was especially renowned for his many statues commemorating the American Civil War, the most famous of which now adorns Boston Common across from the statehouse: a bronze bas-relief that honors the 54th Massachusetts Volunteer Infantry Regiment, which, on its way south to join the fighting in 1863, marched down the exact stretch of Beacon Street on which I began my bicycle journey more than thirty years later. The statue took its place on Beacon Street in May 1897, the first public monument in the United States to honor the courage of Negro soldiers.

But Paris, too, had its hard edges. It was in Paris that my decision to call myself Londonderry seemed prescient, for anti-Semitism was spreading like a virus through Parisian intellectual life. The notion that Jews had certain hereditary flaws that rendered them incompatible with other ethnic groups started to take hold among French intellectuals in the 1880s and by the 1890s was widely embraced and often openly expressed. Though many Parisians were well-to-do, poverty afflicted many others. Anarchists, too, were shaping Parisian life in the 1890s; less than a year before my arrival an anarchist named Émile Henry detonated a bomb at the café next to the Gare Saint-Lazare that killed one person and wounded dozens more. Life in Paris was gay, enlightened, and lively, but not without its dark side.

As Catherine and I walked the city, in her broken English she told me some of her life story, and I found her to be kind and interesting, if a bit needy. A provincial girl, she had come to Paris in her early twenties, drawn by the poets, writers, painters, and other artists who congregated in the city. She soon met Victor, a mechanical engineer by training, and a few years older than she. As the bicycle took hold of the French imagination in the 1880s, the mechanically inclined Victor opened a small bicycle shop selling and repairing various French wheels and, just a year before I arrived, began importing the Sterling, which was quickly acquiring an international reputation for its superb engineering. Catherine was now thirty-five years of age, Victor close to forty, and the great sadness of their life was their inability to have children.

I have to confess to you, dear Mary, that both Victor and Catherine grew quite attached to me during our three weeks together. It would not be an exaggeration to say both, each in their own way, fell in love with me. I would receive many letters from them en route after leaving Paris and even when I returned home, plaintive letters written in Catherine's hand but most written from both of them, pleading with me to respond, which, I am somewhat ashamed to say, I did only once. They dreamed of me, they said, they were desperate to hear from me, to know if I had returned home safely to Boston, to have me return to Paris.

In one letter Catherine wrote of hard times. Victor was trying to make his own brand of bicycle and apparently invested much of his capital in the effort to little avail. In my one letter to them, written in October 1895, about a month after I had returned home, I explained my lack of communication with a white lie: that I had never received their earlier posts. I had, in fact, received several letters from them sent to American consulates along my route, but I was indisposed to respond as I found them cloying.

Not long after receiving my letter Catherine replied, but her letter was mostly a litany of burdensome bad news that arrived as I was coping with my return to family problems of my own. My sister, Rosa, in ill health in New Jersey, was pleading constantly with me for money and making unreasonable demands for my presence, all as I was trying, with considerable difficulty, to reenter domestic life with Grandpa and the children.

"You can't believe that since two weeks ago, I was every night dreaming of you," Catherine wrote that fall, "that you were coming to Paris and my husband who says he never dreams, did, too, about two or three times this week. We hope you will come again soon, how happy we would be all together, you would interest us so much."

The closer Catherine tried to draw near, the more repelled I was, but it was her hinting that they needed some financial help that convinced me I had no interest in sustaining the relationship, not in Paris and not via the mail. Catherine wrote that since I had left Paris less than a year earlier, they'd had to surrender their flat and move into "a little room" near the bicycle shop.

"We are so happy together," she added, "but we have much trouble in the business due to that cursed money." She also mentioned that they were still unable to have a child and were "sorry about it," but there was little I could do or say that would have been of help. The letter was signed "yours forever, C. Sloan."

As much as the Sloans, especially Catherine, had shared with me in Paris, how little I shared with them you can imagine, for her letters to me were addressed to "Miss Annie Londonderry." They never so much as learned my real identity, because I never revealed it. They never learned I was married or that, unlike them, had, by the age of twenty-three, three children of my own. Though they gave me no reason to believe they were anti-Semitic, I don't know how they might have reacted had I shared my real name with them. My circumspection was not so much a matter of deception but of necessity. Especially now that I was on foreign soil, I was completely immersed in my new identity; the farther from home I got in time and distance, the more thoroughly I had become a new woman whose past I could invent as easily as my future. My joy in this new skin was *delicious*, and I steered clear of conversation that would puncture the illusion of the gay, liberated, globe-girdling wheelwoman, Mlle. Londonderry.

I made sure, of course, that the Paris newspapers learned of my presence in the city. Paris was the bicycle capital of Europe. Cycling was a bona fide craze and an intense passion for almost all Parisians. One Paris writer, noting the popularity of the bicycle among all classes, wrote, "No class of the community is free from the passion, the workers as well as the butterflies." How I loved that turn of phrase: "as well as the butterflies"; it so perfectly described the socialites for whom the bicycle was little more than a status symbol.

It was without difficulty, therefore, that I was able to arrange for the scribes of Paris to spill considerable ink about me and my venture. I believed that all press is good press when your aim is notoriety, so it didn't bother me to have the French reporters describe my physical appearance quite differently than I was accustomed to in America, where I was repeatedly flattered as being good-looking or attractive or as a worthy representative of the fairer sex. But a dour and pompous correspondent for *Le Figaro* took it a bit far. After referring to France's "fragile and delicious maidens," he wrote:

> Truth be told, Miss Londonderry is not of their race, not even their sex. She belongs to that category of neutered beings, single women without a husband or children. Such women resemble neutered worker bees whose superiority of labor is the result of infertility. And the suppression of love and maternal function so profoundly alters in them any feminine personality that they are neither men nor women and they really constitute a third sex. Miss Londonderry belongs to this third sex. It is enough to see her masculine traits, her muscled physique, her athlete's legs, her hands which appear strong enough to box vigorously, and everything masculine which emanates from her energetic being.
>
> (*Le Figaro*, December 7, 1894)

What a hoot! I have to admit, though, he wasn't far off when it came to "maternal instinct." I had, of course, become more muscular riding from Boston to Chicago and thence to New York, but, truly, I had a good laugh when Catherine, with the help of one of her friends whose English was more fluent, read this article to me from the newspaper. Catherine, though, was mortified.

In interviews I repeated many of the stories about my history that I had conjured from whole cloth aboard *La Touraine*; you just would not believe how gullible were the newspapermen who sat on the edges of their seats, giving me their rapt attention as I spun gold from dross. One wrote, "Her adventures? We would need an entire book to describe them. Attacked by a tramp in New York whom she shot and nearly killed next to a railroad track where she had fallen off her bicycle onto the rails at the moment a train was coming with phenomenal speed. It was truly a miracle that she escaped death and saved her bicycle." Ha! To this day I remember sitting knee to knee on two chairs in Victor's cramped showroom where this handsome young reporter had called on me, his piercing blue eyes innocent and wide, his attention rapt as I let my imagination run wild.

Illustration from *Le Figaro*. Those are advertisements pinned to my pant legs.

Having received considerable attention in the newspapers in the week or so after my arrival, I found it relatively easy to collect adverts from local merchants in the neighborhood where the Sloans lived, much as I had started doing in earnest in Buffalo, in the form of banners and patches of fabric I could pin to my riding costume.

Though the Sterling had yet to arrive from Le Havre, I borrowed one from Victor's bicycle shop, a model not unlike my own. When Catherine and I were not walking the streets of the city, or I was not out walking alone, I would spin my way through the city and became quite the rage as an advertising medium. Nothing breeds success like success, and I soon found I had more offers for this novel brand of advertising than I could accommodate, for within a week's time there was nary an inch still available for rent; I was covered from head to toe with adverts for everything from dress shops to apothecaries to restaurants. To repay Victor for the loan of a bicycle and for my lodging (remember, I was to accept nothing gratuitously), I placed on my back a large advert for his bicycle shop and rebuffed offers from his competitors, which, in a city as bicycle-crazy as Paris, were many.

As luck would have it, my stay in Paris coincided with the magnificent Salon du Cycle, one of the largest bicycle exhibitions in the world. Bicycle makers from all over Europe and America, including Sterling, came to show off their wares, and I was engaged at the handsome sum of fifteen dollars American a day for three days to appear in my riding costume and talk with visitors about the virtues of the Sterling wheel. It was also arranged there for me to deliver a lecture, in English, of course, because the only other language I had any practice in was Yiddish, and I drew a large crowd of curious onlookers, dressed as I was in my pantaloons and men's riding jacket still covered with adverts.

I don't know how many who came to catch a glimpse of the woman billed as "Mlle. Londonderry, Globe-Girdling Girl Extraordinaire" spoke English, but it didn't seem to matter. Every few minutes I would shout, "*Vive la France!*" and the crowd would go wild! In a phrase that could be a motto for my entire modus operandi, I told Victor and Catherine when I returned to their flat that night, "I found out what they liked and gave them plenty of it!" I was discovering that I was, among other things, a show-woman at heart, and this trip had become the movable stage on which I produced the greatest show of my life.

As I said, the Sterling, *my Sterling*, arrived in Paris from Le Havre two days before Christmas, a welcome holiday present, for I had grown quite fond of my own wheel during the miles from Chicago to New York. I could have continued on a substitute if necessary, but a woman and her wheel that have traveled together through rain and wind and cold form a bond. My Sterling now felt as much a part of me as my left arm or right leg.

I set my departure date from Paris as December 30. The Sloans and I spent a quiet Christmas together. Aware that I could carry little with me, the Sloans gave me a gift of a jeweled pin I could fix to my lapel; I had a local artist make a fine sketch of me in my riding attire, which I signed and gave to them as a memento of our time together.

After Christmas I called on the American consulate in Paris for I needed the signature of the consul there, or some other official, to prove I had reached Paris. There I received a surprise gift from the consul general, a New Yorker with an Irish brogue named O'Rourke: an American flag of fine silk on a staff about two feet long.

"Display it prominently, Miss Londonderry," he said. "It will protect you wherever you go."

I thanked him, quipped that I would rather have expected to encounter him in Dublin than Paris, and assured him I would take his advice, and I did. I immediately realized how traveling with the Stars and Stripes affixed to my wheel would heighten the spectacle.

That evening, with Victor's help, we affixed a small mount that would allow me to fly the flag from my handlebars when desirable, though I would most of the time keep it tied tight to the top tube with twine.

Before sailing for France from New York I had dispatched several telegrams back to Boston: one to Alonzo Peck, who, though I was no longer riding the Columbia wheel, I felt obliged to keep apprised of my progress, for the colonel still had a vested interest in my success or failure; one to my brother Bennett; and another to Susie. I apprised each that should they wish to reach me by post or telegram in Paris, I would be at the Sloans and provided the address. Three days after Christmas the postman delivered a small packet of letters postmarked in Boston a few weeks earlier.

Alonzo wrote a brief note of congratulations for my having reached France, assured me that switching my mount from the Columbia to the Sterling had done nothing to diminish his admiration for me or his fervent hope that I would succeed in my venture. He said nothing about the colonel, though, and I wondered if I had burned an important bridge with my switch to the Sterling.

From Bennett I received the usual news of the children's activities, that all, along with his own children, had suffered with a cold that exhausted Baila and him around Thanksgiving, but that all was well now. The letter was, happily, free of any recriminations about my absence, a welcome sign that he was done trying to persuade me to cut the journey short and return home. My persistence, I surmised, had worn down any hopes that he might, as he would have said, "talk some sense into me." He enclosed a little drawing Mollie had done of me on a bicycle with the Eiffel Tower in the background; she was old enough to understand where her mother was, but I am sure by that point, six months gone, I had become something of an abstraction. Still, deep down, I was cheered to see that she seemed to have some vague understanding of what I was doing even if it was terribly unfair to her.

From Susie I received a letter that, in truth, I had been expecting for some time. She was, she told me, engaged to be married. It was a letter received with some sadness, but mostly resignation and understanding. Few women, especially society women of Beacon Hill, no matter their feelings for other women, could forever resist the pressures all around them to conform their lives to the expectations of family, friends, and neighbors. In her late twenties, Susie was already, by the standards of the day, what we called an old maid, well past the age when most respectable women had already found a husband and settled into a life of domesticity, tending to babies and young children and ensuring a peaceable and well-kept home for the man of the house. Her letters were, as I said, among the relatively few I saved in my life: I understood that this one in particular was a letter of moment, one that I might, in the years ahead, want to revisit, if just to remember how near impossible it was for such a love to survive in those days. I am enclosing it here for you to read so that you will better understand just how hard it was (and still is) to live true to oneself.

> December 5, 1894
> My dear Annie,
>
> In the nearly six months you have been gone, you have never left that special place in my heart that will always, always belong to you. My feelings for you have never changed and never will. But when we next see each other, the terms of engagement, if you will, will have changed irrevocably. As an astute and keen observer of life in all

its complexity you know well the harsh reality of love between two women in this rigid society of ours.

When I received your last telegram sent from New York, it took me several days to reckon with how to tell you the news this letter bears, news that will, I suspect, not entirely surprise you but which, I fear, will pain you as it does me.

Not a week has gone by since I turned 18 when my parents, my siblings, my friends, and my acquaintances haven't asked me when I would finally settle down, marry, and start a family. My seeming disinterest, badly hidden beneath rote recitations that it would be "soon," was a puzzlement to all, but to my knowledge none suspected that the reason for my apparent apathy was that I was not in the least attracted to men, they are mostly a boorish lot, but keenly attracted to brilliant, independent-minded women, an attraction that found its ultimate fulfillment in you.

For reasons I cannot fully articulate or fathom myself, the pressure to conform to the expectations of all around me, and to the social mores of this stodgy old town, have worn me down. I have searched my soul for the reason and believe it is this: there is within me a maternal instinct I have long suppressed but which age has teased from me. If it were possible to have a child without the assistance of a man I should be glad to do it!

Back in October I chanced to meet a nice, gentle, shy man of about 30 at a party on Joy Street. His family, too, was constantly pestering him about his bachelorhood at an age when most men have married. I found him quick-witted in conversation, well read, and industrious; he is an attorney engaged in the practice of maritime law at a firm in Boston, hails originally from Brookline, graduated from Boston Latin, Harvard College, and Harvard Law School. And, you will certainly appreciate this, he is an avid rider of the wheel. Why he never married I have never asked, nor has he asked the same of me. He will be a good husband and father, though I expect my feelings for him, which I would describe as fondness, will never come close to rivaling those I had, and still have, for you.

We will, of course, renew our friendship on your return, though on different terms. I am to be wed in the spring, so when you return I will be Mrs. Alfred Constable. My dear Annie, I think I know you as well as I have anyone in my life and you, me. So I say with confidence that this news, though it will be accompanied by some despair, will be met with even greater understanding, for few understand as you do what it means to be a woman in 1894.

Do write whenever you have the chance. I peruse the newspapers every day for the short items that keep me apprised, more or less, of your progress, and read every newspaper clipping you send me from the road, which I beg you continue to do. It would mean the world to me to hear from you directly as often as you can, for what remains unchanged is my deep and abiding love for you.

Forever yours,

Susie

Though Susie accurately predicted my emotional response to her letter, I found my reaction more muted, and less debilitating, than one might have supposed. I was now so thoroughly inhabiting the character I had created, out of both necessity and by choice, that Annie Kopchovsky seemed like a remote cousin whose pain I empathized with but felt with greatly diminished impact. Perhaps, I thought, this abrupt and unwelcome change in my life would be felt with more immediacy when I returned home. For now, here in Paris, nothing, as a practical matter, had changed. Susie had not been a part of my day-to-day life for six months, and I expected to be gone and away from her presence for another nine. It was surprisingly easy to put this news aside, into a little invisible compartment, to be dealt with, if at all, many months hence. I wasn't angry, and when I allowed myself to think about it at all, my love for Susie was, like hers, undiminished. Indeed, though she passed away almost ten years ago, it never did extinguish itself entirely, though I saw her again only a handful of times after the trip had ended and before I moved our family to New York in 1896. After the move, we never would see each other again, though we corresponded from time to time. Susie's marriage to Alfred, whom I met but once early in 1896, lasted until his death in 1930. To her everlasting regret, Susie was never able to bear a child; several pregnancies resulted in miscarriages. It was one of the great sorrows of her life.

The day before my departure south I gave my final Paris interview to a writer from the newspaper *Matin*, which means "morning" in French. I really pulled out the stops for this one, telling the reporter I was born to wealth but had temporarily lost the fortune in a family lawsuit. Nevertheless, I said of the prize money I was trying to claim, "winning money preoccupies me little. What I want is to show what a young American who has the will and the resolution can do with very simple resources." I claimed to be a doctor of law and an accomplished pianist, but refused to make use of these skills to help finance my journey because that would be too easy. And to ensure that some mystery lingered behind me, I closed the interview by saying that Miss Londonderry was my stage name, and a pseudonym I used as a journalist. "My real name," I said, "is much more beautiful and of course more well known, but I can't tell you for the moment. You will know it if I succeed." There is an old adage in show business, dear: Always leave them wanting more!

On the morning of December 30, 1894, I bid Catherine Sloan adieu. She sobbed, something I found awkward, for the depth of her feeling for me was not matched, though she was kind and agreeable and I was fond of her. Victor, who tried to be stoic, looked crestfallen, though he would, along with his brother James, cycle with me for some distance out of the city.

The weather was cold and wet as we stood in front of the Porte Doree café on the Avenue Daumesnil from which we would depart. With Catherine's help, we had on a small piece of cloth written in French, "Miss Annie Londonderry from Boston (America) is traveling around the world on her Sterling bicycle, built like a watch, with only a penny. Please show her the way to Marseille." On the inside breast pocket of my riding jacket, I sewed the piece of cloth in case I needed help along the way.

As in America, nearly every village and town in France had a wheelman's club, and as I had on my trip to New York from Chicago, I planned to alert the local papers along my route as to my impending arrival, knowing that such news would likely be seen by the local cyclists who might escort me into and out of their towns and, in turn, alert other clubs along my way. Such was the extraordinary popularity of the wheel in France, I knew I could count on an enthusiastic reception wherever I rode in the country and make some money to boot. Indeed, the major newspapers and magazines in Paris had devoted so much space to me during my stay there that I had already achieved a high level of celebrity throughout the country.

As in America, few roads outside of some in the cities were paved, and wet weather often turned the dirt thoroughfares into slick, muddy messes. And so it was for the twenty miles from Paris to Lieusaint. Victor, James, and I often had to dismount and push our bicycles along. In dry conditions the ride might have taken two hours, but on this horrid day it took twice as long.

We took a break in Lieusaint to dry off and get a bite to eat before slogging on through the dense, magnificent, and mysterious forests of Fontainebleau, and finally to Nemours where, relieved, we checked into Hôtel de l'Ecu de France. In nine hours of riding we had covered fewer than fifty miles, slow progress even by the standards of the day, but it felt good to be on the road and moving once again.

I fell asleep shortly after dinner, exhausted by the difficult cycling we had done that day, a deep and satisfying sleep.

The next morning, the last of 1894, dawned cold and snowy, but I would not allow the inclement weather to slow my progress. It was, after all, winter in France, and I expected to confront unfavorable conditions.

The Sloans had been kind and congenial hosts, but I felt smothered by their constant solicitousness. My element was now to be on my wheel and moving forward pedal stroke by pedal stroke. It was here that I bid farewell to a downcast Victor and his brother James. Victor was such a forlorn, down-on-his-luck fellow; his bicycle shop was struggling, he and Catherine were trying without success to have a child, and he seemed daunted that he now had to ride the return fifty miles in the wintry weather. James suggested they take the train, but Victor, perhaps embarrassed at the prospect of riding in the warmth and comfort of a railcar as I journeyed south by wheel, rejected the idea.

A crowd of several dozen townspeople gathered outside the hotel to see me off. I shook many hands, signed autographs, and gave brief remarks in English, of course, which they politely pretended to understand. Two employees of the local bike shop arrived on their wheels and offered to be my escort for the day, an offer I gladly accepted.

Within an hour the weather turned positively frightful; the wind picked up (a headwind from the south, unfortunately) and the snow grew heavier. It was dark by the time we arrived in Montargis, a mere twenty miles from where we began the day. Bundled up as I was in every piece of clothing I had, and some loaned to me by my companions, freedom of movement was constricted and the pedaling hard. Yet my spirits were high that New Year's Eve in Montargis, where, it seemed, half the town came to the hotel where we were staying to celebrate the arrival of the "globe-girdler, Mlle. Londonderry," now a fixture on the pages of newspapers throughout the country. To the French I was a real celebrity, if an eccentric one; a bright light on a dark midwinter's night as the calendar turned to 1895.

It was a new year, but the same old dreary weather as I rode south along the national highway for Cosne-Cours-sur-Loire, where I arrived in a very good state but covered in mud. The temperature, hovering just above freezing, had softened the road surface, and with each turn of the pedals mud from the front wheel spattered my pants from the waist down, and mud flung up by the rear wheel covered my back. In La Charité-sur-Loire the local representative of France's largest cycling organization, the Union Vélocipédique de France, beseeched me to take the train to Lyon, some one hundred and seventy miles south, because of the deplorable state of the roads ahead. To this suggestion I was not averse, for the clock was ticking, and given the state of the roads it might well take another full week to reach Lyon at the rate I was traveling. I told the gentleman I would ponder the question overnight.

The next morning, the Sterling and I boarded the train for Lyon, where I took a room at the Hotel de l'Univers. That evening, a local reporter called on me, an occasion that was by now commonplace wherever I landed for the night. To this credulous fellow I related a version of a story that I continued to tell with some frequency and which grew with each telling a little more dramatic, for what's the fun in repeating the same story over and over and over again? I was, I told the reporter, attacked by a tramp in upstate New York. "Miss Londonderry, with unusual energy and a vigorous push, rid herself of the miscreant. She just had enough time to get up and throw herself and her bicycle aside as a train went by at full steam," read the report in the next day's paper.

France was in the midst of one of its most severe winters in years, and I lingered for a couple of days in Lyon hoping for a break in the weather that never came. Unable to idle any longer, on the morning of January 6 two Lyon wheelmen met me at the hotel to continue the journey south.

The ground was icy, and as I exited the hotel I slipped and scraped my ankle. A little blood started oozing from the wound. It was minor, really, but much fuss was made and the hotel doctor was summoned. In a small private room off the lobby he took some bandages from his little black satchel, lifted the cuff of my pants, and began wrapping the minor wound as those outside anxiously awaited word as to the severity of the injury. Never one to settle for a molehill when a mountain could be had, I told the doctor to liberally wrap the wound and to extend the bandage from my ankle to my knee.

"But, Mlle. Londonderry," he said in heavily accented English, "it is not badly cut."

"I know," I answered, "but it will look so much more impressive if I mount my wheel appearing to have suffered a serious wound. It will be proof of my extraordinary willpower and determination. Of what interest is a scrape when a nearly severed artery has far greater dramatic possibilities?"

The doctor looked at me with weary resignation.

"As you please," he said, and proceeded to apply a heavy bandage from ankle to knee.

"We must wait here a few minutes," I said to the doctor when he had finished. "It would be impossible to treat so serious an injury in so little time."

The doctor sighed, resigned to sitting with me in silence until I deemed the time elapsed sufficient. When we emerged from the hotel, the crowd outside had grown to nearly a hundred. I rolled my pant leg up over my knee so all could see the heavy bandage.

"The good doctor has informed me that the wound is quite deep and serious," I announced, having enlisted the hotel proprietor as my translator. (I did not want the doctor doing the translating, for unlike the proprietor, he knew what I was about to say was at variance with the truth.) "I nearly severed an artery. The doctor has advised me not to continue until the wound is completely healed lest I reopen it. It required more than twenty stitches to close."

The doctor, standing with his head bowed ever so slightly, rolled his eyes, but he dared not contradict me.

"He wanted to use anesthesia to save me the pain of the suturing, but as I am resolved to continue on without delay, I suffered the needle without it," I went on. "Never, the doctor told me, has he treated a patient with such tolerance for pain. I assured him that in my journey so far I have endured far worse."

Not a soul seemed to doubt my story, and there was, when I finished, a hearty round of applause and a chorus of good wishes.

"Thank you all for coming this morning to see me off toward the south and thence to the exotic lands of Africa and Asia," I said. "I will remember your kindness."

And with that, I slung my bad leg over the bicycle frame, being sure to wince as I did so, and my little party of three rolled out of town as a dry, light snow fell in the freezing air. A mile or so out of town we stopped, and I removed all but the smallest bit of bandage and stowed the material in my saddle bag, for it would, I was sure, come in handy later. My companions were puzzled at first, but as they saw that my leg had suffered only a minor scrape, it dawned on them that they, too, had been gulled; their smiles, now that they were in the know, were smiles of approval for my cunning and showmanship.

A midday luncheon, courtesy of the local bicycle club in Vienne, was a pleasant break from the cold, and from there we continued on to Saint-Rambert where I spent the night.

By the next morning my ankle wound, superficial as it was, was cranky; I had also bruised the ankle bone apparently, but it was little more than a nuisance. A group of Saint-Rambert cyclists escorted me to Valence, a short ride, where we arrived late in the morning. Knowing that my companions had arranged for us to be welcomed by a group of Valence cyclists, I decided to milk my injury for all it was worth. With my wounded leg propped on the handlebar, I rounded the roadway into town pedaling with one foot to the delight of the assembly.

I spoke briefly upon our arrival with a local reporter, who wrote in the next day's paper, "Her endurance is remarkable. She took only four days to go from Paris to Lyon never sleeping more than two hours a night."

Every good illusionist works through misdirection, Mary dear, and while it was true that it had taken four days to travel from Paris to Lyon, I was mum about the many miles I had covered by rail. People see what they want to see, and France wanted to see a brave American heroine of the wheel. Why should I disabuse them of the illusion they so eagerly craved?

While resting at the Hôtel Tête d'Or in Valence that afternoon, my leg began to ache more seriously, no doubt because I had allowed it no time to rest. A hotel doctor was again summoned, and he surmised that my Achilles tendon was inflamed. Though not nearly as serious as I had pretended the day before, the injury was more serious than I had first assumed. Rather than risk aggravating it further and make riding impossible, I resolved to remain a few days in Valence and do what I could to further my celebrity there.

The escorts who were accompanying me in relay fashion across France were all male riders, eager to be in the company of a celebrity. Newspapers across the country were reporting daily on my progress, and wherever we went people seemed well aware of who I was and my purpose. Being the center of such attention was exhilarating, and I saw each day as another performance of my one-woman show.

For the most part my escorts were respectful and friendly, even if most spoke, at most, only a bit of English. There was little conversation as we rode, both because the exertion made conversing difficult, for we were often breathing heavily, but also because of the language barrier. That barrier did not, however, deter one or two from hinting at amorous intentions, which I laughed off.

In Valence, during my brief idyll there, I had many callers who simply wanted to shake my hand, secure my autograph, and share a few words of admiration, and I tried to oblige them all. I gave interviews to local reporters where I opined on everything from my impressions of French men (favorable) and French women (not so much—they smoked too much, at which I feigned shock). For a woman dressing in man's riding clothes and generally intent on making a spectacle of myself, the notion that I found the idea of a woman smoking was ironic. With all the descriptions of me as masculine, boyish, muscular, and even of a neutered "third sex," I was, I suppose, trying to reclaim my femininity by allowing that I favored French men over French women.

The layover in Valence did little to reduce the discomfort from my ankle injury, but I could idle no longer. A group of eight cyclists from the Valence wheel club met me on the morning of the tenth of January to help me continue south. Because of the tenderness of my injury, one of them, a Mssr. Paul Seigneuret, had secured a tandem bicycle for us to ride together and a volunteer to mount my Sterling.

I greatly enjoyed this gentleman, for he had a lively manner and a good sense of humor. The plan was for this group to travel with me to the village of Montélimar, some thirty miles south. But such was the good cheer of the group, despite the frigid weather, that we continued past Montélimar toward Orange, another thirty-five miles distant. To cover so many miles in a single day in the conditions we encountered was quite a feat, but such was the camaraderie that our spirits remained high all day. It is best described in a dispatch Mssr. Seigneuret arranged to publish in the *Messager de Valence*, a copy of which reached me by post when I arrived in Marseille and which I had translated there.

> She possesses an unheard-of energy, laughs continuously, and does not stop singing. On the hills, she pushed her pedal leg with her hand and breaks out in laughter once she has ascended the slope. She is always gay and we arrive at Montélimar without even noticing the route. To explain to you how, having departed to accompany Miss Annie to Montélimar, I went to Orange, will be difficult because I am not aware myself. As we climbed a steep slope at Bel Air, we were forced to dismount and walk to the top before beginning a fast descent into the village of Donzère. On the way down, one of the riders lost control and was pitched into a snowbank. We saw a snow-covered head poking out of a hole in such an amusing way that we didn't even notice his legs, which were desperately kicking in the air! Miss Annie and I avoided a near collision ourselves, but we avoided the accident, and with a burst of laughter from Miss Londonderry, we got back on our route.
>
> (*Messager de Valence,* January 12, 1895)

Dare I say that one of my talents was holding eager and enthusiastic young men under my spell? I was nothing if not beguiling.

Exhausted, cold, but invigorated, our party arrived in Orange, where we gathered for dinner. I playfully implored my companions to accompany me to America via Bombay, Calcutta, and Yokohama.

"It is a temptation, Miss Annie," replied Mssr. Seigneuret, "but perhaps too ambitious for men with jobs and families to support.

Why don't you return to Valence next year and we shall have a reunion?" I promised to do so, but it was just one of countless promises I made in my life that I would never fulfill.

Late that evening my companions departed to catch the last train back to Valence, leaving me and my Sterling to spend the night alone in Orange.

Avignon was just a short way down the road, and two escorts from the cycle club there rode to Orange early the next morning to accompany me south. I learned from my companions that the local newspapers there had been trumpeting my impending arrival for several days; they had brought with them a handful of the clippings.

"Miss Londonderry will pass through Avignon on her bicycle tour of the world!" said one. "Hip! Hip! For the courageous bicyclist," proclaimed another. It was a measure of my success in making a celebrity of myself that few would have needed an explanation of who Miss Londonderry was at this point.

The reception I received in Avignon did not disappoint. People were lined up along the streets for well over a mile to my destination in the city, the home of a Madame Boyer, a woman of about thirty and a cycling enthusiast. There the entire group from the local wheel club crowded in and jockeyed for position in the parlor of Madame Boyer's charming house, where tea and cake were served to all. I told a few stories of my travels, and Madame Boyer, who spoke nearly fluent English, translated.

"What will you do when you return home to Boston, Mlle. Londonderry?" I was asked.

"I have nearly completed my medical studies at Harvard," I replied, "and I suppose I should finish and become a doctor."

"What about marriage, Mlle. Londonderry?" asked another. "Surely a woman of your accomplishment would have no trouble attracting many suitors."

"Who do you have in mind?" I shot back with a grin. "Perhaps you have come prepared with a ring?"

This brought forth gales of laughter and reddened the face of my interlocutor.

"What will be your route upon leaving France?" asked yet another. This question was asked of me a lot, and it always elicited an improvised response, for the point was to impress, not inform.

"From Marseille I expect to travel by ship a short distance to the Italian coast," I answered, "for the terms of the wager I have been selected to settle permit me an allowance of a thousand miles by ship and train." That I was traveling on a wager was widely reported in the French press, so that part required no further explanation. But there was no allowance for ship and train travel specifically, only the requirement that I cover ten thousand miles by wheel. "From there I shall go overland to Budapest, Constantinople, Teheran, and Calcutta. I expect crossing China to be the most formidable challenge."

Heads nodded and approving glances were exchanged.

"But I have no fear. I fully expect to be back home in Boston come the autumn."

Around midafternoon, Mssr. Geo, one of the Avignon cyclists who met me in Orange, and I bid the assembly adieu, and all gathered outside to give us three hearty cheers as we pushed off for Salon-de-Provence. As we were now well south, the temperatures were more moderate, and the riding more agreeable. By early evening we had reached our destination for the evening. Mssr. Geo was an amiable companion and a true gentleman. After ensuring that I was comfortably checked in to my hotel for the night, we shared a light dinner before he wished me a smooth and safe journey and headed for the rail station.

"If I were not a married man, mademoiselle, I think I would be inclined to propose to you myself," he said in his thick French accent, with a wry smile that let me know he was flattering me, not flirting with me. "It has been a great honor to pedal all these kilometers with you today. You will make a success of this venture, I am sure." And with that, he extended his hand, which I took firmly in mine.

"The pleasure has been mine, dear sir. Until we meet again."

I was now just a short thirty-mile ride from Marseille, where the land mass of France meets the Mediterranean Sea. The cycle clubs had been so abuzz about my travels through that country, and the interest of the press so keen, that I knew Marseille would be preparing a large welcome. That evening I sent telegrams to the Marseille clubs and to several of the newspapers saying that I expected to arrive in the city on the morning of the thirteenth of January, two days hence. I could have made the ride in a single day, but for the sake of spectacle I knew that a daylight arrival in the morning hours would be preferable to arriving in the darkness of evening. My plan was to spend the night on the city's outskirts and to pedal into the city early the following day.

I almost didn't make it. The next day, a few miles from Salon-de-Provence, near Lacone, I was ambushed by three masked highwaymen. They sprang at me from behind a clump of trees, and one of them grabbed my bicycle, throwing me heavily. I had my revolver in my pocket within easy reach, and when I stood up, I had that revolver against the head of the man nearest me. He backed off, but another seized me from behind and disarmed me. They rifled through my pockets and found just three francs. They were magnanimous enough to return that money to me, but my shoulder had been badly wrenched by my fall, and my ankle sprained, but I was able to continue my journey.

Well, that was the story as I imagined it that night in my hotel room in Salon-de-Provence. I wanted to make a dramatic entrance there and knew exactly how to do it.

A short distance out of Salon-de-Provence I retrieved the bandages I had set aside in Valence, the ones I insisted the doctor apply from my ankle to my knee after the small mishap there, and again wrapped my leg from ankle to knee. When a small group of Lacone cyclists met me for the ride into Marseille I told them in breathless terms of the assault I had suffered the day before, how I had feared for my life but managed to fend off my attackers. Fortunately, I told them, I had bandages with me for just such an eventuality and was able to bandage my leg, which had been injured in the assault. I was *very* convincing.

As we approached Marseille I begged my companions to stop for a few moments so I could add another flourish. Until now the American flag given me in Paris and the short pole to which it was affixed had been wrapped around the top tube of my bicycle and secured with heavy twine. I removed it from its usual place and inserted the pole into the receptacle Victor had rigged up on my handlebars in Paris for just this purpose. I would ride into Marseille with the Stars and Stripes waving in the wind and my bandaged leg propped up on the handlebar, pedaling with one foot! What a sight I was! A spectacle to be sure, and sure to be remembered by all who saw it.

A delegation of about a dozen local wheelmen joined our party for the procession through the city. There must have a thousand people or more lining the main route into the city center, and how they did cheer at the sight of the famous lady cyclist from America, with Old Glory flying in the breeze, and undaunted by injury! Confetti in copious amounts was thrown as we passed all along the route to the hotel where I had arranged to stay in the city.

Marseille was a bustling port city, the harbor seemingly filled with more ships than it could possibly accommodate, steamers and sailboats, the masts of which, with their sails dropped, were reminiscent of a forest in winter. Goods of all kinds in boxes, barrels, and wooden containers jammed the docks, the task of sorting them all a major logistical challenge day in and day out. One could hardly walk along the docks without being jostled by the stevedores hauling freight this way and that. And because it was a major port city, as at home in Boston's West End, you could hear dozens of languages spoken during a day's walk by the North Africans, the Asiatics, the Spanish, and the Europeans either on brief shore leave or who worked the docks or in the offices of the various shipping lines that crowded the waterfront.

Thanks to my own efforts and those of the wheel clubs all along way from Paris, I was now a true celebrity, at least in France. The night of my arrival a large reception was arranged at the city's famed Crystal Palace, packed with people in a celebratory mood. I made my entrance astride the Sterling, my leg still bandaged, and rode through the crowd, which parted like the Red Sea as I slowly passed through the hall. I was begged for a speech and happily obliged, though few in the throng would have understood my English. But I made sure every few moments to again shout, "*Viva la France!*" and each time the audience thrilled to it!

I would spend a full week in Marseille, where I was offered more advertising contracts than I could accept, riding through the streets adorned, again, with all manner of adverts for this and that. The stream of admirers who called on me at the hotel seemed never-ending, so much so that the local papers obliged me by publishing visiting hours. During my time there I called on the U.S. consulate to secure the signature of the consul to prove my presence in the city.

On January 20, a week after my arrival, it was time to press on. I had booked passage on a mail steamer, the *Sydney*, bound for the Orient. I had to make my way through thousands of onlookers who had crowded the docks to see me off. I would, months later, receive a clipping from *Le Petit Provençal*, one of the Marseille newspapers, that described the scene. The assembled masses "resembled a huge swarm of ants," they reported. "The Soufre Pier was equally invaded. Along the quay, privileged hundreds came to make their goodbyes to the intrepid Miss Londonderry."

As the ship, flying the French and American flags (in my honor), maneuvered through the port, the captain made a final pass close by the pier so the crowd could get one last look at me. Standing with my Sterling on the port side, I waved my riding cap until the pier, and France herself, slipped from view. I was prepared for a few days at sea by myself and looked forward to enjoying some peace and quiet after weeks in the company of others. But just a few minutes after Marseille had disappeared, I would get the shock of my life.

Eleven

There are two versions, well, many more, really, but two principal ones, of how I reached the eastern shores of China and then Japan from Marseille, and I told both of them, sometimes to different reporters on the same day in the same city, depending on how much time I had and what struck my fancy in the moment. There was the long story and the short one, but in truth the longer one was conjured during the shorter one. I can tell you this: I sailed from Marseille on the twentieth of January 1895, and arrived in Yokohama in early March of that year.

For those paying attention, this was a remarkably fast passage for a woman supposedly riding a bicycle across Europe, through Persia, Palestine, South Asia, and China, but it was filled with adventure. The ride from Bombay to Calcutta was made miserable by insects. I hitched myself to a royal hunting party and spent three days pursuing the great Bengal tiger. In the hinterlands of Asia, where many had never even seen a bicycle, I was mistaken for a flying squirrel, an evil spirit, or, on one occasion, a visitor from Mars. Many times my life was in mortal danger, my escapes always narrow, and my courage, and my spirits, always high. On several occasions warning shots fired from my pistol sent natives who wished me harm fleeing in fear. In eastern China, where war raged between China and Japan over control of Corea, as they spelled it then, I met up with two journalists and a missionary and traveled with them to the front lines of the conflict, at one point falling, with my Sterling, through the ice on a frozen river. When we reached the front, we were fired upon by Chinese troops, and I took a bullet to the shoulder, causing a wound that took a full month to heal. Our Japanese guide was killed on the spot. Mr. Moffatt, the missionary, was also shot, and his wounds proved fatal; he died a few days later. The fields were littered with war dead, sometimes packed so closely I had to roll my Sterling over the bodies. Now traveling alone, I was arrested by Japanese soldiers and thrown into a prison cell where, right before my eyes, I saw a Japanese soldier kill a Chinese prisoner and drink his blood while his muscles were yet quivering. Upon my release, thanks to a legion of French soldiers who arrived and demanded my freedom, I rode up to Siberia where I was witness to the cruelties of the Russian prison system, at one point passing forty prisoners being forced to march fourteen hundred miles. Some of this may sound familiar, for many of the stories I made up as a young woman of twenty-three made their way into bedtime stories I told you when you were a little girl.

The war between China and Japan over control of the Corean Peninsula had been front-page news around the world for nearly a year, even in America, where the outcome had little relevance for most Americans. Yet the dispatches from the front were so dramatic, the battles so pitched and brutal and bloody, that the conflict became yet another serial entertainment told in almost daily installments to readers eager for a taste of adventure. I knew that stories, seen firsthand, or at least told as if they were, would be of keen interest to American audiences, and most would hardly care if the storyteller were on the level as long as the accounts set them on the edge of their seats.

Oh, Mary, dear, so much happened in those six weeks between my taking leave of Marseille and my arrival in Yokohama! I confess, I don't know whether people believed these stories or simply reveled in them regardless, but they became a staple of the repertoire I was developing for my eventual return to America, where, I reasoned, I would find a public eager for tales of high adventure. I was living, dear, on the knife-edge between fiction and reality and needed an account of my travels more interesting than could be had on a mail steamer making its way from Marseille to Hong Kong.

The *Sydney*, like most mail steamers of the day, carried passengers, but it lacked the amenities of *La Touraine*. Far from a luxury liner, the *Sydney* was a more modest affair, a working boat that belched black smoke from its stacks day and night. It accommodated some two hundred passengers, ninety in first class, forty-four in second class, and seventy-five, me among them, well belowdecks in steerage.

Right after Marseille had disappeared from view, I went to my tiny cabin to take a nap and prepare myself mentally for the long voyage ahead, when there was a gentle knock on my door. I told you earlier that after receiving in Paris the letter from Susie explaining that she was soon to be wed, I saw her but a handful of times after my journey and before moving to New York. But I saw her one other time, as well, for when I opened the cabin door I could scarcely believe the sight before me. It was Susie, and I was unable to mutter so much as a word for the shock was complete. I could no more have imagined opening the door to find President Cleveland in his pajamas. Susie embraced me, but I felt my body go rigid, for I was too stunned to make sense of what was happening.

I recognized her, of course, but to the woman whose character I had come to inhabit she was a complete stranger. The sight of her had the effect of wrenching me without warning from one world, the one I was now living in, into another that was as far away and flat as photographs from a distant past. Susie took a step back and placed her hands on my upper arms.

"Are you not pleased to see me, my dear Annie?" she asked, her eyes pleading. She didn't seem hurt, just curious. I believe she understood the profound sense of dislocation her sudden appearance had caused. Without a word I backed up slowly and plopped down on the bed, unsure that what I was seeing was real. I don't know how much time passed before I spoke at last; I suppose it was the time it took for Annie Kopchovsky to swim up from the depths and reclaim her place inside me.

"But how . . . how . . . I mean, why . . ." I could hardly arrange words into a coherent sentence or question. "I am so confused," I said, shaking my head as my feelings started to organize themselves. It was a rare moment when I did not feel completely in control, and here I was, flummoxed as never before.

"How did you find me here? I mean, I am happy to see you, of course, but I don't understand. I received your letter in Paris, the one about your engagement. I cannot believe it is you, here, now, in the flesh."

Susie came and sat beside me. She knew I was relying on her to help me make sense of her sudden reappearance in my life, especially far from Boston aboard a mail steamer sailing away from Marseille and across the Mediterranean, the last place on earth where I might have expected to see anyone I had known in my previous life.

"After I posted that letter to you in Boston, I immediately felt I must see you before my wedding, to speak to you, hold you, and, I hoped, to share my love for you one more time," said Susie. "I told Alfred a white lie, that I was traveling to New York and Washington to visit with friends for several weeks. But I had already arranged for passage to Le Havre from New York. Once there it was easy to determine your whereabouts. Every newspaper in France seemed to be tracking your progress! In Paris I learned you were riding south to Marseille and traveled there by train. I arrived two days ago resolved to surprise you, but there, for the first time, I feared you might not welcome my intrusion. I know I have been terribly selfish coming here like this, but when I read that you were to sail on the *Sydney* I impulsively purchased myself a ticket to Alexandria. I will make my return from there. Oh, my dear Annie, I hope my impetuousness has not made you unhappy. I am so very pleased to see you."

In all the time I had known Susie, throughout those years in which we shared the most intimate parts of ourselves with each other, I don't think I had ever felt angry with her, or disappointed in her, or confused by our love for each other. It always had such *clarity*. But sitting there on that small bed in a cabin in the belly of a French mail steamer off the French coast I became aware of an unfamiliar feeling rising up from the depths. As the shock began to subside, when I was able to grasp that this was no apparition, I was angry . . . angry to have been taken off guard, to have been ambushed (unlike the ambush near Salon-de-Provence, this one was quite real and quite injurious), and with no way to escape, for we were now well out to sea in more ways than one.

Perhaps I should be more precise. The anger was Miss Londonderry's, not my own. Now, I don't want you to think I had taken leave of my senses, was suffering from a malady of the psyche, or had lost touch with my real self. That was not the case. I was well aware of who I really was. But in the six months since I had left home, with every mile I put behind me, I had grown accustomed to my new role, and it was one I was taking great delight in. I was no longer the downtrodden Boston housewife and mother who put bread on our table caught in endless days of domestic drudgery. I was a free woman unsaddled with the weight of the life I had left behind. Susie's abrupt appearance was forcing me out of my new shell, my new *armor*, which was protecting me from regret, second thoughts, and guilt at, well, let's face it, abandoning my family, *your* family. I was terribly afraid that if I allowed myself to retreat from the new woman I had become, and was still becoming, I might lose the fortitude to continue on, and I had very much determined that I would, indeed, carry on to the very end.

There was yet another irony I confronted in that brief moment when I was buffeted one way by the winds of my past and another by the winds of my future. In the six months I had been traveling I had undergone a metamorphosis. I left Boston in the most ladylike attire, adopted the bloomer costume in Chicago, and was now doing my riding in a man's riding suit of wool pants and short jacket (with warmer overlayers as necessary). And my body had changed, too. As the French press had been quick to point out, I hardly conformed to French notions of femininity owing to the more muscular build acquired by my exertions on the wheel. My legs were more taut and sculpted, my waist thinner, and my upper body a bit broader. My skin, once soft and supple, had been weathered by the elements; my hands were rough and the skin on my face made me appear older than I was. Yet, ironically, as my appearance gradually became more "masculine," I found myself less attracted to the women I encountered, and when I saw Susie I felt, for the first time, no physical attraction toward her. None at all.

Susie seemed to sense all of it in an instant.

"Oh, dear, my dear Annie. I have a made a terrible mistake, I can see it in your eyes and I can feel it. You are not pleased to see me. I thought this would be a delightful surprise, but I can see that I have badly misjudged the situation."

I was unsure what to say, for Annie Kopchovksy still loved Susie very much, but she was indeed breaking a spell, so to speak, that left Miss Londonderry shaken. I took her right hand in mine, gave it a slight squeeze, and let go.

"I think I need a moment to collect my thoughts," I said. My feelings seemed beyond corralling. "Please sit. I am in a bit of shock, to be honest."

"Oh, Annie," she said, "I do understand. Perhaps I should have told you, or asked you, before making this long journey to see you. It was terribly impulsive on my part, I know."

I nodded, trying to figure out what to say next. The air in the cabin suddenly seemed stale and stifling.

A few awkward moments passed in silence.

"It's a fine day," I said at last. "Come. Let's take a stroll on the deck and catch the Mediterranean breeze."

And there, as we walked, I tried to put into words all the feelings I just conveyed to you.

I felt like a fish trying to explain life under the water to someone whose life was lived on land.

It was not Susie's intent to remain with me for long. She had already booked her return passage to Marseille from Alexandria, the *Sydney*'s first port of call, but that was yet five days away. For better or for worse, we would be on this boat together for the next five days, five days during which the love I felt for Susie as Annie Kopchovksy would wrestle uneasily with the displeasure I felt as Miss Londonderry for having had the veil I had drawn around myself pierced without warning. It was a struggle that left me bewildered, disoriented, and distressed.

Let me be plain. Miss Londonderry carried the day. Our conversations were frequent, sometimes awkward, but mostly limited to the mundane. Susie had no news of my family, for she didn't really know them and traveled in different circles. The winter in Boston, she said, had been particularly frigid, the skating pond on the Common crowded for weeks. Much snow had fallen. In all these conversations I could see the pain in Susie's eyes; she had traveled a great distance and incurred considerable expense for what she hoped would be one last romantic interlude before her marriage, but the woman she expected to meet had run off somewhere, her body inhabited by a harder, more distant, far less accessible woman. Truly, I felt sorry for her; I took no pleasure in her pain but was unable to assuage it. We dined together, walked the deck, and sometimes caught the rays of the sun in the chairs set out for passengers, but we slept in our separate cabins. Those five days, as the *Sydney* made its way east across the Mediterranean, passed with excruciating slowness. I was ready to fully reclaim my new identity and to be among people for whom Annie Kopchovsky did not exist, where I would be a stranger among strangers and free to be whomever and whatever I chose to be.

As you can imagine, our parting at Alexandria was likewise awkward and painful. I could only apologize to Susie for being so distant, for disappointing her so, for causing her any pain at all, for the real me trembled at the thought of all those things. I begged her to understand, to forgive me, and the look in her eyes told me she was trying, truly trying, but had not fully arrived at that destination. I allowed myself to give her a genuine and prolonged embrace, hoping that she would at least feel the *sincerity* of my apologies, though I also felt the apologies she offered me were indeed quite necessary.

The very next day, after a brief stopover at Alexandria, I was relieved to once again be alone. After Susie's departure, the sand quickly filled in the hole she had dug. I gave her intrusion little thought.

The *Sydney* sailed on to Port Said, a major coaling station at the northern end of the Suez Canal, where the ship would be refueled and lay over for two and a half days, just enough time for me to fulfill my dream of seeing the holy city of Jerusalem.

Passenger boats moved regularly between Port Said and Jaffa, a voyage of about ten hours. A narrow gauge railway, built in 1892, ran from there to Jerusalem. Though just some forty miles distant, the rail trip to Jerusalem took a painstaking three hours. Once there I had just several hours to see some of the sights; the view of the city from the Mount of Olives, the Wailing Wall, and the al-Aqsa Mosque. Although the city was nominally divided into quarters—Moslem, Armenian, Christian, and Jewish—Moslems were the majority population in each. Most streets in the city were paved and cleaned with regularity, unlike the thoroughfares in many American cities, which were usually gritty and dirty. Regular garbage collection kept the streets looking tidy and welcoming, and even in winter it felt more like springtime at home. Important landmarks such as al-Aqsa and the Dome of the Rock had undergone major repairs in the 1870s and been kept in good condition, so that overall, despite its ancient history, Jerusalem felt fresh and orderly and very civilized. Jerusalem, birthplace of the world's three great religions, was not the contentious place it is now in 1947. I do hope, before I die, to see the birth of the State of Israel; in 1895 it was not even a notion.

In a photography shop in Jerusalem I purchased a large collection of lantern slides for the slide show I was putting together for my lectures. Once I reached the States, it was my plan to make good money lecturing about my journey as I made my way from California to Chicago. No sooner had I arrived in Jerusalem than it was time to leave and make the long trip back to Port Said. I could ill afford any delay lest the *Sydney* depart without me but with my precious Sterling.

As luck would have it—bad luck, that is—on the return trip the train stalled an hour from Jaffa owing to some unexplained mechanical failure. As the delay wore on I became increasingly alarmed, a concern that proved to be well founded. By the time the train lurched into motion again we had been stuck for well over two hours, and I missed the boat I had planned to take back to Port Said. The next scheduled departure was eight hours hence, which would have put me back in Port Said two hours after the *Sydney* was scheduled to sail. I was apoplectic: I had no plan B and had no idea what I would do if the *Sydney* sailed without me. Normally cool and collected, I started to panic.

Along the docks many fisherman sat mending nets and tending to their boats, and I tried desperately, frantically in English, to explain my predicament, hoping to find one adventurous and brave enough to take me back to Port Said. I struck most of them, judging by the expressions on their faces, as a slightly daft, excitable foreigner trying in vain to make myself understood. Knowing glances were exchanged among them, glances that made it clear they took me not at all seriously; jokes made in an Arabic dialect were, I surmised, being made at my expense.

I had just about given up hope of making it back to Port Said in time when an elegant, well-dressed gentleman approached me, having seen from a distance what must have seemed the comical sight of a woman, increasingly panicked, try to make sense to a gaggle of rough-hewn, dark-skinned fishermen who could make neither head nor tail of her pleadings.

"Good day, madam," he said. His accent was strongly and properly British. "You seem to be in a state of considerable distress. May I help you?" He extended a hand. "My name is Winchester. Bradley Winchester."

"Oh, thank goodness," I replied, and then breathlessly spilled out the details of my predicament. "Can you be of any help to me, Mr. Winchester? My name, by the way, is Miss Londonderry, Annie Londonderry, from America."

"*The* Miss Londonderry?" he asked. "The famous globe-girdler? I have read of your adventures in the papers. But I certainly never expected to make your acquaintance, especially not here."

"Nor did I expect to find myself stuck here with my bicycle nearly two hundred miles away aboard a ship, the *Sydney*, that is likely to depart Port Said without me unless I can figure out a way to get back in the next fourteen hours," I replied. "I was hoping one of these fishermen would take me, but I cannot make myself understood."

"Well, Miss Londonderry, good fortune is shining upon you today. You see, I am here on business of the Crown. I work in the Foreign Office on maritime affairs, and as your luck would have it, I am about to sail for Port Said myself aboard the HMS *Balfleur*."

Mr. Winchester pointed behind me to a large and fleet fighting ship, larger than the *Sydney*, docked in the distance.

"If you had persuaded one of these ruffians to take his life in his hands to take you to Port Said, you'd either have drowned or missed your ship by several days," said Mr. Winchester. "Neither they nor their boats are equipped for such a journey. The *Balfleur* sails in an hour and will take but nine hours en route. You will be back with a few hours to spare. If you accept my invitation to be my guest, that is. She's a magnificent ship, Miss Londonderry, put into Her Majesty's service just seven months ago. Please, rest assured. We will have you on board the *Sydney* in plenty of time to continue your voyage."

Needless to say, this was an enormous stroke of luck, perhaps the only chance I had to make it back to Port Said in time, and if I had failed, my entire venture might well have gone up in smoke. I gladly accepted Mr. Winchester's offer.

"May I carry that package for you, Miss Londonderry?"

He was referring to the box that contained some two dozen images of the holy city that I had purchased from a vendor there. Glass lantern slides were sold like postcards back in those days.

"Thank you, Mr. Winchester, but I am, as you would imagine, used to being quite self-reliant. It's a small burden and I can carry them myself, thank you."

Mr. Winchester seemed a bit put off by this. He was, after all, a very proper British gentleman and was no doubt surprised that I did not accept his offer to carry the package. It was an affront to his British sensibilities.

"As you wish, Miss Londonderry," he said.

Given that my passage on the *Balfleur* owed itself entirely to the graciousness of Mr. Winchester, I knew I would be beholden to him for the next nine hours or so, and he proved himself to be both a bit of a dilettante and a minor nuisance, for he refused throughout the voyage to give me any privacy or to allow his prattling to subside. But being "saved" by Mr. Winchester drove home something of which I was generally aware, but that really came into focus as we walked toward the *Balfleur*: a trip like this depends very much on the kindness of strangers and the goodwill of most people, for here I was alone and working without a safety net. Who could I call on in times of trouble? No one but strangers who might or might not even speak the same language. I suppose when one undertakes a journey such as this it is a declaration of faith in one's fellow man (or woman).

After we had boarded the ship, Mr. Winchester invited me (and I could not refuse, of course) to sit with him on the deck. It was a warm, sunny day, and the view from the bow of the *Balfleur* was quite magnificent. The sea was an azure blue. A light breeze was blowing on shore.

"You know, Miss Londonderry, I have been aware of your venture for many months now," said Mr. Winchester, at the beginning of what proved to be a rather lengthy monologue. "I am an avid wheelman myself, and I chanced to be in New York on business last July when you arrived there from Boston. I saw many articles in the newspapers about you. I must admit that I would have put the chances of your making it all this way to Jaffa at nil. It sounded as if you had done little to prepare for such a journey."

"That is indeed so, Mr. Winchester," I answered. "But I have found that most men find it very easy to underestimate a determined woman."

I would have been happy to leave the conversation at that, but it quickly became clear that silence was not among Mr. Winchester's virtues. The interrogation, it seemed, was destined to last as long as it took the *Balfleur* to reach Port Said.

"And do I recall correctly that your name is assumed, that you are married with children, and that you are allegedly traveling on a wager?"

This, I have to say, took me by surprise. I had been annoyed when the *New York World* published an item during my stay in New York with these details, details I would have preferred to keep out of the newspapers, which I did with success for most of my journey.

"You have a keen memory, Mr. Winchester. Yes, those details were published in New York." I was eager to drop the subject.

"If you don't mind my asking, Miss Londonderry, what does your husband think about this jaunt of yours?"

I did mind, but I owed my presence on this ship to Mr. Winchester and I was obliged to talk much while saying as little as possible.

"I can assure you, Mr. Winchester, that I would not have embarked on such a journey without his support and understanding." This, of course, was false, but it was the answer least likely to take the conversation in unpleasant directions.

As I was deflecting a fusillade of similar queries, the ship's horn blasted several times, indicating that we would be easing away from the port momentarily. But I feared the next nine hours with Mr. Winchester might seem longer than the ride thus far from Chicago. Halfway to Port Said I think I learned all there was to know about the childhood, the marriage, the four children—three boys and a girl—and the career—distinguished, he assured me—of Mr. Bradley Winchester.

"So tell me, Miss Londonderry, it is clear you will be remaining on board the *Sydney* through the canal. For a woman wheeling around the world you seem to be spending quite a few days at sea." From the tone of his voice I knew that Mr. Winchester, perhaps unsatisfied with my businesslike demeanor, was challenging me, albeit politely.

As I often did when confronted with such questions, I told him that the terms of the wager allowed me, in addition to passage across the Atlantic and Pacific Oceans, which were, after all, not passable by bicycle, one thousand and five hundred nautical miles at sea. The numbers I dispensed varied for my own convenience, but it was a stock answer that allowed me to deflect challenges to my endeavor.

"Once you have traversed the canal, what is your plan?" he asked.

As I so often did, I said the first thing that came to mind.

"I shall stay on the *Sydney* through the Persian Gulf to Aden and from there wheel my way across the Arabian peninsula and Persia and thence to India." Geographically this made little sense, as such an overland journey would have been much shorter from Jaffa. Starting from Aden would have added perhaps a thousand miles of treacherous riding. Mr. Winchester, being a man of the British admiralty, surely knew this, but rather than challenge me directly, he simply looked at me knowingly. It was clear from his expression he thought I was full of baloney.

"Well, Miss Londonderry, you have surely chosen a difficult path. I shall be interested to know if you make it through safely or perish somewhere in the blast furnace of the endless sands of Arabia."

We had reached, it seemed, a mutual understanding of the nature of my journey. Mr. Winchester was at heart a chauvinist just like the rest of them, and he was not the first, nor would he be the last, to see through the veil. Such skeptics were of little concern to me at the moment, however. I was right where I wanted to be, doing just what I wanted to do. I was living, for the time being anyway, on my own terms.

By the time we reached Port Said I had grown quite weary of Mr. Winchester. He was pedantic, arrogant, and self-involved. I must have listened to him discourse on Britain's maritime history for close to three hours when the docks at Port Said came at last into view.

"You have saved my journey, Mr. Winchester, and I am most grateful to you for that," I said, as the ship reached its mooring.

"It has been my honor, Miss Londonderry. You are certainly a determined woman, if not the most transparent. You will make your mark for women by hook or by crook!"

I took his choice of words to be quite intentional and bristled at the idea that what I was doing was somehow crooked. I was hardly the first person on earth to take a little license with their own story and would surely not be the last. Mr. Winchester himself seemed a bit of a peacock himself.

On the pier we shook hands, I thanked him profusely, said goodbye, and set off to find the *Sydney*. She would be sailing through the Suez for the Persian Gulf in just a few hours.

I told you, Mary dear, that I left Marseille in late January and arrived in Yokohama in early March, so it is plain that I had no designs on riding across the Arabian desert for Persia. It was a vast, sparsely inhabited territory with no true roadways to speak of. It was not my destiny to perish in the sands.

There were about eighty passengers among the mail on board the *Sydney*, but I mingled little. The surprise encounter with Susie, and Mr. Winchester's slightly menacing skepticism, left me a little unsettled. I wanted to keep my own company for a bit.

A little more than a week after leaving Port Said the *Sydney* arrived in Colombo, the major port on an island that had for a century been a British Crown colony. Such British outposts, scattered the world over, had the odd effect of being both exotic and familiar at the same time. So firmly had the British made their stamp on the local cultures of these colonies that one could feel they had not set foot outside of English-speaking Britain. Thus, the impact of what might otherwise have felt strange, alien, foreign, mysterious, and intriguing was blunted by the determination of the British to make every locale feel like an extension of London or Liverpool. Colombo, with its dark-skinned, mostly Buddhist native population, was no exception.

It was early afternoon on the seventh of February when the *Sydney* docked at Colombo, where she would remain overnight. Being a British outpost, and with the bicycle as much a phenomenon in Britain as it was in France and the States, it was not surprising that there was a local cycling club in the city. With help from the officials of the Crown who met the ship I quickly made contact with them, and by midafternoon a small gaggle of wheelmen and women had met me on the docks, from which we set out on a thirty-mile spin around the city and its outskirts, followed by a supper at a guest-house frequented by British bureaucrats dispatched from London on government business. Of greatest interest were the ancient Buddhist temples in the city, several of which we stopped to examine as we wheeled around the city.

The very next morning we were out to sea again, another one-week stretch during which there was little to do but refine the stories that would become a staple of the lectures I would give when I returned to America. The next stop was Singapore, where upon arrival I gave an interview to a local reporter.

The next day I received a slap in the face from the Singapore *Strait Times*, and wondered if Mr. Winchester, for reasons known only to him, had set out to expose me as a fraud and ensure that I would never see the prize money I had been chasing for more than seven months. I was being a bit paranoid, but my concerns were not unfounded. News sometimes traveled slowly in those days, but travel it did, and it was entirely possible that a story in the *Strait Times* would appear a week or two later in a newspaper in San Francisco, Chicago, or even Boston.

A WOMAN ON WHEELS, read the headline, 50,000 FOOLS AT MARSEILLE. The story described me as "a crank from that land of marvelous wagers and remarkable exploit," the "50,000 fools" a reference to the throngs that saw me off in Marseille, hoodwinked, the paper suggested, into believing I was authentic. That number, of course, was my own count, and it did not impress the ink-stained wretches at the *Strait Times*. "But we fancy she exaggerates," read the story. "Some women do."

"Singapore has been reached," the story continued, "by the easy method of a French mail on the cheap. To the chagrin of the wagerers, she will be in Boston once more with the $5,000 legitimately earned according to the terms of the contract. Miss Londonderry, then, fortunately for journalism, retires on her laurels, and writes a book. Miss Londonderry has had experiences, of course, but they are reserved for the volume which a waiting world is bound to buy."

The press in Singapore wasn't all negative, however. "Miss Annie Londonderry," reported the *Free Press*, "the lady cyclist who has been seen cycling around near the Borneo Wharf, had dispensed with any superfluous outer garment or skirt above the knee and wears a pair of knickerbockers calculated to effectively display a pair of advertisement garters, advising everybody to 'Ride Somebody's tyres,' or perhaps to wear 'Untearable Twills.'" It was all quite risqué! The story continued: "The textual accuracy of the quotations is not vouched for, our representative (who is a modest man and fears to be misunderstood) not caring to appear as if gazing too intently in that quarter."

Oh, Mary, your old grandmother was quite a sight in those days, not above using a little sex appeal to advance myself!

I didn't fully realize it then, but the prize money was starting to loom ever larger in my thinking. When I undertook the challenge, it was, of course, one of the attractions, but secondary to my insatiable desire to leave one life for another. Now that I was more than halfway around the world from Chicago, and traveling toward home rather than away from it, it's importance was slowly growing. Ten thousand dollars was a queen's ransom in those days, especially for a family always trying to outrace borderline poverty, and it would help me atone for a multiplicity of sins, first and foremost abandoning the family. The notion was slowly gaining even more traction in my mind that it might be the only way I could justify—to Grandpa, the children, and Bennett and Baila, and perhaps to myself—having torn a wide hole in the fabric of our family. Were I to fail to claim the prize and, still worse, be exposed as some kind of charlatan, the entire family would be humiliated, and they had already suffered the profound humiliation of my leaving in the first place.

There was no way, I knew, to conceal the timeline of my travels, for anyone willing to do a little digging would surely realize I wasn't covering so much ground, or water, on a bicycle. It occurred to me that any claim I would have to the prize money would lay not in my strict adherence to the terms of the wager, but in becoming enough of a cause célèbre that the colonel would rather grant me the prize money than endure the costs of the adverse publicity his refusal would generate. It was, therefore, more important than ever that as I got closer and closer to home, I build my celebrity and fix myself in the public eye, especially the eyes of women, as a symbol of their struggles. For it was women, after all, that were still the great untapped market Colonel Pope had his eye on.

Until now I had been met with little skepticism and more than a little adulation by the press wherever I had landed. But that story in the Singapore *Strait Times* dripped with sarcasm and contempt and branded me, in not so many words, as a fraud, pure and simple. It was a harbinger of things to come.

Though I would not know it until I returned to the States several weeks later, as I was making my away across Asia on the *Sydney*, some negative notes about me were starting to appear in the American press, too. A few observant reporters scouring the news dispatches about me recognized that for a woman supposedly astride a bicycle I was popping up in cities quite distant from one another in a relatively short time. Many found my unabashed storytelling and willingness to sell myself to advertisers vulgar. But they were missing the point. Fame and notoriety, and hopefully the riches that would follow, though welcome, were not my primary ambitions. I was after the freedom of being a woman about the world, liberated from the pedestrian and soul-crushing demands of wifery and motherhood. And in all of this I was succeeding beyond my wildest dreams!

After a brief stopover in Saigon, that beautiful French colonial city, it was just a couple of days' sailing to Hong Kong and then four more to Shanghai, where I informed the editor of the *Celestial Empire* newspaper that I was engaged by twenty-two American newspapers to send dispatches about my travels (good luck finding any!) and that ten thousand people, quite a drop from the fifty thousand I'd boasted of earlier, and a brass band had seen me off at Marseille.

Just ten days earlier the Chinese had surrendered the Port of Weihaiwei to the Japanese. The brief and bloody war between them over control of Corea was all but over, but I was witness (wink, wink) to the most horrible atrocities while traveling to the war front, though it would have taken a more powerful set of binoculars than ever existed for me to see the battlefield from the *Sydney*, which left Shanghai on February 26, arrived in Nagasaki on the 27th, Kobe on March 3, and Yokohama on March 4 with yours truly aboard at each port of call.

My stories of the war front, spun from whole cloth, were honed on the two-week voyage from Yokohama to San Francisco aboard the *Belgic*, a lumbering ship over four hundred feet long and equipped to sail or steam. The raw material for those war stories I "borrowed" from a handsome war correspondent I chanced to meet on the quay while waiting to board the ship the morning she sailed, March 9, 1895.

The *Belgic.*

I was standing with my Sterling, my American flag wrapped tight and tied to my bike frame, in what was now my standard riding attire, a short jacket worn over a plain white shirt and men's trousers acquired in Paris. Newspapermen are curious by nature, and since I cut an unusual figure in my male riding costume and holding on to my cream-colored wheel with the Stars and Stripes, a man, very striking-looking, made his way through the crowd to introduce himself.

"You are, I assume, Miss Londonderry of Boston," he said. "I read about you in the *Weekly Mail*." The *Weekly Mail* was an English-language newspaper published in Tokyo and read throughout Japan.

"Indeed, I am," I replied. "And to whom do I have the pleasure of speaking?"

"My name is Johnson," he answered, extending a large, strong hand. "Mark Johnson. I'm a war correspondent for the *Call* of San Francisco. Heading home after two months at the front."

I have to tell you, dear Mary, that Mark Johnson was probably the most beautiful representative of the male sex I had ever seen. He had dark hair, a sly but friendly grin, a thin moustache, bright blue eyes, and stood several inches over six feet tall. He was about my age, maybe a couple of years older. His manners were impeccable. Decades later, when Errol Flynn became a big movie star, I could have sworn he was the son of Mark Johnson. The resemblance was uncanny.

"Well, Mr. Johnson," I said, "we will have two weeks to spend as prisoners of this ship. Hopefully, you will share with me stories of the war, of the horrors you have seen. I would be most interested to hear them." But I was really interested, as I said, in *borrowing* them.

"Likewise, Miss Londonderry," he replied. "It seems you have been on quite an adventure of your own. I should be interested to hear details of your journey, too. You see, I am an avid wheelman myself when I am not making my way through a war zone."

As Humphrey Bogart says at the end of *Casablanca*, it was the beginning of a beautiful friendship and quickly became something more. I hope I do not shock you with these confessions, dear, but you are a grown woman now, wise, I hope, to the ways of the world, and I want someone to know my story, blemishes and all. I am an old woman now, but back then I had an abundance of git up and go, and there is nothing wrong with exploring the sensual side of life. You are just sixteen now but will be thirty if you open this when I intend. Perhaps you will be married and have children of your own. Or perhaps a career. Wherever life has taken you, I do so fervently hope you have had your share of adventure and romance, and romantic adventures. Most men have. Why should we women be deprived?

Only in hindsight do I understand how, still so in love with Susie despite our ill-fated meeting aboard the *Sydney*, I was able to fall so easily under the romantic spell of Mark Johnson. It was, after all, not Annie Kopchovsky who fell for him but Annie Londonderry, an emancipated woman meeting a man on her own terms. We were both adventurers in a far-off corner of the world and we met as equals. I sensed it and he sensed it, and he engaged me as such in every way. He was, for a man, well ahead of his time, just as I suppose I was ahead of mine for a woman. Here was someone who could well understand my thirst for adventure and not be at all threatened by it.

For the next two weeks, Mark Johnson and I took nearly every meal together, spent countless hours walking the deck swapping stories of our adventures, and, to be plain, falling in love. The relationship turned romantic about halfway across the Pacific, and by the time we reached San Francisco I had all the raw material I would need to make considerable hay of my "experience" at the war front as I made my way lecturing from California to Chicago, and for the first-person account of my travels I expected to write for the *New York World* upon my return.

Thanks to Mark and the telegraph operator aboard the *Belgic*, all the San Francisco newspapers were primed for my arrival back in the United States. And, as I would learn from reading the stories they published about me, I had become a symbol for an entire generation of women and a symbol of the struggle for women's equality. The press across the country had been reporting frequently on my whereabouts during the four months I was away from American soil, and the inconsistencies in my story, and my rather fleet passage from France to the western Pacific, were mostly drowned out by coverage more favorable to me, the grand scope of the adventure overwhelming the smaller details.

To anyone paying close attention, making it from the southern coast of France to San Francisco in two months' time on a bicycle was an impossibility, and some *were* paying attention. But for most, the sheer novelty of my enterprise, indeed just a woman traveling alone, was enough to wash away doubts. I sowed considerable confusion about my own travels by telling wildly inconsistent stories about them, sometimes, as I said, to different reporters on the very same day, as I did when I arrived in San Francisco.

I told the reporter for the *Examiner* a version closer to the truth, that I had mostly been at sea since leaving Marseille, making short tours on my bike at the various ports of call. The wager, I told him, required only that I procure the signatures of American consuls in Colombo, Singapore, Hong Kong, Shanghai, Nagasaki, Kobe, and Yokohama, that "it did not matter how I reached those places, so long as I made the circuit with my wheel in tow."

Later the next day I met with a reporter for the *Chronicle* and dished up another story altogether. In that version I had ridden across India and endured a long and dangerous slog across China to the Pacific coast.

But the most effusive account of my travels appeared, not surprisingly, in the *Call*. Not only was I flattered with a description of my physical beauty (unlike the *Chronicle*, which called me "short and stout" and said I had "sacrificed personal appearances for comfort" during my journey), but I was brave, beautiful, and brilliant, and had overcome obstacles few women could have surmounted. Perhaps it is needless to say, but who knew more about me and my journey than Mark Johnson, war correspondent for the *Call*, who had just spent two weeks listening to my story, sometimes in the comfort of my bed! And who better to write a story for the *Call* than he? You might say he had an exclusive!

People were always wanting to know the answer to two other questions: how many miles had I ridden and how much money had I earned thus far, because it was widely reported that I was required to travel ten thousand miles by wheel and earn five thousand dollars in order to win the wager. My answers to those questions, like my descriptions of where I had been and how I had gotten there, were also all over the map, so to speak!

But so great had my fame become, and so effusive the accolades for what I was doing, that few were looking closely enough to notice that my answers weren't always consistent, in fact far from it. Not that it was of any concern to me anyway. Freedom and fame were what I was after, and I had achieved both and, in the process, was now seen as a champion of the female sex, of the "New Woman," and of women's equality. My story was so well known in America, thanks to the interest of the newspapers eager for a great story, that when I arrived back on American soil many of the headlines simply read, ANNIE IS BACK! I had become the shining star of my very own one-woman show.

Twelve

San Francisco. Mary, dear, if you haven't already, I do hope you will someday travel to San Francisco. There isn't a lovelier, more beautifully situated city anywhere in the world, and I would know. Sometimes called the "Paris of the West," the city was expanding over the entire peninsula by the 1890s. It was a vibrant place of 300,000 people, many coming and going from points in Asia, and it had all the virtues (and vices) of a port city, a crossroads where people of all stripes mingled.

Golden Gate Park, a park to rival Central Park in New York, had been established several years before my arrival. The city's famed cable cars were newly in operation, the clanging of their bells part of the city's infinite charm. There were many Chinese laborers in the city and a bustling Chinatown that felt like a miniature Shanghai. Throughout the city bicyclists jockeyed for position on the streets along with the wagons and streetcars, for the bicycle craze was in full flower in this city sandwiched between ocean and bay.

The weather had already turned to spring when I arrived and would remain sunny and beautiful most of the days during my stay. Mark and I took in the views of the great bay from Nob Hill, walked the beaches of the Golden Gate, though there was no bridge across it then, and admired the Seal Rocks from the newly constructed Cliff House on the city's northwest corner.

That the newspapers in the city made much of my arrival turned out to be good fortune in more ways than one, for my celebrity there would soon open the most unexpected doors.

I settled into quarters at the Palace Hotel on Montgomery Street, the city's first luxury hotel, and what a fine hotel it was. Never had I stayed in such a sumptuous place, nor since, covering the cost of my lodging in return for a short series of lectures about my travels for the guests. I would stay in San Francisco, at the Palace, for a little more than two weeks. Shortly after my arrival I learned that three other people of considerable fame were expected in the city within days and, as improbable as it may seem, my path would soon cross each of theirs, much to my benefit.

A national women's convention was to open two days hence, and I was thrilled to read that the keynote address was to be given by the great Susan B. Anthony. Though in her mid-seventies, she was still traveling the country rallying women to the causes of suffrage and social equality. Never married, she had been a major figure in the movement for more than forty years, a bold and outspoken force of nature, and widely revered by women across the country. I was determined to have an audience with her, if even briefly, and was sure that my story would have great appeal to her.

And just a week after the convention, the greatest show on earth was scheduled to open at the fairgrounds just south of the city center and along the bay. No, not the Ringling Bros. and Barnum & Bailey Circus; a show far more original than that, a show that traveled the world for three decades and made its namesake founder the most famous American in the world, even more famous than the American president, a show called "Buffalo Bill's Wild West and Congress of Rough Riders of the World." That was the full name, but mostly people just called it Buffalo Bill's Wild West Show. It was an enormous spectacle that included reenactments on a grand scale of scenes from the American West. In addition to several circus-sized tents, at one end of the open field where part of the show was staged was a huge canvas, more than four hundred feet wide and forty feet tall, on which was painted a finely detailed western landscape. And within that canvas were cutouts, barely visible from a distance, through which dozens of men on horseback, whether portraying a cavalry or an Indian war party, could gallop, with the painted canvas providing a realistic backdrop in a reenactment of, say, Custer's Last Stand or some other historic battle. It was absolutely thrilling according to all those who saw it.

One of the stars of Cody's show was the sharpshooter Annie Oakley. Remember when I was shown the advertising card in Chicago of Oakley on a Sterling? Well, we now had something in common. My image was being used to promote the Sterling wheel, as was Miss Oakley's. She was such a skilled marksman she could, in rapid succession and with nary a miss, hit a dozen airborne targets in just a few seconds.

I made up my mind to try to meet Buffalo Bill and Annie Oakley, too, and to try to talk myself into a cameo role in the show while it was in San Francisco. I had learned a few bicycle-riding tricks and now had some celebrity to trade as well. And I thought Bill Cody would understand me, for he and I had something in common, too. Though many of his daring exploits were real, Bill Cody, with the help of the dime-store novelists, was a masterful creator of his own myth. Everyone read those books, including me, and as a young girl in my late teens, enamored of Bill Cody and the American West, I read as much about him as I could.

At the age of fourteen he had become a Pony Express rider and later a scout for the Union Army during the Civil War. He earned his nickname hunting buffalo for crews working the Kansas Pacific Railroad, where he became an expert shot and earned the name Buffalo Bill. He won a Congressional Medal of Honor for his valor in the Indian Wars. Just three weeks after the fall of Custer, Cody's regiment encountered a group of Cheyenne, and Cody killed and scalped a Cheyenne named Yellow Hair to avenge Custer's death. Over the years his legend grew, and he became a favored subject of pulp-fiction magazines that glorified and exaggerated the exploits of those who roamed the plains, both the good guys and the bad guys, and this eventually led him to portray himself in a stage production that featured a reenactment of his scalping of Yellow Hair. That's where the notion of a Wild West Show on a grand scale took root in Cody's imagination, as did greatly exaggerated versions of his encounter with Yellow Hair. He claimed his small group of cavalry confronted more than eight hundred Cheyenne, but no reports of the battle mentioned more than thirty. He described his confrontation with Yellow Hair as a duel where the two horsemen charged at each other as in a medieval joust, but the Cheyenne never fought like that. He claimed he and Yellow Hair knew each other, but it was not true, and he described Yellow Hair speaking to him, challenging him, and claimed to have understood, though he spoke not a word of Cheyenne. But Cody did understand, as did I, that the stuff of legend sometimes has to be sewn from whole cloth. Where Bill Cody the man ended and Bill Cody the legend began no one really knew.

But it wasn't just our mutual interest in mythmaking that drew me to Cody. He was, improbably, an early champion of the rights of women. In 1868 he had declared, "If a woman can do the same work that a man can do and do it just as well, she should have the same pay." And he practiced what he preached: the women performers in his Wild West Show were paid the same as men who did similar work, whether they were trick sidesaddle riders, experts with a rope, sharpshooters, or actors.

And so I determined that I would, while in San Francisco, make myself known to Buffalo Bill Cody if I could, a task made all the easier by the copious amount of press I started receiving in the city within hours of my arrival. To a man like Cody, the story of a woman adventurer making her away around the world alone on a bicycle should have irresistible appeal, I thought. The only issue was how to make contact with him.

Coincidentally, Miss Anthony checked into the Palace Hotel the day after I arrived. I was in the lobby when she came striding in, accompanied by several assistants, young women about my age. It was impossible not to be impressed and, rare for me, in awe of this iconic and powerful woman. Fifty years my senior, she was controversial, outspoken, and a force to be reckoned with. She was as famous a woman as lived at the time. She had a regal bearing and, even at seventy-five, a spring in her step. She had a prominent chin, high cheekbones, a large, angular face, a masculine nose, narrow, wide-framed glasses behind which her flinty blue eyes sparkled, and straight gray hair parted in the middle, pulled back, and held in place with a small bow. A white shirt with a frill collar and a velvet, ankle-length black skirt gave her the appearance of an ancient British royal or one of the Founding Fathers, had one of them been a woman! I expected her to be taller, perhaps because of the magnitude of her celebrity, but she was just two or three inches taller than me, though heavier. For a woman so far ahead of her time she appeared as if from an earlier, more austere age.

I did not approach her as she crossed the lobby that day; I was, in truth, intimidated by her serious and imperious bearing, but I lingered close enough to learn that she was staying in a suite on the second floor. That night I pondered how best to make my attempt to gain an audience with Miss Anthony. Mark devised the scheme that evening, one of many we spent together in my room at the Palace.

"It is quite simple, Annie, but I am surprised that you of all people are intimidated by anyone, let alone an elderly woman," Mark said to me. "I will write her a note on the letterhead of the *Call*, enclose a copy of my story about you, and offer to make the introduction. You are the embodiment of the New Woman. Why wouldn't she welcome the chance to meet you? I'd wager she already knows who you are—so many do—but just in case, my story will make it clear. We can leave it for her at the front desk. I will ask that by return note she let me know if an audience would be possible."

It seemed as good a plan as any, and I agreed. The next morning Mark left the envelope at the front desk as we left the hotel to ride our bicycles along the bayfront, where we would meet up with friends of his, members of the Olympic Club, an athletic club of which Mark was a prominent member. Cycling was a popular pastime among the men of the club, and it was from his colleagues that I learned Mark was, perhaps, the best-known and most accomplished wheelman in San Francisco, capable of riding more than one hundred miles in a day, which he had done many times. He was too modest to tell me so himself. Members of the club had arranged for a luncheon on the beach where the bay meets the ocean. It was a splendid spring day and I was the object of much interest to the dozen or so wheelmen who had joined us.

We returned to the hotel late that afternoon, and Mark asked the clerk at the front desk if there were any messages for room 302, the room where I was making my home for two weeks. The clerk handed him a folded piece of paper, and I watched as he opened and read it. I could tell from the grin on his face that it was a note from Miss Anthony and that she had replied favorably to his query.

"Miss Anthony has invited us to join her in her suite after dinner this evening," he said, his smile growing bigger every second. "Seven thirty. She apologizes in advance that her schedule is so full she can only afford us a brief audience, but says she is looking forward to making the acquaintance of such an adventurous young woman."

I could scarcely believe it and I was truly nervous. I had been at times alone at night on forsaken roads in distant places, risked highwaymen and injury and even death (well, perhaps I exaggerate a little), but never had my stomach been aflutter as it was now.

"Oh my," I said to Mark, "whatever will I say to her?" The brave, intrepid Annie Londonderry who could talk rings around nearly everyone was suddenly at a loss.

"I have a feeling that won't be a problem," said Mark with a smile. "Be yourself."

But that was precisely the problem. Who was I? I had said nothing to Mark, despite the intimacy we shared, about Annie Kopchovsky. As far as he knew, the woman he had met on the quay at Yokohama, the famous globe-girdler Annie Londonderry, *was* the real me. But behind that façade was a Boston housewife and mother, and she occasionally pushed herself to the surface, as she did now. I had to push her back down.

"I suppose," I said. "But imagine . . . Susan B. Anthony."

"It will be fine," Mark reassured me. "Her note is filled with warmth. I am surprised you seem intimidated. It's quite unlike you."

That was true. Even as Annie Kopchovksy I had acquitted myself quite well with the likes of Colonel Pope, as imperious a figure as one could imagine. And he was a man! A friendly courtesy call with Miss Anthony was, I told myself, nothing to fret over. Still, I remained unconvinced.

I declined Mark's suggestion that we take dinner in the hotel restaurant before the meeting. The butterflies in my stomach made eating out of the question. Instead, I suggested, despite our long day of riding, that we walk down by the wharf. Fresh air, I said, would calm my nerves.

At seven thirty sharp Mark knocked lightly on the door to Miss Anthony's suite. One of her young aides answered and bid us to come in.

"Miss Londonderry," said the young assistant, "I have been following your journey since you left Boston last June. I spent my early years in Dorchester. You have been a real inspiration to me and many other women. Miss Anthony is excited to meet you. My name is Liza."

This put me more at ease. I realized that my anxiety about meeting Miss Anthony was rooted in my fear of being exposed as some kind of fraud. After all, some of the newspapers were beginning to suggest as much. But, as I've said, the details were of far less importance than the big picture. Whatever liberties I was taking with my own story, whatever shortcuts, could not dim the larger fact that I was a woman alone making her way around the world, relying on her own resources and wheeling thousands of miles in the process. Nine months ago

I was a cloistered housewife and mother. Now I was world famous. That was no small feat in itself.

"Please," said Liza. "Miss Anthony is in the sitting room. We have set out tea. You will enjoy meeting her as much as she will, I am sure, enjoy meeting you." Liza succeeded in easing my anxiety.

And then, almost like an apparition, she was before me, rising out of a rich leather armchair with a broad smile and her arms spread wide.

To my astonishment she wrapped her arms around me and gave me a brief hug before taking my hands and a small step back to take in the sight of me.

"Miss Londonderry," she said, "this is an honor for me. I have been hearing bits and pieces about you for several months. Liza is one of your biggest fans. That we should find ourselves in this city at the same time is good fortune. Please sit." And she gestured to a chair that had been set a few feet in front of hers.

"And you must be Mr. Johnson," Miss Anthony said. "A pleasure, sir. Please . . ." And she gestured to another chair that had been brought aside mine. Mark smiled broadly, and I knew he was smiling for me. All of my worry was for naught.

As Liza poured tea, I was vaguely aware of perhaps another half dozen women scurrying about the suite, all aides to Miss Anthony.

"So, my dear," she said, "do tell me, will you make it back in time to claim victory in your wager?" She had, from Mark's article and perhaps others, acquainted herself with some of the details of my journey.

"Of that I have no doubt, Miss Anthony," I replied. "There are not quite six months remaining on the wager clock, giving me plenty of time to make Chicago."

"Tell me, Miss Londonderry, what plans do you have once you return home to Boston? You are, I believe, from that city."

"Well, I can't say that I know for sure." It crossed my mind that perhaps she had read one or two of the rare newspaper stories that reported I was a married mother of three, but if she had she didn't betray it. "I suppose I might write a book of my adventures, or perhaps take up newspapering. I think being a reporter would suit me. I have long admired Nellie Bly."

"As have I," said Miss Anthony. "Well, whatever life has in store for you, I hope you will continue, as you have, to be an inspiration to women everywhere."

Three years later I would read a letter Miss Anthony had written to the editor of *Sidepaths*, a cycling magazine, and recognized it as very similar to something Miss Anthony said to me that evening.

"The bicycle has done a great deal to emancipate women," she said, "and you, Miss Londonderry, are proof of that. I stand and rejoice every time I see a woman ride by on a wheel, though I am too old to give it a go now. It gives a feeling of freedom, self-reliance, and independence. The moment she takes her seat she knows she can't get into harm while she is on her bicycle, and away she goes, the picture of free, untrammeled womanhood. It helps to make women equal with men in work and pleasure and preaches the necessity of woman suffrage. Don't you agree, Miss Londonderry?"

"Indeed, I do, Miss Anthony." I knew too well it was quite possible to get into harm on a bicycle, but I kept that thought to myself. Before I knew it, the half hour allotted for our meeting was coming to a close.

"Miss Londonderry, Mr. Johnson, thank you for this visit. It has been most inspiring to meet someone who truly embodies the spirit of the New Woman. I have another meeting in a few moments, but I bid you to stay just a bit longer for I would like to introduce you to the gentleman who will be calling here shortly. He has been quite outspoken on the subject of equality for women and I think you will enjoy meeting him. I am quite sure you will recognize him for he is famous the world around."

I wondered if it might be the famous orator and abolitionist Frederick Douglass; he often spoke at large national women's conferences on the subjects of racial equality and equality between the sexes. (I had not yet heard that he had passed away just a few weeks before.) A grin crossed Miss Anthony's mouth and her eyes twinkled.

Then, promptly at the stroke of eight o'clock, there was the jingle of a bell announcing a caller at the door. Mark and I glanced at each other wondering who in the world we were about to meet. Mark shrugged his shoulders as if to say, "I have no idea." Miss Anthony knew presidents and congressmen and all manner of famous and powerful people.

A moment later, Liza, the assistant who had escorted us into the parlor to see Miss Anthony, returned with another guest. You could have knocked me over with a feather.

The man standing before us was of middle age and solidly built. I put his height at about six feet. He had obviously spent a good deal of his life out of doors, for his skin was brown and weathered. He had a striking mane of graying hair that, in back, he wore well beneath his shoulders. His handlebar moustache, turned up at the corners, complimented a prominent, well-trimmed goatee. He wore a dark Stetson hat at a jaunty angle, the brim rakishly upturned on the right side. Though usually seen in a tan buckskin coat that dropped to mid-thigh and adorned with tassels that hung from both sleeves, this day he was attired in a more conservative dark gray overcoat and a matching vest. His neckwear was a string tie adorned with a small clip made of the turquoise favored by the Navajo. He was instantly recognizable.

"Miss Anthony," he said in a powerful voice as he strode confidently across the room. "It is a fine thing to see you again."

Miss Anthony stood up to greet him, and he kissed her, European style, first on her right cheek and then on her left. It was obvious there was genuine affection and mutual respect between them.

"Bill, please allow me," she said, gesturing with an outstretched hand. "This is Miss Annie Londonderry of Boston. Perhaps you have read of her. Making her way around the world by wheel."

The man grinned approvingly, and his eyes widened.

"Yes, indeed, I have been reading the local newspapers since I arrived."

The man extended his hand to me. He needn't have introduced himself. He was one of the most famous men on the planet.

"Bill Cody, Miss Londonderry. This is indeed a pleasure," he said.

I don't know how long it took me to respond. I was dumbstruck, but I suspect a man of Bill Cody's fame was used to that. And without even trying, the second person I had hoped to meet in San Francisco had, in a manner of speaking, simply fallen into my lap.

"The pleasure is all mine, sir," I managed, trying not to sound as nervous as I feared I looked. "Mr. Cody, this is my friend Mark Johnson," I continued, holding out an open hand in Mark's direction. "He is just back from the war front in Asia as a correspondent for the *Call*." They shook hands, two strapping men who had both seen plenty of violence in their day.

"Miss Londonderry has just been sharing some of her adventures with me, Bill," said Miss Anthony. "She has quite a story to tell and is quite a determined young woman. Please, everyone, sit, sit."

"Bill and I met two years ago," Miss Anthony explained, for the look on my face must have conveyed a mixture of confusion and curiosity about how the two knew each other. "I was attending the World's Columbian Exposition in Chicago. Bill's Wild West Show had quite a run there, as you probably know. I was giving a talk to a group of clergymen when I suggested that to accommodate workingmen and -women, many of whom worked six days a week, that the fair should remain open on Sundays. Of course I knew this would be scandalous to such a group, and when one of those present rose to question me and asked, 'Would you approve of your own son's attending Buffalo Bill's Wild West Show on the Sabbath?' I shot back, 'Of course I would. In fact, I think he would learn more there than from the sermons preached in some churches!'"

"Well, needless to say," Miss Anthony continued, "all the newspapers in the city reported on this the next day. Bill read the accounts and invited me to attend the show the next afternoon, which I did with a dozen suffragist friends. Bill is a true friend to women, you know. He pays the women in his show the same as men for equal work. Anyway, he made his usual grand entrance into the arena on horseback, rode up to the VIP section where he had arranged for us to be seated, stopped his horse, stood in his stirrups, and gave us a gallant wave of his Stetson and bowed deeply. I stood, bowed in return, and waved my handkerchief. That elicited quite a cheer from the thousands in attendance."

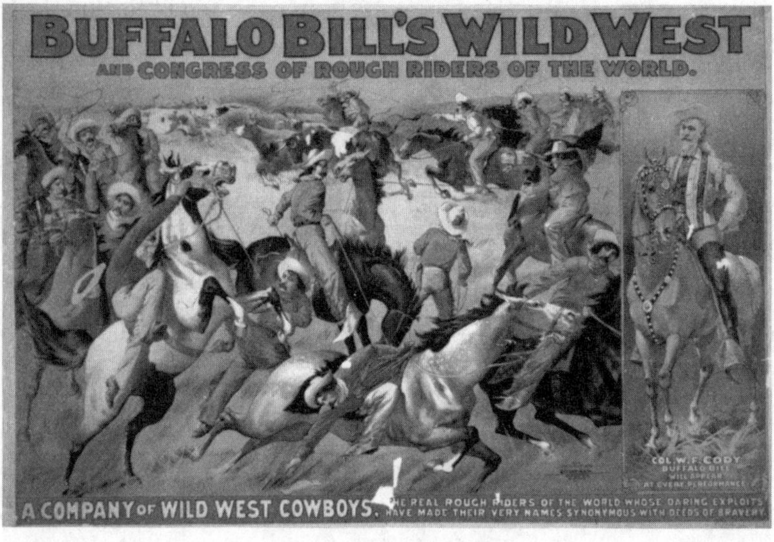

Cody, evidently enjoying Miss Anthony's reminiscences, smiled broadly and nodded as if replaying the scene in his head. As the conversation proceeded I was trying to screw up my courage and find a polite way to inquire about making a cameo appearance at Cody's show, but he beat me to the punch just as we were about to take our leave.

"How much longer do you expect to be in town, Miss Londonderry?" asked Cody. "I do hope you and Mr. Johnson will be my guests at the show. We open in three days' time."

"We would love to, Mr. Cody, that is very kind of you. I expect to be here for another two weeks or thereabouts."

"Even better, then," said Cody. "Perhaps you would be willing to make an appearance in the show? We would be honored if you would do so! I am sure we can devise a way. Your notoriety is already well established. I imagine people would thrill to the opportunity to see you make an appearance on your wheel. Indeed, of late, Miss Oakley—I am sure you know of her—has been doing some sharpshooting while pedaling a wheel. Maybe there is way for you appear with her. Would that be of interest?"

I was, truly, almost speechless now. It was exactly what I had hoped. More, in fact. I could scarcely believe my good fortune.

"It would be an honor and a thrill, Mr. Cody. To be honest, I was planning to try and arrange a meeting with you to propose such an idea. Lady Luck appears to be looking down on me today."

"Where do you stay in the city?" he asked.

"Right here at the Palace," I replied. "One floor up."

"I will speak with Miss Oakley tomorrow and send one of my men to call on you the day after. Would 10 A.M. be convenient?" He was a kind and courteous gentleman. Very dignified.

"I will make it a point to be in the lobby at that hour," I answered. "Thank you. I couldn't be more excited, and I am most pleased to make your acquaintance here thanks to Miss Anthony." I looked toward her, and she was beaming, as if she had made a match found only in heaven.

"Thank you, Miss Anthony," I said, reaching out to shake her hand. "Meeting you has been the honor of a lifetime." She took my hand, stood up, and embraced me again.

"The honor has been mine, Miss Londonderry. You may not realize it now, but you are striking a solid blow for women with this tour of yours. If I do not see you again before I leave the city, Godspeed. I will be looking at the papers for news of your progress and, I expect, your eventual success, which, I believe, is assured."

Mark made his goodbyes, and we exited Miss Anthony's suite. We stood in the hallway looking at each other, half stunned, half elated, and fully in disbelief at what had just transpired. We had to walk more than an hour in the chilly night air—it felt more like walking *on* air—before I felt like I had returned to earth. Mark made sure that my meeting with Miss Anthony and her favorable words about me appeared in the next day's *Call*, thus cementing my bona fides as a champion of the rights of women, and I would make sure that a copy of the article reached the desk of Colonel Pope by mailing it immediately to Alonzo Peck in Boston. I was sure he would see the reason for my doing so. I was paving the way to lay claim to the prize money. With the article I enclosed a brief note saying that I expected in a few weeks' time to be at the Hollenbeck Hotel in Los Angeles if he wished to reach me.

True to his word, Colonel Cody dispatched a messenger. I was waiting in the hotel lobby when he arrived promptly at 10 A.M. and gave me a handwritten note inviting me to come to the fairgrounds at four that afternoon with my Sterling. "Miss Oakley," read the note, "is as delighted as I am to welcome you as a special guest in Buffalo Bill's Wild West Show." It was signed "Col. Bill Cody." I felt as if I were dreaming.

Mark and I decided to ride out to the fairgrounds together, a short trip of only a few miles. It was another lovely spring day. When we arrived it seemed everyone already knew who I was and were expecting me. We were directed to Colonel Cody's "office," a small white tent set up adjacent to several of the larger circus tents used for parts of the show. Miss Oakley was already there, recognizable from the many photographs that had appeared in newspapers and magazines over the years.

"Ah, Miss Londonderry, Mr. Johnson. Good to see you again!" said Colonel Cody, as he came out from behind his mahogany desk to greet us. He could not have been warmer or more gracious. "Let me introduce you to someone who needs no introduction. Miss Londonderry, Mr. Johnson, allow me. Miss Annie Oakley."

Annie Oakley had for years been one of the brightest stars of Buffalo Bill's Wild West Show. A true legend. One of her nicknames was Little Miss Sure Shot, but for some reason it had never dawned on me that the word "little" was being used literally and not figuratively, for women were often, regardless of their stature, referred to back then as "little," a way of belittling their significance. So I was quite surprised to see that Miss Oakley was in fact a tiny woman, barely five feet tall and small boned. She stepped forward, shook Mark's hand briefly, then took both of mine in her own and held them for a good minute or more. Her hands and her gaze were as steady as I had ever seen. No wonder she was a marksman, or should I say, marks*woman*, without peer.

"I have been following your journey for many months now," said Miss Oakley. "I have the utmost admiration for your grit and perseverance. What good fortune that we have a chance to meet."

In the past two days I had met three of the most famous Americans alive. It was quite a heady experience.

"Please, the honor is truly mine," I replied. "It is like seeing someone step off the pages of a dime-store novel. When I received my Sterling in Chicago and agreed to appear in some adverts for them, I was shown the publicity card of you aiming your rifle while astride a Sterling. I could hardly fathom that I was in such famous company. And, now, meeting you face-to-face . . . well, I hardly know what to say."

"Please, everyone, sit," said Colonel Cody. "We have business to discuss!"

And so it was decided that for the week the show was in town, I would appear briefly during Miss Oakley's sharpshooting demonstration and be paid the generous sum of two hundred and fifty dollars for doing so. Miss Oakley had many routines, each seemingly more impressive than the next. She was capable of shooting half a dozen objects tossed simultaneously in the air in a matter of two or three seconds, of hitting a target with precision at a distance of two hundred feet even while standing with her back to the target by holding a mirror to get it in her sights and shooting over her shoulder. She could split a playing card held edge-on from a distance of thirty feet, hit dimes tossed into the air, shoot cigarettes from a man's lips, extinguish a candle flame with a speeding bullet, and knock the corks off bottles without damaging the glass. How I could contribute to her act was beyond me, but she had an idea.

"Can you steer your wheel steadily using just one hand?" she asked.

"Yes, Miss Oakley, I have often found myself steering single-handedly when the paths have been smooth."

"Would you have the nerve to allow me to shoot a target you held in your other hand?"

My journey had been filled with dangers, but this seemed to be a danger of another order. I wasn't sure and gave Colonel Cody a nervous glance. He was grinning like a Cheshire cat.

"Miss Londonderry, let's step outside and allow me to show you something," said Miss Oakley, sensing my apprehension. "Bill, will you serve as my assistant?" Cody smiled broadly. I had the feeling he had been through this routine before.

Outside, rifle in hand, Miss Oakley motioned for the colonel to walk a ways from the tent. When he'd walked about fifty feet she called out, "Right there. That will do." Without another word, Colonel Cody removed two coins from his pocket and held one in each hand between his thumb and index finger. He extended his arms, then bent them up at the elbow so that the coins, glinting in the sun, were about a foot away from each ear. With no other word spoken between them, Miss Oakley raised the rifle, looked down the barrel and without so much as a second's hesitation fired off two shots that blew the coins right out of the colonel's hands. He didn't even flinch. His trust in her was absolute. Her faith in her aim was absolute, as well.

Mark and I stood in stunned silence.

"I never miss, Miss Londonderry," she said with a wry smile. "Your life will not be in my hands, but in yours. Here is what I suggest. We will each be on a wheel in a ring circling in opposite directions. You will hold a small piece of plywood, about a foot square, on which will be painted a target. Hold it in the hand closest to the outside of the ring, out in front of your body. When we are on opposite sides of the ring I will put a hole in that target. I won't fire unless I am sure I have a clear shot. But we will need to practice. Are you game? Believe me, this is easy as pie for me. The novelty is only in the bicycle."

What could I say? For months I had been hailed as a woman of remarkable courage and pluck. I had been presented with an extraordinary opportunity to build my fame, earn a tidy sum of money, and would have a story I could tell for the rest of my life. I couldn't say no, but I had misgivings aplenty. The colonel approached.

"The last thing I would do is put you in danger, Miss Londonderry," he said in a kindly voice. "For Miss Oakley this is about as difficult as hitting the side of a barn from ten paces. But I understand your concern. Think it over and, if you are ready, come back tomorrow morning so you and Miss Oakley can prepare. The show opens in two days."

You won't be surprised to learn that the next morning I had ridden back out to the fairgrounds. We started simply enough by riding our wheels in opposite directions around a ring; I was to keep to the outside, riding counterclockwise, allowing Miss Oakley, riding clockwise, to pass inside to my left. Once comfortable doing so, she asked me to continue but steer only with my left, inside hand. I hardly noticed when she took hold of her rifle and began circling, steering with her left hand, the rifle in her right by her side. We did this for perhaps an hour when she then produced the first of a couple of dozen plywood targets that had been prepared by the show's carpenters.

"This is just for practice, Miss Londonderry," she said reassuringly. "I want you to be accustomed to steering with your left hand while holding the target in your right well in front of you and facing across the ring. If you are steady, during the show, by the fourth or fifth pass I will fire. It will happen so fast you'll hardly notice. I will not signal you as that will only have the effect of making you tense up and raise the risk of injury. The longer we circle each other, the more the suspense will build for the audience."

I must be crazy, I thought. But I could hardly back down now and maintain my self-respect. We practiced for close to two hours.

Then, without warning, during one of our practice rounds, as I concentrated on keeping my bike steadily moving in a circle while extending the target in front of me, I was startled by the report of the rifle and nearly lost control of the wheel. But there was a method to Miss Oakley's madness that I recognized straight away. By the time I heard the shot, the bullet had pierced the precise center of the target and lodged itself somewhere in the densely packed hay bales that surrounded the ring for exactly that purpose.

I brought the wheel to a stop, the target firmly in my hand. My grip was so tight from fear I had trouble releasing it! Miss Oakley pulled alongside and put one hand on my shoulder.

"If you knew I was going to fire, you would have been too tense. This way, there was no time to react. I wanted you to see that you could do it, and, Miss Londonderry, you did it!"

Basking in the approval of a woman of Miss Oakley's fame, I felt a surge of confidence, in myself and in her. We practiced another dozen times, and each time it became easier as she shot a hole right through the center of the target without exception. I was ready.

Since I was to be with the show for two performances a day for six days, Colonel Cody suggested I stay at the fairgrounds with the rest of the troupe and that I spend a last night at the hotel, pack my things, and return the next day. He said he would dispatch one of his men to retrieve my steamer trunk in the morning. I readily agreed.

It would be hard to exaggerate the enormity of the logistics in running the Wild West Show. There were more than two hundred performers, including dozens of horsemen. Some were former U.S. cavalry officers; others were experienced cowboys from all over the West. There were, of course, dozens of Indians—Cheyenne, Sioux, Mandan, and Apache. The famous Chief Sitting Bull himself had joined the cast for a few months back in the mid-1880s! But there were also riders from all parts of the world where horseback riding was a great tradition: Cossacks from Russia, Mongols, and Arabians. And it took an army of laborers and other staff to support the show. There were carpenters, cooks, ditch diggers, manual laborers, a couple of nurses and a doctor, wranglers, farriers, messenger boys, laundresses, costume makers, and even a barber and, for the women, a hairdresser. More than four hundred people and perhaps half as many animals, mostly horses, that needed to be fed, tents and cots to sleep on, blankets, cookware, latrines, water troughs, saddles, stirrups, and ropes, countless hay bales, rifles, tomahawks, headdresses, costumes, and the huge canvasses on which Western backdrops had been painted in meticulous detail. Though Colonel Cody was a modern thinking man, sleeping tents were segregated by sex and race. Dozens of them were set up in rows, forming a small, temporary village. Each slept about ten to twelve; privacy was the one thing in short supply. And all of this, the equal of a small city, had to be taken down whenever it was time to move on, and set up in the next town. And imagine that the show wasn't just an American hit, but popular all over Europe, as well!

When I saw Mark that evening, he was excited for me and had no reservations about my taking up Colonel Cody's offer to stay on the fairgrounds. In fact, I think he was a little bit jealous. But he promised to come to at least two of the shows. We were both aware that right after my stint in the show it would be time for me to return to the road, for time was a-wasting. And though neither of us had said so much as one word about it, we both knew I would not be leaving San Francisco by myself. Unspoken, we had a mutual understanding that we would ride together south toward Los Angeles; exactly how long we would remain together was a question yet to be answered.

Lest you wonder why my plan was to head to Los Angeles and not directly east toward Chicago, the reason is simple. Though the mileage would be longer, the riding would be easier going around the Sierra and Rocky Mountains than over both of them, especially since wintry weather can afflict both at the higher elevations well into summer. And so I had decided my route would take me south, then east across the desert to El Paso, where I would turn north and ride along the eastern slope of the Rockies. Somewhere near Denver I would find the best route east toward Chicago.

The next morning, after one of Colonel Cody's men had hauled my trunk off from the hotel, I headed downstairs to retrieve my bicycle for the short ride to the fairgrounds. Mark was with me, and to our delight, there in the lobby was a poster and handbills advertising the Wild West Show with a hand-drawn depiction of me on my Sterling holding the plywood target in my right hand and steering with my left:

COME SEE MISS LONDONDERRY,
THE PLUCKY GLOBE-GIRDLING
WHEELWOMAN FROM BOSTON, SPECIAL GUEST OF
COL. BUFFALO BILL CODY, AS SHE PERFORMS AN ACT OF
DEATH-DEFYING COURAGE WITH
"LITTLE MISS SURE SHOT"
ANNIE OAKLEY!

I learned that the Wild West Show even included a portable print shop capable of turning out handbills in just a matter of hours. They were all over the city that morning. You can imagine the thrill of seeing myself portrayed in such a way as part of the greatest show on earth!

The six days I spent with Buffalo Bill's Wild West Show exceeded even my highest expectations. The crowds loved the routine Miss Oakley had devised for us, and my confidence grew with each performance. It seemed everyone knew who I was, and the favorable press continued day after day. Everyone treated me like a star, and Colonel Cody generously added to my purse beyond what he had promised when we met for the last time in his tent to say goodbye. It all seemed like a most pleasant dream. But the time had come to leave the beautiful city between the bay and ocean. It was now the second week of April.

Before leaving San Francisco, I arranged with Taber Studios, a professional photography studio, to have some photographs taken and turned into lantern slides that I could use to spice up the lectures I planned to give as I made my way east, another way to earn money. I had purchased dozens of such slides in Jerusalem and at the various Asian ports and taken them with me aboard the *Sydney*. Some were depictions of the bloody battles of the Chinese-Japanese War, some of exotic people, and some simply scenic. All together I had about a hundred, plenty around which to build my lectures. Taber Studios provided two actors, employees of the studio, actually, for this one, which, I was sure, would be hit.

No time I spent traveling was more enjoyable, more deeply pleasurable, than the time I spent in San Francisco. Appearing in Buffalo Bill's Wild West Show cemented the fame I had longed for, and added generously to my purse, as well. Whether I conformed precisely to the terms of the wager, I was increasingly hopeful that the pressure would be on Colonel Pope to make good on the prize money or face a backlash of bad publicity. And I was quite in love with Mark Johnson. We'd been together for several weeks since leaving Yokohama and were kindred spirits. He placed no burdens on me and embraced my independent, rebellious nature. Like Susie, he seemed to understand me as few others ever had and always treated me as his equal. Meeting, in short succession, three of the most famous Americans alive, thrilled me no end. When each of them died in the ensuing years—Miss Anthony in 1906, Colonel Cody in 1917, and Miss Oakley in 1926—I mourned as news of their deaths transported me back to the finest, most exciting hours of my life.

Los Angeles is, in a direct line, less than four hundred miles from San Francisco. The roads in California were generally better than in most of the country, and a strong rider such as Mark could, even if riding leisurely, have made the trip on a bicycle in less than a week. Even a less experienced rider could easily have made it in less than two. For reasons I leave to your imagination, we arrived in Los Angeles on the tenth of April, six weeks after leaving San Francisco. We did not seek the most expedient route nor the straightest one. Spring in California is positively intoxicating. The hills, which brown in the summer heat, are lush green. Wildflowers proliferate. The sun kisses the cheeks nearly every day, all day. Romance is in the air.

I had a commitment to deliver my first lecture since arriving back in the States, save for the more informal talks I gave to earn my keep at the Palace Hotel in San Francisco, at the opera house in Stockton on April 11. I arranged for my trunk to be shipped by rail the day before our departure from San Francisco.

Our first day of riding, we crossed to the east side of the bay by ferry, covered more than fifty miles by wheel, and spent the night in the small town of Tracy. The next day I suffered an accident on the Niles Canyon Road that was very nearly disastrous.

We were coasting downhill at a smart clip, came around a bend, and found ourselves face-to-face with a runaway horse pulling a small wagon coming from the opposite direction, forcing both of us into a fence trimmed with barbed wire lining that section of the road. Mark, a far more experienced rider than I, managed to break his fall by rolling onto his shoulder. I made the mistake of trying to break my fall with my arms outstretched, but I could not keep my face from striking the ground, which left me with several small cuts and bruises. Our bicycles were luckily undamaged, and after collecting ourselves and cleaning the cuts with a small cloth, we were able to continue. It could have been so much worse, and I knew straight away that there would be mileage in making it worse!

Upon reaching Stockton we found a local physician, who examined me for signs of any internal injury. A rarity in the day, the doctor was a woman, a Dr. Lomax, and when I introduced myself, she gave a wave of her hand and said she had been reading about me in the papers for weeks. And apparently she'd been paying close attention. With a knowing grin, she looked at me and said, "You are almost a doctor yourself, are you not, Miss Londonderry? Trained at Harvard, I have read." She clearly knew it was a crock. "But they say the doctor who treats himself has a fool for a patient, so I'd better have a look."

After looking me all over for signs of bruising and removing a few small stones that had embedded themselves in my upper lip, which had started to swell, she rendered her verdict.

"I think you will be no worse for wear, Miss Londonderry," she told me. "But I recommend a day or two of bed rest just in case. You don't want to aggravate your situation."

"But I am scheduled to lecture at the opera house this evening," I replied. "Hundreds of people will be there. I can't disappoint them."

"Well, I do not recommend it, but I suspect my recommendation will not deter you."

She was right, of course. Sporting a black eye and some facial bruises, my body sore and my lip swollen, I delivered my lecture to a full house that evening, beginning with an explanation of why I looked the way I did.

"There was not one vacant seat," read the story in the next morning's paper. "The audience was composed almost entirely of men and the majority of them seemed to take more interest in Miss Londonderry—who is a shapely young woman—in her abbreviated cycling habit than they did in the images that were thrown on the screen," a reference to the lantern slides I showed using what we called a "magic lantern" back in those days. It's a device that used an electric arc as a light source capable of projecting images from glass plates onto a screen.

After the weeks in France in which I was repeatedly described as manly or masculine, or even as neither male nor female but some "third sex," I was happy to be back in a land where men (and women) might appreciate my womanhood again!

But by the next morning, it wasn't only my face that was bruised. Bruises appeared on my torso, too, and I felt unwell. Mark and I returned to Dr. Lomax's clinic, located in her home. By then I was also running a fever, and I accepted Dr. Lomax's recommendation that I recuperate there. Mark lodged with a friend he had made at the lecture the night before.

Prior to leaving San Francisco I had tossed into my steamer trunk a stack of letters bound in twine that had made their way to me at the Palace Hotel. I was too preoccupied to open them, and honestly, I wasn't keen on reading letters from home anymore. I wasn't interested in anything that would take me backward; I was only interested in pedaling forward. I had no longing for home, not even, I admit to you with some sorrow, for Grandpa and the children. I was, despite my current condition, happy to be in a little bubble into which my old life would not intrude. But, bored and with nothing to do as I took bed rest at Dr. Lomax's, I asked Mark to bring me the letters the next day. There must have been close to a hundred of them, far more than I had realized, and most, many dozen, were proposals of marriage from men I had never met! Some had read about me in the papers, some had seen me at the Wild West Show, and in each the writer made his case for matrimony. Men who claimed to be rich promised a life of luxury. Some professing their love of wheeling promised adventure. Some, more backward than the rest, said that a woman as attractive as me should not go through life without a husband and children, and promised a large, happy family. A few were alarmingly forward about their desires. All of these letters made a rapid trip into the dust bin.

I was relieved that there was no letter from Susie. I felt badly about our last encounter and hoped we would at some point move beyond the sadness that accompanied it, but I didn't want the intrusion. There were, of course, letters from Grandpa and my brother Bennett, letters filled with little bits of news, assurances that the children were well, and the like. But I read them dispassionately and with considerable ambivalence. After all, with every day that passed, I would be riding closer and closer to the inevitable return to the very life I had been so desperate to escape, utterly unsure of what the future would bring and how, or if, I would manage to slip back into my old life and pick up once again all of the burdens I had happily dropped nine months ago.

On the morning of the eighteenth of April, the fever gone and my bruises almost entirely healed, we left Stockton for San Jose, joined by a group of San Jose wheelmen Mark had invited along.

An interview I gave to the *Daily Mercury* there was the first opportunity I would have to embellish my account of the accident in Niles Canyon. Like the fisherman telling the tale of the one that got away, in each subsequent telling of the Niles Canyon accident, the ball of yarn would grow bigger and bigger. In San Jose I reported that the spill had knocked me unconscious and that I lay in a coma for two days in the hospital. When I awoke, I coughed up a good deal of blood and was told by the doctor that I would never make a complete recovery.

"But here I am!" I told the astonished reporter. "And what's more, I intend to complete the journey."

After leaving San Jose, Mark and I spent several days riding purely for pleasure in and around the hills west of the city before making our way across the flat terrain to the southeast, past Morgan Hill and Gilroy to Salinas. There we chanced to meet another long-distance rider, a meeting I would come to regret.

His name was Thomas Winder, a newspaper editor from Warsaw, Indiana. Winder was in the midst of what the *Salinas Weekly* called "the longest ride ever undertaken on a bicycle." Winder's game was to win a one-thousand-dollar prize by riding the entire border of the United States, some twenty-one thousand miles in all, Winder told the paper. This was preposterous. The circumference of the United States is, depending on how you figure it, somewhere between eight thousand and eleven thousand miles. Not that Winder's making more of himself than he deserved would have bothered me; I was doing the same. But when he called me "a hustler" in a story published the day after we met, accused me of making my journey entirely by steamship, described my lecture tour (which at this point had consisted of just the one lecture in Stockton) as "a dismal failure," and warned the public that I intended to write a book that would be fiction, I was riled. Our encounter had been pleasant enough. Why he chose to disparage me this way I can only surmise—he saw me as a competitor for the attention and affections of the public. Negative publicity rarely bothered me. It only added to my growing fame. But I resented that Mr. Winder saw fit to be the source of such mischief. However, I took to heart that I would likely find myself the subject of increasing skepticism as I closed in on my goal of reaching Chicago by mid-September, and that the prize money I hoped to claim might be put beyond reach if Mr. Winder's view of my endeavor became the dominant one. And, it seemed, the trend was in that direction. The articles that began to find their way to me from various newspapers and magazines were now filled with words such as "allegedly" and "supposedly."

Cycling Life, a magazine that had been following my journey and had run advertisements for the Sterling wheel with my image, wrote snidely, "Smart girl, Annie Londonderry, but much too fresh to be touring the world as a representative of American womanhood in any shape or form. To read of the hair-breadth escapes of this young woman, to say nothing of the hair-breadth escapes of the people who make her acquaintance, makes our eyes bulge with astonishment."

The *Sandusky Register* in Ohio wrote, "as she left Marseille, France, sometime in January, her trip across Eastern Europe and Asia must be considered a record-breaker from a cycling standpoint. What are you giving us, gentle Annie?"

"According to original plans, Miss Londonderry should be in the wilds of some savage country instead of delivering lectures on the West Coast," reported the *Chicago Tribune*.

The fact is, I wasn't making much of an effort to conceal anything. Yes, I told stories about places I had never been, contradictory accounts of how I had reached Japan from Marseille, and it should have been obvious, as it was to some, that no one on a bicycle could have covered such a great distance in so little time. But the lesson I learned was this, Mary: never underestimate the power of the mind to see what it wants to see and to believe what it wants to believe. Yes, the chorus of skeptics was growing, but for the most part people wanted to believe, and so they did. Perception has a way of becoming reality.

My idyll with Mark Johnson continued down to Paso Robles, San Luis Obispo, Los Olivos, and Santa Barbara, where we arrived on the thirteenth of May, almost a month after leaving San Jose. I gave a few lectures along the way and was quite the draw wherever I appeared. Mark and I knew that our time together was growing shorter with each passing day, which explains why our daily progress was so modest. The spring air, the ubiquitous wildflowers, the beauty of the mountains and the sea were thoroughly intoxicating, and our affection for each other, already strong, grew by the mile. Yet, as close as we had grown, Mark still did not know my real identity, or that I was married and had three babies at home waiting for their mother to come home. If he had somehow learned that I was not who I appeared to be (by reading some of the earliest accounts of my travels, perhaps), he never mentioned it, and that he would have been silent had he known seemed wildly improbable to me. And if anyone was expert in the improbable it was me.

I do hope, Mary dear, that at some point in your life you have known passion like this, that you have had that one impossible love affair, preordained by circumstance to come to a close (after all, Grandpa and the children awaited), but, which, while it lasted, carried you away on its wings.

Since recovering from my injuries in Stockton, the riding was without misfortune, but our luck changed for the worse some twenty-four miles from Los Angeles. The Sterling suffered a tire puncture, and the repair kit we had, when opened, was missing the glue we needed to affix the patch. We had no choice but to walk our bicycles all the way to the city. It was dusk, but the moon rose full, and for the next ten hours we walked in the silver light and watched the sun rise from the hills just north of the city.

You would not recognize the Los Angeles into which we walked that May morning. As I write, the population of Los Angeles is approaching two million people, and by the time you read this it will surely have multiplied by leaps and bounds. Hollywood was the name of a place, not an industry. The Los Angeles of the mid-1890s was home to a mere forty thousand souls. Still, it was large enough for a cable car and had paved sidewalks and many paved streets.

Mark and I took a room at the Hollenbeck Hotel. Exhausted from our long trek into the city, we slept like logs from late afternoon until the following morning. Mark inquired at the front desk of the whereabouts of a bicycle shop that could repair my broken tire. There was one just two miles away, and we walked our bicycles there after breakfast. With the wheel repaired I set out for the newspaper offices to introduce myself, and Mark made his way to the Los Angeles Athletic Club and arranged for me to lecture there later in the week.

At the Hollenbeck I received a telegram from Alonzo Peck. He knew me to be a cunning woman and understood immediately the reason for my sending him a copy of Mark's story recounting my meeting with Miss Anthony. He wrote:

> My dear Mrs. K. Am, as you know, your biggest cheerleader. But Col. increasingly perturbed. Unhappy you switched wheels in Chicago, but acknowledges oversight that Columbia wheel not specified for entire journey. Now skeptical of your swift passage France to California. Believes it impossible you will cover required 10,000 miles. Prize money in doubt as he expects to lose wager. Will do my best but be prepared. Yours, "Capt." A.D. Peck

I was not at all surprised or even deterred by this message. It's what I would have expected. And it's precisely why I was laying the groundwork to make it more costly for Colonel Pope to refuse me the money than to pay it. It would all come down to whether I could outmaneuver the naysayers, especially in the press, who were now nipping at my heels.

The ten days we lingered in Los Angeles were bittersweet, as you can imagine. Mark wanted me to return to California when the journey had ended, and I could not honestly explain why that would be impossible. My evasiveness on the subject bewildered him. Given the intense passion we had shared for six weeks he was confused by my inability to promise him straight out that I would return. And then, the night before we had agreed that I must restart my journey east, he asked me to take his hand in marriage. I was speechless. I couldn't possibly say yes, of course, but saying no would have been a devastating blow, and an ending utterly out of drawing for what had been a beautiful six-week dream.

I told Mark I was very flattered, of course, that our feelings were mutual, and that I would use the time remaining in my journey to consider his proposal. My family, I told him, without being specific, was all back in Boston, and a move to California would be hard on my aging parents, who were, in reality, long dead. Disappointment was written all across his face, but he said he understood, that it was a large commitment, and that he would await word after I had returned home.

And so, on the morning of the twenty-eighth of May, we embraced one last time, and I watched as he pointed his two wheels north.

My heart was heavy as I pedaled on toward San Bernardino, some fifty flat miles east, across a largely uninhabited landscape on a roadway that skirted the foothills of the San Gabriel Mountains. Because I had lingered so long in San Francisco and with Mark on the ride south, I now had less than four months to make it back to Chicago to meet the deadline that had been so widely reported. I was confident it was possible, but I also knew I was beginning what would surely be the most difficult, dangerous, and challenging stretch of the journey, for El Paso was about eight hundred miles distant, and I would be crossing hot, dry, sparsely populated desert with far more rattlesnakes and scorpions than people. I would soon learn roads were little more than lightly worn paths that often petered out in the middle of nowhere, and the emptiness was so vast it was possible to ride thirty or forty miles and feel that one had not moved at all.

Adding to my woes, the newspaper notices were, with increasing frequency, growing more and more dour. The *Daily Sun* in San Bernardino said I was not "good looking" and "not much to admire in a white sweater, a light brown skirt, and a boy's hat and cap to match," yet another outfit for riding I had acquired in Los Angeles. "Yes, she is interesting," the story read, "evidently well-educated, charming in conversation, and makes a good story out of any one of a hundred incidents in her journey." And the *Los Angeles Times* wasn't impressed either: "Annie Londonderry, who is supposed, from her own story, to be going around the world on a bicycle, arrived in San Bernardino yesterday, and is working the town for what she can earn for her exchequer. She may realize enough to pay her fare on the Southern Pacific to Yuma, and thus avoid the dangers and dust of wheeling through desert sand."

Two days later I made the short ride to Riverside, where the local notices were more favorable and lifted my spirits. "Smart as a whip and an excellent conversationalist," said the *Daily Press*.

I also found a new and novel way to earn money. A large bicycle meet was underway at the athletic park, and between races I was invited to display my skills on the wheel. Though some races featured many racers competing head-to-head around the track, some were simply timed sprints, some from a standing start and some from what was called "a flying start" where the racer was allowed to build up speed as he approached the starting line. I was, by this time, very fit, and covered an eighth of a mile in fifteen and a half seconds, a quarter mile in just over thirty-three seconds, and with a fellow I met at the track, a tandem mile in two minutes and twenty-eight seconds, collecting ten dollars in all for finishing in the top tier.

I had shipped my steamer trunk from Los Angeles, and I selected the clothes I would wear for my desert crossing to Yuma: a light, white blouse with billowy sleeves, bloomers, stockings, and, to keep the sun off my head, a cap with an ample brim. I availed myself of the hospitality of the local wheelmen's club for two more days, and on the morning of June 2, with several male and female club members as an escort for several miles, pedaled south and east for my next destination, Yuma, in Arizona Territory (Arizona was not yet a state then), one hundred and sixty-five miles away. When my escorts bid me farewell and headed back to Riverside, I was, for the first time in months, truly alone, and I confess to you, more apprehensive than at any other time in my entire journey.

Thirteen

"Follow the railway tracks!"

That was the advice of the Riverside wheelmen. It was the only way not to get lost in the vast, hostile environment of the Southern California desert, they said. By day at that time of year temperatures were almost always close to one hundred degrees, the sun unrelenting, and water scarce. Without the advice of the Riverside wheelmen I'd have been a dead duck in the desert. They marked on a hand-drawn map the locations of freshwater springs and told me to avail myself of the shelter of the "section houses" immediately along the railway route, rudimentary but sturdy enclosures the size of a large tool shed where canned goods, water, and other provisions were stocked for the train crews. Whether in the searing heat of midday or the chill of the desert night, these section houses afforded nourishment and escape from the elements. They were, I was told, spaced about thirty miles apart and were always unlocked, for no one, save the crews or a daft cyclist trying to cross the desert, would have any use for them. That wasn't quite true, for I quickly learned they were a refuge for rattlesnakes also seeking relief from the sun and, in one case, a weathered and taciturn Indian man who told me he was walking all the way from Winslow in Arizona to Los Angeles to visit his sister.

The logic of following the railway tracks was unassailable. Every mile across this vast landscape looked like every other mile in every direction. Getting lost in this punishing environment could quickly turn fatal. Following the tracks was not only the way to avoid getting lost, but, in the event of illness or mechanical failure, one could at least count on a passing train for help, though one never knew if the wait would be four hours or four days. But, like most advice, this proved easier given than followed for the simple reason that the ground alongside the slightly elevated tracks was often littered with sage, rock, cactus, and other obstacles that made riding virtually impossible for long stretches at a time. I had learned back in New York State, when we had to take to riding between the elevated rails and over the ties to avoid the thick mud that accumulated alongside the tracks, that as impractical and improbable as it seems, it was often the only way to ride when the railway beds were the only alternative, and in the desert, roads were nonexistent. Bumping over endless railroad ties was bruising and exhausting, not to mention hard on the bicycle, especially the tires, but it was, across the desert, sometimes the best of bad choices.

About sixty miles from Yuma, on my fourth day out of Riverside, my tires had had enough, and the front one simply wore out. The Sterling was no longer rideable. Of course, I told the newspaper reporters in Yuma that I had pushed the broken machine across sixty desert miles, but the *Los Angeles Times* didn't get it wrong when they wrote, "if certain railroad men were asked how she crossed the desert, they would wink their other eye."

With fewer than two thousand souls, Yuma was, nevertheless, one of the largest towns in the Arizona Territory. Tucson, the territory's capital, was a city of five thousand, and Phoenix had a population of barely three thousand. You can imagine how sparsely settled this vast area was in those days. Yet, the railway links were expanding, connecting these towns to each other and to other parts of the West. But still, these were remote outposts in the middle of the desert, relatively isolated, which made the arrival of a woman from Boston making her way around the world on a bicycle a novelty like no other and one I was well prepared and eager to exploit.

Once my tires were replaced in Yuma, a man named Art Bennett, the editor of the local newspaper there, the *Yuma Times*, proposed to ride with me all the way to Phoenix, eager for an exclusive about having ridden nearly two hundred miles with the first woman going around the earth on a bicycle. Bennett was a mild-mannered man of middle age who had been in Yuma since he was a child. His horizons didn't extend very far beyond Arizona, and so he was particularly charmed by my stories of exotic places such as the jungles of India and the rugged countryside of China. Though I would soon become accustomed to various newspapermen making their advances, Bennett was too modest to be inappropriate in any way. He was an experienced wheelman, had made the trip to Phoenix by wheel several times, and was therefore familiar with the rigors of desert riding. He knew the locations of several freshwater springs along the way, how to get water from a cactus, and was accustomed to spending nights in the section houses along the Southern Pacific Railroad. At night, to keep ourselves safely above the poisonous critters that often, as we did, used the section houses for shelter, we had to clear the heavy wooden shelves that held canned goods and water jugs and miscellaneous equipment, and sleep on them or, if there was a table inside, on that. And each morning, or in the middle of the night if we had to relieve ourselves outside, we had to carefully scan the floor to be sure it was safe to put our feet to the ground. More than once I was terrorized by the rattle of a snake's tail, and I was lucky to escape the desert unbitten.

It was hot and dry during the daylight hours, but we were able to cover about fifty miles each day, mostly riding alongside the tracks, sometimes on the ties as I have explained. The sunsets were breathtaking, and I found the isolation and utterly still quiet of the desert very agreeable. It was possible to believe, watching the fiery sunsets turn the hills, the cacti, and the sagebrush into a surreal, dreamlike landscape, that there wasn't another person anywhere on earth.

When we reached Phoenix, Mr. Bennett escorted me to the hotel and then headed directly to the train station for the return trip to Yuma. I never heard from him again, and whether he ever wrote up a story I do not know. I assume so!

Before we left Yuma, Mr. Bennett had sent a telegraph message to the Valley Cycle Club in Phoenix, and they made a nice fuss about me for the two days I passed there. I spent part of the first day walking about the town in my bloomers with a local reporter from the *Arizona Gazette*, and though bloomers were by then a common sight in, say, Chicago or New York or San Francisco, they were a novelty in a remote town like Phoenix, and I turned quite a few heads. The reporter captured one encounter with a woman who was startled to see me in such an outfit, though he embellished a bit, and why not?

Upon seeing me in bloomers, he wrote, this woman "threw up her arms in horror and bemoaned the depravity and boldness of the nineteenth-century girl. 'Wal if that ain't queer doin's now-a-days. I jest seen a woman wearin' men's pants!'" The reporter, so the story went, explained that they were bloomers. "'Balloons, did you say! Wal if ever ketch my darter wearin' balloons, I'll jest, I'll jest . . .'"

I was, in my outfit, challenging every preconception folks in those parts had about masculinity and femininity and rather enjoying it!

I also called on the local Sterling agents, whom I had telegraphed from Yuma, and they used me and my bicycle as an attraction, taking out a large advert in the *Gazette*:

ANNIE LONDONDERRY,
THE LADY WHO IS RIDING AROUND THE WORLD
ON HER STERLING, IS IN TOWN—HER WHEEL WILL BE
ON EXHIBITION AT PINNEY & ROBINSON'S

As in France, the local wheelmen's clubs delighted in serving as escorts and helping me make contact with other clubs down the road. And so, with an escort of about half a dozen wheelmen from Phoenix, I spent two days getting to Red Rock, where an escort of Tucson riders met me for the ride into that city.

The Tucson club had seen to it that my arrival in the city would be well noticed, and as we reached the outskirts of town another twenty riders or so joined the procession, including a famous trick rider from Los Angeles, Claude Leslie, who made his living traveling the West giving demonstrations of his unique skills. He could ride for distance balanced on his back wheel, ride backward while standing on his saddle, and had all manner of entertaining but otherwise useless cycling skills. He was a funny fellow, though, with a large personality, a booming voice, and a stable of silly jokes he used during his routine. I took a shine to him right away; not in a romantic way, as he wasn't a terribly attractive man, though he was a physical specimen. He just seemed to take delight in everything.

The people of Tucson were giddy with anticipation about my arrival. One group positioned itself in a bell tower with binoculars hoping to catch a glimpse of me and my posse as we came over the horizon.

"All the Tucson riders unite in testifying to Miss Londonderry's ability as a rider," reported the *Daily Star*, though they noted I was a bit wobbly as I rode into town. Riding in the company of two dozen men, and with no trees or other obstructions in the empty desert, I had no chance to relieve myself for several hours, which accounted for my "wobble."

We had just enough time to check into the Orndorff Hotel, have a quick dinner, and make our way to the opera house, where arrangements had been made for me to lecture about my trip and for Leslie to demonstrate some of his skills on the wheel, though the small stage severely limited his repertoire.

To understand why my lectures were so popular in these small, remote cities, you have to understand the isolation of life there in the 1890s. Yes, they were connected by train to other cities, but most people lived almost their entire lives within a few square miles. Rarely did I meet anyone in these remote towns who had traveled overseas, or even to Boston, Chicago, or Los Angeles, so it was easy to fill their imaginations with stories of hunting for tigers in the jungles of India, exotic geishas in Japan, and bloody battlefronts in China. The characters who inhabited my stories would, figuratively speaking, have been at home in a circus sideshow or a Jules Verne novel: Japanese laborers with bodies completely covered in tattoos, Bedouins, opium merchants, and royalty. I'm not sure if half my stories were believed by even half my audiences, but they paid, usually twenty-five or fifty cents, for an evening's entertainment, and that's what I gave them—my best one-woman show. The lantern slides I had collected with images of exotic people, distant countrysides, and bloody battles gave life to these stories and left people quite satisfied that they had gotten their money's worth.

My sights were now set on El Paso, the largest city I would see between Los Angeles and Denver. Back then, El Paso was a lively town of more than ten thousand and, I figured, one of my last chances to make a big splash. I started sending telegrams and telegraph messages to the bicycle clubs and the newspapers there ten days before I expected to arrive, and my efforts paid handsomely, for my impending arrival was well reported as early as a week before I reached the city.

On the morning of June 21, Bert Orndorff, the owner of the hotel in Tucson and a passionate wheelman himself, organized an escort to accompany me east toward Willcox where a telegram from a man named Jim Williams of the El Paso wheelman's club reached me, detailing the rousing reception that was being planned for me there.

"Expect delegation of El Paso cyclists to meet you in Strauss," he wrote, referring to a town in New Mexico about fifteen miles north of El Paso. "Have arranged for lecture at McGinty Club, meetings with most important newspapermen of city, and special appearance at bicycle races on Fourth of July. Pray we can induce you to remain in El Paso until then."

I was excited that such a reception was planned and determined to make as much hay as I could in El Paso, known then as "sin city" because it was a magnet for outcasts, outlaws, desperados, women of ill repute, and all kinds of unsavory characters. It did not disappoint.

Sometimes traveling by wheel, sometimes by rail, I arrived in Lordsburg, New Mexico, on June 23, where I received a telegram from the *El Paso Daily Herald* containing a series of questions, which I answered by return telegram. Some of my answers were true (the toughest roads I had ridden were indeed across the desert and the most hospitable people in France), some were not (I was not shot by the Chinese and I was not refused a drink of water in Yuma after pushing my broken-down bike sixty miles across the desert), but no matter. Then, on the afternoon of June 25, exactly one year since my formal departure from Boston, I stepped off the train in Strauss, and the stationmaster sent a telegraph message to the *Daily Herald* stating that I was there and awaiting my escort into the city.

About three hours later they arrived: Jim Williams, Joe Mollinary, Randolph Terry, Herbert Bishop, and a *Herald* reporter named Patrick O'Leary, who attached himself to me like glue during my stay in El Paso, a persistent and often cloying presence who was, to tell the truth, lovesick.

After introductions were made, a light dinner was spread out on tables in the railway station, and I regaled those assembled with stories of my travels, a preview of the lecture I would soon give in El Paso. It was too late to ride into the city, so the men slept on the station floor while I was afforded a small private room with a cot normally reserved for the stationmaster. I was, after all, the only woman present.

By the time we set out the next morning, more riders, having learned of my arrival in Strauss, joined those who had cycled out the night before, and with every mile the escort got larger and larger until we were close to a hundred strong pedaling through the streets of El Paso. Arrangements had been made for my lodging at the Vendome Hotel where several hundred spectators had gathered to welcome me. Not since Marseille had I seen a reception so large and enthusiastic. Since so much (ten thousand dollars' worth) was dependent on my creating a counter narrative to combat the skeptics and the naysayers, this greatly cheered me.

Mary, dear, the days in El Paso almost defy description, but I will try. In several conversations with the reporter, O'Leary, both in Strauss and the day after my arrival in the city, I filled his head with a grand and sensational account of my journey thus far. He was so utterly credulous that he eagerly shared my account almost verbatim in a big story in his newspaper the next day. So smitten was O'Leary that when he inquired about the terms of my wager, I felt obliged to add one—that I not contract matrimony during my trip—heading him off at the pass, as they say, to deflect his amorous intentions.

"The necessity of this condition," he wrote, "is patent, from the fact that she has received nearly 200 offers of marriage and written refusals to 147 of them." (Perhaps I exaggerated just a bit!) He then added: "Any horrid man who says she is not good looking ought to be taken out back of a cow shed and knocked in the head with an axe."

Having my physical appearance commented upon, for better or for worse, was generally tiresome, but a constant of the newspaper coverage wherever I went, as if it was somehow relevant to the story of my journey. At least in America it was mostly flattering, unlike in France, where I had, for all practical purposes, morphed into a man!

O'Leary gave a breathtaking account of my hunting the Bengal tiger in India, of being attacked by "Asiatics" who wanted to stick knives in my tires, voracious insects that nearly ate me alive in Hindustan, and my rattling the tar out of some Chinese soldiers with my pistol. Not only had I nearly made it around the world on a wheel, but I was a certified war hero to boot! It was all my way of teasing the public to come to the lecture I was to deliver at the McGinty Club a few days hence.

My lecture was a huge success, every seat sold, and my repertoire of stories took on a life of their own. I cast quite a spell that night in West Texas with the carnival absurdity of some of my stories!

Our bicyclist visitor gave her lecture last Saturday night on the McGinty Club grounds before an audience of about 100 people and was well-received. The fair lecturer detailed some of her experiences. On reaching Chicago she had but three cents. She made the windy city, 1,235 miles, in six weeks. En route mademoiselle had to sleep in a barn, and fell through from the loft onto a horse's back. But in eighteen days she traveled 1,030 miles to New York and earned $835 in carrying advertisements.

When in France she was not allowed to talk French, according to the terms of her contract, which made it embarrassing for her, and landed in Paris with only seven cents in American money so she earned $1,500 by carrying advertisements about town and working in stores. Miss Londonderry was six days in riding to Marseille, during which time occurred the hold-up racket already detailed in the *Herald.* Ludicrous mistakes were made in trying to make people understand her necessities. Miss Londonderry tried by signs to ask for meat to eat, and a beefsteak was given her in a shoe. She wanted mushrooms and was given an umbrella. Then the cyclist tried to make a woman understand that she wanted a place to sleep by lying down on the floor, whereupon the woman thinking it was a case of fainting threw a pitcher of water in her face. In Marseille Miss Londonderry was treated royally so that in four days she earned $1,000. Thence she went to Egypt, Bombay, and Calcutta. The Hindoos seemed afraid of the bicycle, thought it an evil spirit, so that the rider had to pay priests to pray for her in the temple, and a knowledge of this kept the natives at a more respectful distance. While in India, she visited a museum of freaks. She saw one man with a foot like a chicken, another with a leg shaped like that of an elephant, while there was one woman with a wen on her neck like a Saratoga trunk. Miss Londonderry was afraid that if she remained there much longer she would see some such sight as a man with an extra pair of legs dangling lightly from the sides of his neck, or some of the lovely creatures treated of in *Gulliver's Travels*. So she beat a precipitous retreat.

Miss Londonderry went to the battlefields of Wei Hai Wei where even little children were killed. She was favored with a guard by the French consul, but had the sleeve of her coat carried away by a bullet and was captured by the Chinese with two war correspondents and a doctor of divinity who were locked up in jail where neither food nor water was furnished. But for the snow water they would have died from thirst. The French consul finally sent forty gendarmes to release them. The lecturer said that the dead were unburied from the battlefields. The clergyman finally died from wounds he received and exhaustion from crossing a frozen river and breaking through the ice where the party came near drowning. The best they could do in the way of burial was to lay the poor man in a trench and cover him up with dead Chinese. In one shack where the party crawled in to sleep they had to brush aside the dead bodies to make a place to lie down.

The lecture concluded with the stereopticon exhibition with views taken by Miss Londonderry herself in Asia and elsewhere en route. The audience went away very much pleased.

(*El Paso Daily Herald*, July 2, 1895)

The audience laughed and guffawed and when it was over gave me a standing ovation. All that mattered was that they were entertained, and were they ever! But it was after the lecture, at a reception, that one of the most chilling episodes of my fifteen months on the road unfolded.

All who attended lined up to shake my hand and exchange a few pleasantries or have an autograph signed. Standing with me was a woman of my age who had come to call on me at the Vendome the day after I arrived, a woman who became a fast friend: Euphreisa Sweeney. She knew many of those in attendance and was able to make many introductions.

Near the end of the line stood a sturdy middle-aged man with a female companion, and when my eyes first caught his I felt a shiver go down my spine. He was serious but cordial and complimentary of my lecture, but never had I seen eyes as dead as his. It is said that the eyes are the window into the soul, but I swear that no soul lay behind those eyes. You know the phrase "if looks could kill." His gaze was stone cold.

Euphreisa Sweeney.

“Hardin is my name, Miss Londonderry.” His hand was clammy and lifeless. It was like shaking hands with a cadaver. “And this,” he said, gesturing toward his companion, “is Miss Helen.” I didn’t know if Hardin was his first name or last, and he gave no last name for his companion.

“How do you do, Miss Londonderry?” Helen chimed in. “We greatly enjoyed your lecture and are happy to have you in El Paso.”

“The pleasure is mine, Miss . . . ”

“Mrose, Miss Londonderry. Helen Beulah Mrose.”

"Miss Mrose, then," I answered. "Thank you for coming tonight, and I am delighted to be in El Paso. It's a long way from Boston to be sure."

The Hardin fellow seemed very distracted. He said a few more perfunctory words, and then he and Miss Mrose bid me good night and nodded in the direction of Euphreisa.

After they'd gone I turned to her.

"Well, he seems an odd fellow," I said. "You don't know him?"

"I do not, Miss Annie," she replied, "but there isn't a soul in El Paso who doesn't know *of* him, and a fair share are afraid of him, and with good reason."

"Afraid? Why afraid?"

"His name is John Wesley Hardin. Have you ever heard of him, Miss Annie?"

"I have not," I replied. "Whatever he may be known for, word surely hasn't traveled as far as Boston."

"Well, Miss Annie, in his younger days he left a trail of dead men in his wake. He's a legend throughout these parts, and one of the deadliest shots west of the Mississippi. Folks say that even Annie Oakley wouldn't have stood a chance against Mr. Hardin."

"Is that right?" I answered. I knew firsthand, of course, of Miss Oakley's skills with a firearm.

"Killed at least two dozen men between the ages of fifteen and seventeen, but brags it was many more," she continued. "Finally, the Texas Rangers caught up to him, and he was sent away to prison for twenty-five years, where he learned the law. When he was released last year he came here and opened a law practice. Fancy that. An outlaw turned lawyer. But he has little business. Spends most of the time gambling and drinking in the saloons."

I was nonplussed to say the least. That explained the odd demeanor and the stone-cold stare.

"Well, he gave me the chills," I said to Euphreisa. "Who was the woman accompanying him? It was not his wife, I assume, for they don't share a last name."

"Of late, Mrs. Mrose, not Miss, has often been seen on the arm of Mr. Hardin," she replied. "They are not hiding their relationship even though Mrs. Mrose's husband, Martin, is very much alive and presently in Juarez, just across the river. He's never amounted to much. A horse thief with a fondness for drink. Word is he's in Juarez avoiding the authorities."

"Come, walk me back to my hotel," I said. Together we strolled through the moonlit streets and said not another word about Hardin or Helen or Martin Mrose. But it turns out Martin Mrose was not in Juarez, as Euphreisa thought, but in El Paso, and he was not very much alive. He was very much dead, though his body was still warm. This I would learn only when I returned home to Boston in late September, where a letter from Euphreisa was waiting for me. Please save it, for it is a piece of history.

August 22, 1895
My dearest Miss Annie,

I trust this letter will find you safe and sound in Boston, and that you made a success of the final part of your journey. I do miss having you here to talk to.

You will scarcely believe what I am about to tell you. It has been the talk of the town for weeks. The same day you left our city, some workers at the town dump, just a mile or so from the McGinty Club, found a body, and from the looks of it, it had been there for a few days. The undertaker was dispatched to bring the body into town where Chief Milton identified it as that of Martin Mrose, the husband of the woman who accompanied Mr. John Wesley Hardin to your lecture in El Paso. I have no doubt you remember them. He'd been shot at least half a dozen times, twice in the neck and four times in the chest.

Well, it didn't take long for suspicions to attach to Mr. Hardin, since he'd been seen around town often in the company of Mrs. Mrose, and when the newspapermen gathered up the courage to ask Mr. Hardin what he might know about Mrose's murder, he proclaimed to know nothing about it. Witnesses who encountered Mrose heading to the dump right around the time of your lecture said he told them he was to meet a man there who had a business proposition involving some ranch land right nearby. That fixed the date of the murder. Pressed further, Hardin stated that he could not have killed Mrose that night for he was attending your lecture, and because of his notoriety, there were about one hundred witnesses who could attest to the truth of that assertion, including me.

Soon enough, though, someone involved, someone likely under the influence of drink, went bragging, and within days the whole scheme, and the events leading up to it, was known. You see, Helen Beulah first met Mr. Hardin when she was looking for a lawyer to represent Martin on a charge of cattle rustling, and their affair began straight away. When Martin learned of it he got two friends to send threatening letters to Mr. Hardin daring him to come to Juarez to come face-to-face with Martin. He did, but Mr. Hardin had company when he traveled to Juarez, Police Chief Milton and U.S. Marshal George Scarborough. When they arrived at the meeting place, Martin was absent, but a fistfight ensued between Hardin's and Mrose's men, the ones who had been threatening Mr. Hardin. Mr. Hardin pulled a gun, but Marshal Scarborough intervened, and the party left. Miraculously no one was killed.

Furious that Martin had been too cowardly to show up, Mr. Hardin decided to get his revenge. But he didn't do the deed himself. He made a plan with Chief Milton, Marshal Scarborough, a Texas Ranger named Frank McMahan, and another man named John Selman, to lure Martin to El Paso with the prospect of a business deal involving some land and then up to the dump the night of your lecture. There was already a $1,000 reward for Martin's capture or killing on the cattle rustling charge, and Mr. Hardin proposed the five men split the reward plus whatever money was found in Martin's pockets.

Remember how distracted Mr. Hardin seemed the night we met him after your lecture? Well, I'm sure his mind was on the events he hoped were unfolding over at the dump. But there's more.

After the killing, because of the complicity of someone from every level of the law in El Paso, no action was taken against any of the conspirators, and Helen Buelah, now a widow, moved in with Mr. Hardin. But in the weeks after the killing Mr. Hardin became more ornery than ever. He threatened to kill several of the men he would gamble with, he was almost always drunk, and according to Helen Buelah he even threatened to kill her.

On the night of August 19—I am writing you just three days later—Mr. Hardin was at the Acme Saloon gambling when Constable John Selman, father of one of the men who killed Martin Mrose, burst through the saloon doors and shot Mr. Hardin three times before Mr. Hardin could even move. Now, no one knows why Constable Selman killed Mr. Hardin, but rumors are all over town. Some say the junior Selman and Mr. Hardin argued over the reward money, that Mr. Hardin threatened to kill him, and that the senior Selman was protecting his son. Some say the senior Selman wanted a share of the money taken from Martin Mrose's pockets. No one seems to really know.

So, Miss Annie, you can see that it has been anything but dull here in El Paso since you left town on your wheel. Do write me a letter from time and time and tell me of your life. No one here will soon forget you.

Fondly,
Euphreisa Sweeney

It's quite a story isn't it? Imagine your little old grandmother making the acquaintance of one of the Old West's most notorious outlaws!

After the lecture I spent a few more days in El Paso, implored by nearly everyone to remain through the July 4 holiday, when part of the celebration would include bicycle races. There, several men took turns riding on a tandem bicycle with me, but few could keep up as I took the lead seat and pedaled furiously. One of my favorite bits from the newspapers described what happened when a man named Bart Allen decided to take a turn.

"The way Miss Londonderry pulled Bart Allen around the track on that tandem greatly amused the crowd," wrote the *Herald*. "She pulled him along so fast that it was all he could do to keep his feet on the pedals." The *Herald* predicted a tremendous welcome when I reached Boston and that I would then select "the fortunate man upon whom she will see fit to bestow her fair hand." Little did they know.

Three days later, on the seventh of July, an escort rode with me back up to Strauss, and from there I headed north alone, following the tracks of the Santa Fe.

Fourteen

Chicago was eighteen hundred miles ahead of me, and I had just over two months to get there if I wanted to lay claim to having satisfied at least one of the terms of Colonel Pope's wager, that I make the circuit in fifteen months. But I immediately ran into some bad luck.

Near Anthony, a short way across the border with New Mexico, I suffered a tire puncture and had to wait until the next morning for a repair kit to arrive from El Paso. No sooner was I on my way again than a deluge struck; it rained cats and dogs all day as I struggled along muddy roads to Las Cruces, thirty miles of the worst riding I had yet encountered. The rain did not relent, forcing me to spend three days in Las Cruces, three days I could ill afford if I were to make Chicago in time.

Without realizing it, I had also ridden straight into the middle of a bitter feud between the editors of the town's two newspapers, the *Independent Democrat* and the *Rio Grande Republican*. Their rhetorical battle over my authenticity would soon be joined by other newspapers in the New Mexico territory, and rage for weeks in my wake. It was a kerfuffle, really, but you'd never have known, judging by the intensity of the war of words and the cross fire in which I soon found myself thanks to a lecherous drunk named Allen Kelly, editor of the *Democrat.* I suspect the battle was so intense because the stakes were so small!

Kelly met me at my hotel for an interview shortly after my arrival in Las Cruces. Fifteen minutes into our conversation, during which his hands shook so badly he could barely take notes, those same trembling hands started to wander where they did not belong, and I delivered a solid smack to the side of his face. He reeked of alcohol and was clearly drunk, and I demanded that he leave the premises immediately, which he did, though not in a straight line. The next day, stung by my refusal to let him have his way with me, he published a lengthy screed in which he denounced me as a fraud and used many other libels. Sensing an opening to discredit their rival, the following day's *Republican* came to my defense.

> With the usual disregard for veracity, and the usual eagerness to fill up blank space, the *Independent Democrat* devotes nearly four columns to Miss Annie Londonderry, the lady cyclist passing through Las Cruces. While purporting to roast Miss Londonderry, the writer succeeds only in making a clown of himself. Such buffoonery is probably a relic of bear-training days, and it was thought those antics would please the readers of the *Democrat.* The people of our town, however, have become very tired of this kind of thing. When it is fiction they want, they know where to

find something readable and less nauseating. While not hoping for a reform in this line from our contemporary, we cannot but think how refreshing it would be to at least see an attempt made at something near the truth once in a while.

(*Rio Grande Republican*, July 19, 1895)

Now, the imbroglio grew because I fertilized it. A couple of weeks later, when I reached the town of Las Vegas, New Mexico, and was asked by a reporter from the *Optic* about Mr. Kelly's attacks on me (word travels, especially in newspaper circles), I told the reporter, and he duly reported, that Kelly had been on a "whiz" when he met me and that his beef was that I refused to go buggy riding with him. I told a reporter from the *Santa Fe New Mexican* the same thing.

Mr. Kelly simply could not let the matter go. A whole month after I'd left Las Cruces, Mr. Kelly, having read my version of events in the other papers, defended himself in print and demanded retractions from the *Optic* and the *New Mexican*.

The *New Mexican* ran Mr. Kelly's letter demanding a correction for what he deemed "a stupid slander," but wasn't willing to put the matter to bed just yet. Next to Kelly's letter was a delicious response from the editor.

Allen Kelly has been sloshing around in his editorial mudhole for over a year, butting his cranium against nearly everything and everybody in sight, emitting copious quantities of splenetic nastiness. He ought to be more careful whether dealing with his brethren of the press or with an unprotected female bicycle agent.

(*Santa Fe New Mexican*, August 5, 1895)

The *Optic*, however, had come around to Mr. Kelly's side by the time I left that city.

> Her declarations about Allen Kelly were spread all over town by Miss Londonderry. The *Optic* doubted its truth at the time, classing it with many of her traveler's yarns. Since then this paper has become assured of its falsity. Mr. Kelly, it has been learned, is not a whizzer in Miss Londonderry's sense of that term, nor does he invite strange women to take buggy rides with him. He was convinced of Miss Londonderry's unreliability, as were a large majority of those who came in contact with her, and with a fearlessness and a plainness of speech which has won him a distinguished position in New Mexico journalism, he told his convictions to the world. Miss Londonderry, unable to answer his charges, attempts to besmirch his character.
>
> (*Las Vegas Optic*, August 6, 1895)

Still not content to let the matter drop, Mr. Kelly had more to say on the subject in his newspaper.

> The alleged female person in nondescript apparel who went through here on a wheel some weeks ago claiming to have ridden around the world, did not succeed in fooling the editor of the *Las Cruces Independent Democrat* as easily as she did some others, and he exposed some of her extravagant pretensions. The libel is the assertion

that we wanted the jade to go driving with us, but that is mitigated by the allegation that we were drunk at the time. Nobody in his sober senses would have sought the intimate society of the woman, as she appears to have realized that in order to give the appearance of probability to the one assertion it was necessary to prefix the other.

(*Las Cruces Independent Democrat*, August 14, 1895)

I have to hand it to Mr. Kelly; that's one clever piece of writing. I sure stirred up a hornet's nest out there, which was, after all, the point!

But I have gotten ahead of myself, for the journey from Las Cruces to Santa Fe and Las Vegas was not without drama of another kind.

Socorro is about one hundred and fifty miles from Las Cruces, but it took me nearly a week to get there. Part of this stretch is called the "Jornada del Muerto," or Journey of the Dead Man, a broad, flat, desolate valley that in a normal summer bakes in the heat and sizzles when a sudden thunderstorm breaks open. Unfortunately, I was riding into one of the worst stretches of weather the region had seen in years. Violent thunderstorms and monsoon-like rains plagued my trip north. Only the three section houses I passed following the Santa Fe tracks provided escape from the elements over six long and exhausting days when I was often forced to push the Sterling through mud several inches thick. Where I could ride, the going was rough, whether over the ties or alongside the rails. The weather was so bad even the trains had stopped running, for several railroad bridges across shallow arroyos, normally dry that time of year, had been washed out by the raging torrents of water that ran through them. It was the first time during the entire journey that I thought I might perish, alone and far from help of any kind. But for the section houses, I had to sleep on the ground with only the clothing I wore for protection. By smashing some tins of food with a rock, tins found in the section houses, was I able to eat—the only sustenance I had for six days. No part of my journey had been, or would be, as miserable. I began to have serious doubts I would make Chicago in time.

When I arrived in Socorro on the fourteenth of July I was a sorry mess, drenched to the bone, covered with mud, exhausted, and hungry. I had shipped my steamer trunk to Albuquerque from El Paso, but had little faith given the condition of the tracks that it would be there with a much-needed change of clothes. I headed directly to the rail station in Socorro, where my luck improved, as I learned that despite the troubles farther south, the train was running between Socorro and Albuquerque. I inquired of the stationmaster about the likelihood that my steamer might have made it through.

"If you put it on the train a week ago, you can count on it being in Albuquerque," he said. "It wasn't until three days ago that the through trains stopped running."

I was much in need of this dose of good news. The stationmaster was very kind and provided me with towels and a dry shirt from the lost and found. And though I was not supposed to accept any gratuity, he refused payment for my ticket to Albuquerque. I thanked him profusely.

"You have been through quite an ordeal, Miss Londonderry," he said. "That much is obvious. The railroad won't miss your dollar."

"That is very kind of you, sir. I am grateful," I replied. "You know who I am, obviously."

"Of course! They ship the El Paso newspapers north and the Albuquerque newspapers south through here, and I have more idle time in this outpost than I know what to do with. I read them cover to cover. Would you oblige me with your autograph?"

"I will trade it for my train fare," I said with a smile, thus hewing to the conditions of the wager. I signed the back of a discarded ticket for him. "With gratitude for saving a drowned rat," I wrote, "Annie Londonderry of Boston, Spinning Around the World."

He took it in his hand and looked at it for a long moment.

"We don't get many world travelers through Socorro," he said. "This will be a valued reminder of our meeting. Thank you. I hope the remainder of your journey is easier than the last few days have been."

"As do I. As do I," I replied.

"Your train will be arriving from the north within the hour, and then turns around and goes back to Albuquerque," he offered. "Owing to the present condition of the bridges, it cannot travel farther south. Might be a few weeks until repairs are made."

"Thank you. I shall be very happy to get there," I replied. "May I ask one more favor? Please wire and reserve a room for me at the San Felipe Hotel and let the *Morning Democrat* and the *Daily Citizen* know I am on my way?"

"Of course, Miss Londonderry. It will be my pleasure."

He extended a hand.

"I will always remember the small part I played in your story. Godspeed to you."

"And to you, sir. Your kindness has been restorative."

My trunk was indeed at the train station in Albuquerque. At the hotel, I signed the guest register, "Annie Londonderry, Round the World on a Wheel," and after a much-needed bath and change of clothes met separately with reporters from the two newspapers. I spun the usual tales, and I especially liked the description of me offered up by the man from the *Daily Citizen* the next day.

> She is a charming, vivacious talker. The broad rim of a jaunty white straw hat trimmed with black ribbon bent and shook itself in response to her animated movements of the head when speaking. The right leg was thrown over the left, the hands crossed at the knee and from under the bottom of a plain, black skirt a shapely foot was visible. She carries a pistol on her body, and the quick penetrating flash of her dark eyes shows that she would not hesitate a moment to use it. One half of the so-called courageous sex of humanity would not attempt what this brave little Boston woman has accomplished.
>
> (*Albuquerque Daily Citizen*, July 15, 1895)

During my two days in the city, my battered Sterling was displayed in the window of a local store, for which I was paid a few dollars.

The weather improved, and I left Albuquerque on the sixteenth, arrived in Santa Fe on the nineteenth, and, as was now usual for my stops, lectured and raced some of the local riders to show off my strength and skills on the wheel. I stayed just the night and was off the next day for Las Vegas, a bustling town of more than two thousand souls, including, to my surprise, a sizable community of German Jews who had settled in the town decades before. Why they chose this remote New Mexico outpost I don't know, but for the first time since leaving Boston I found myself in a community that had a little taste of home.

The big department store in town was Ilfeld's, owned by Charles Ilfeld, who had come to New Mexico as a teenager in the 1860s and, with his brothers, built a successful business empire. There wasn't then, but there is now a town in New Mexico that bears his name. I met him when I wandered into his store toward the end of the week to see if he might be interested in engaging me as a celebrity salesclerk for a few hours, a way to earn a couple of dollars for me and attract customers for him, not that he needed help. The store was filled with people. One of the clerks led me to his office and introduced me. He knew who I was, for he read several newspapers a day, he told me. I suspected he was Jewish from the name, but the Hebrew prayer book on his desk and tefillin hanging from a hook on the wall left no doubt. I later learned that several years before my visit, Charles Ilfeld was instrumental in forming Congregation Montefiore, the first synagogue in Las Vegas, and had donated the purchase price for the land on which it had been built. But at the time, I knew only that he was the store owner.

The Ilfelds of New Mexico.

"Miss Londonderry," he said, shaking my hand and bowing slightly, "this is a pleasant surprise. There was a rumor that you might be passing through our town. It's a pleasure."

"Thank you, Mr. Ilfeld. Likewise, I am sure!" I replied.

"I have read of your journey in the papers," he said. "It's most extraordinary. Most extraordinary. But I see you are also kicking up some dust here in New Mexico." He said this with a wry grin, suggesting he found it all rather amusing. He was referring, of course, to the row involving the newspaper editor Allen Kelly.

"Ah, yes," I replied. "I suppose I have. But all the attention, good or bad, is good for business."

"Business?" he replied.

"What I mean is that publicity, good or bad, raises my profile and creates more opportunities for me to earn the money I need to finish this trip and win the reward that awaits me when I have succeeded."

"Yes, yes, I have read about this wager of yours. A very clever device, Miss Londonderry!" He was still grinning.

"Device?" I asked.

"Well, as if a solo trip around the world by a woman on a wheel needed any added drama, this wager provides it, does it not?"

I was having trouble reading him. Was he questioning my veracity or merely observing what was obviously true: that the wager turned the whole enterprise into a race against time and, with a woman at the center of it, a defining moment in the debate over women's equality? Before I could respond, Mr. Ilfeld continued.

"Your pluck and determination are to be admired, Miss Londonderry. Tell me, how can I help you?"

I told Mr. Ilfeld I hoped to make a few dollars working in his store and that we could make a festive occasion of it and draw in some extra customers. He was happy to oblige.

I can't tell you what caused me to say what I said next, but perhaps it was a little nostalgia for home, for Grandpa's prayer shawl, the one he left draped over a hook in the front hall, the tefillin he donned daily, and the Hebrew prayer book that was his constant companion.

Funny how details you never give a second thought come into sharper focus when they're no longer in front of you.

"Mr. Ilfeld, I hope you won't mind a personal word," I said. "I haven't said this to a soul since leaving Boston, but I feel comfortable confiding it to you. I am Jewish." It was one of the very rare occasions since leaving Boston when I broke character, as they say in the theater.

Mr. Ilfeld smiled knowingly.

"The name is Irish or English," he said, "but the cast of your face is anything but. I had my suspicions the moment you walked into my office."

His tone turned paternal. He was, after all, old enough to be my father.

"Tell me, dear, what is your true name?"

"Cohen," I said. "Anna Cohen. I am married to a man named Kopchovksy." I said nothing about children. That might well have been a bridge too far for a traditional man such as Mr. Ilfeld.

"Married!" he exclaimed. "That you are Jewish does not surprise me. At least it didn't upon seeing you. But married? That is a surprise! Pray, tell me, what does your husband think of this adventure of yours? It could not have gone down easily."

"I can't say he was happy about it, but, frankly, I gave him little choice," I replied. "I am a very determined woman, and he is a rather passive man."

"Well," said Mr. Ilfeld, "it is not for me to judge the marriage of another man, but that is highly irregular. Bless your husband. I would not have stood for it, but that is between you and him." He wasn't being judgmental, just stating the obvious, for few men of his generation, or even this one, would have stood for it.

"Miss Londonderry," he continued, "or should I say, Mrs. Kopchovsky, I would be glad to have you in our store over the weekend. I'd wager it's been a while since you have had a proper Shabbat dinner. Why don't you join Mrs. Ilfeld, the children, and me at our home this Friday evening? My brothers and their wives and children will be joining us, too."

"I dearly wish I could, and thank you for inviting me, but I have a commitment to lecture at the bicycle club that evening, and a dance in my honor has been arranged for afterward," I answered. "Please don't think me rude. You are very kind."

In truth, I was torn, but glad to have a good excuse not to accept the invitation. The struggle to maintain my new identity was growing more difficult with each passing week as I drew closer and closer to the end of the journey and the eventual return to the home I had been so desperate to flee. Breaking character, as I did with Mr. Ilfeld, was something I fought mightily to avoid. But there was something about him, the prayer book, the tefillin, that caused me to drop my guard. I was just starting to reckon with what it would be like to reenter the life I'd left behind, to assume once again the role of housewife and mother, and to slip into familiar and unwelcome routines.

"The sabbath is very important, Mrs. Kopchovksy, but I understand the impracticalities of being observant while on a journey such as yours. Come back this Friday and Saturday, and we will engage you to work the counter and chat up the customers. And I will arrange for some homemade borscht and a fresh challah to be delivered to your hotel this evening. You look as though you could use some home-cooked food."

"I will be most grateful for a taste of home, Mr. Ilfeld, you can be sure of that. I don't know how to thank you." And, indeed, I savored every morsel when I found it waiting for me that evening.

With that, he walked me to the door and said, "Until Friday, Mrs. Kopchovksy. Come at noon. The store closes early on

Fridays for the Sabbath, but we are open Saturdays. It's our busiest day of the week."

"Thank you again, Mr. Ilfeld. You are most kind."

On Friday morning, as I perused the newspaper in the hotel lobby, I saw this.

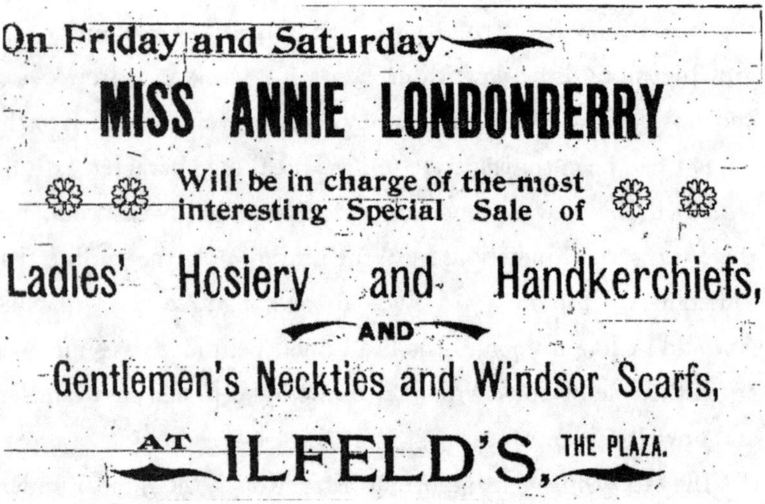

On Friday and Saturday
MISS ANNIE LONDONDERRY
Will be in charge of the most interesting Special Sale of
Ladies' Hosiery and Handkerchiefs,
AND
Gentlemen's Neckties and Windsor Scarfs,
AT ILFELD'S,
THE PLAZA.

After the lecture and the dance on Friday, I paid a long overdue visit to a local barbershop on Saturday morning to have my hair dressed. More than a hundred people gathered outside, peering in the window to watch, and dozens followed me to Ilfeld's, where I took up my position for the second time behind the ladies' hosiery counter.

Though I received a warm and enthusiastic welcome in Las Vegas, skepticism about me and my claims to have wheeled around the world was growing. The *Optic*, the largest paper in town, had welcomed me by calling me "sharp as a tack and as bright as a new silver dollar," but it was very much tongue in cheek. The day after I left, when I was no longer present to defend my reputation, the paper went on the attack, even mocking my name:

> The *Optic*'s conclusion of the whole matter is that Miss Bostonberry is a plucky little woman making a trip to advertise the Sterling bicycle; that she has been around the world, wheeling but little and riding a good deal on trains and ships; and that, like many travelers, she has a vivid imagination, the incidents of travel growing in number and startlingness the farther she gets from their supposed location.
>
> (*Las Vegas Daily Optic*, July 29, 1985)

I had been of the belief that as long as they were writing about me, for good or ill, the press was serving my purpose. But now I wasn't so sure, for all the doubts being raised could be fodder for Colonel Pope to refuse me the coveted prize money. The article left me chagrined.

In the days that followed, I began to regret that I wasn't able to share Shabbat dinner with the Ilfelds. Though I have never been a devout person, there was always some comfort in the old rituals, the familiar words of prayer, and the taste of familiar, traditional foods. It was, whether I wanted it to be or not, part of my life experience; part of *me*.

This regret, this touch of nostalgia for the rituals that were part of life at home, in turn troubled me, for it was a reminder that no matter how far or how fast I pedaled my Sterling, I could not completely leave Annie Kopchovsky behind. It was as if I were riding the front end of a tandem and she was seated in back, shadowing me wherever

I went. The prospect that I would soon be back in Boston, back to the old life I had escaped, bewildered and depressed me. Perhaps my old life, my old self, were, quite simply, inescapable. No matter how furiously you pedal, the occupant of the second seat on a tandem is still right behind you. Each day, as home drew closer and closer, these feelings intensified. I had no idea how I would react to being delivered into the life I had left behind more than a year before, but I was going to find out soon enough.

Fifteen

It was now the end of July. I had six weeks to get to Chicago.

By bicycle I passed through the towns of Springer and Maxwell, arriving in Raton, just south of the Colorado border, on July 30. Then on to Trinidad, Colorado Springs, and Denver, where I arrived on August 12, exhausted and sick with pneumonia. The weather had been stormy for much of the trip north, and I was frequently drenched and forced to sleep wherever a little shelter from the elements could be found. I lost a week to the sickness before deciding that I would have to take the train to Cheyenne and then east to Columbus, Nebraska. I felt well enough to mount the Sterling there and rode to Fremont, where I explained to an inquiring reporter who saw me alight from the train that I was permitted to take the rails provided I secured permission from the parties to the wager, but that was a white lie like so many others.

MISS LONDONDERRY IN DENVER.

The Brave Little Woman is in the Best of Health, and Says She is Enjoying Her Tour Immensely.

COLORADO ROADS IDEAL FOR CYCLING.

Miss Londonderry left Boston last spring for a trip around the world on a wheel. It was a great and hazardous undertaking for a girl; but she possessed the courage, and will win her wager.

Miss Londonderry, before leaving this country, contracted with the

Londonderry Lithia Springs Water Company,

of Nashua, N. H., to use the name "Londonderry" on her journey, and to her great surprise the people of every country she visited were familiar with the name as being connected with the celebrated Londonderry Lithia Water. Thousands of people spoke of the excellency of this wonderful water.

Miss Londonderry has been highly entertained by wheelmen all through her journey. A large delegation of Denver cyclists escorted her into Denver from Colorado Springs. She will remain in the city a few days before taking up her journey eastward.

The Daily News, Denver, Colorado (August 12, 1895).

Though the skepticism I encountered in New Mexico followed me to Nebraska, it didn't dim the enthusiasm of the wheelmen and others who were curious to meet and hear from a celebrity. My lecture in Omaha drew a large crowd, which I regaled with the stories that had become my routine, with a few new twists thrown in for good measure. The *Evening Bee* called me "the greatest lady bicycle rider," and when I was engaged at the Boston Store, a large department store in the city, for a few days, hundreds came each time to talk, get an autograph, and admire the Sterling, which was placed on display.

On September 1, with just two weeks to reach Chicago, I pedaled out of Omaha, through Missouri Valley, Iowa, toward Ames. There was little drama crossing Iowa, so I had to invent some for the local newspaperman who interviewed me when I arrived in Marshalltown on the third. It was a familiar story, I just changed the location, telling him that between Council Bluffs and Crescent I was riding the railway tracks when a speeding mail train came around a curve, forcing me to throw myself and the wheel to the side of the tracks as the train sped by. I was telling these stories with less conviction than before, however, for bit by bit, as I gained on Chicago, I felt the air slowly going out of Miss Londonderry.

But then I had a real mishap, one that threatened my prospects for making it to Chicago in time, and I was sure that failing in that regard would doom my chances of claiming my prize, chances that were already dwindling thanks to my switching to the Sterling and the increasing number of newspapers casting doubt on the stories of my travels. It would be much harder for Colonel Pope to disprove that I had ridden the required ten thousand miles (who was there to keep count?) than that I had made the circuit in the time allotted (the date of my departure from Boston was known to all), so it was essential that I make Chicago by September 25, fifteen months to the day since leaving Boston. The prize money, always part of my motivation, loomed larger and larger the closer I came to the end of the journey. It had become, as I have said, the only way to justify all I had put them through to Grandpa, Brother Bennett, Baila, Rosa, and the children (when they were older, of course). Not least, it was how I was justifying it to myself.

The mishap occurred between Tama and Gladbrook. I was coasting down one of the rolling hills that dot the eastern Iowa landscape when a farmer herding a drove of pigs started across the road. With no brake on the Sterling, I veered to the side, lost my balance, and was thrown from the wheel. I tried to break my fall, but only succeeded in breaking my wrist. The pain was intense, but the farmer, miffed that I had scared and scattered his pigs, made no effort to assist me, and I had to ride fifteen miles to Tama with only one hand on the handlebars to find a doctor to set the fracture. The small cast was a nuisance, and my wrist ached, but riding was still possible. Two Tama wheelmen were summoned to ride east with me toward Cedar Rapids, and when they learned that the farmer responsible for my injury had done nothing to help me, they were indignant and promised that the local L.A.W. chapter would look into the matter, but I never heard a word about it after that.

On the tenth of September I rolled out of Clinton, Iowa, in the company of two wheelmen, Roy Upton and Clarence Rumble, hale and hearty men a little past their prime but excited to be the escort for the final leg of my journey. My broken wrist was still bandaged and sore, but it did not impair my riding. By midday we were halfway to Chicago and stopped in the town of Rochelle, Illinois, where I gave my final interview to the press.

> Miss Londonderry, who has the proud distinction of being the only woman who has circled the globe on a wheel (that is the land portion thereof) was well-equipped in point of education to make the trip, as she speaks six languages fluently.

```
However, this, together with her wheel and a
large share of American pluck constituted her
only equipment. Miss Londonderry was dressed in
knickerbockers and sweater, and carried a
revolver, flask, and cup.
```

(*The Rochelle Register*, September 13, 1895)

The sweater I quickly jettisoned, for an oppressive heat wave struck northern Illinois over the next couple of days.

You would think that with Chicago now in sight that I would be in a celebratory mood. But it was quite the opposite. I suppose I felt like the fisherman who spends a lifetime trying to catch the biggest fish in the pond. When, at last, he succeeds, his excitement is fleeting, for now he must face life without that which has inspired and enticed him for so many years. Barely in my mid-twenties, how would I ever again achieve what I had in the previous fifteen months? What could compare? And there was the nagging uncertainty about trying, like a square peg into a round hole, to fit into the life I had left behind. Every mile that I drew closer to Chicago, the urge to turn that wheel around and do it all over again grew stronger.

I have described for you many times over the years the dazzling hero's welcome that awaited me in Chicago when I arrived on September 12, with two weeks to spare. It was a staple of the bedtime stories I told you when you were a little girl. The resounding welcome was a much-needed lift to my spirits and took my mind off the dread of ending this chapter of my life and returning home.

Thousands lined Michigan Avenue for a parade arranged by the mayor's office and the Sterling Cycle Works. Thousands more crowded windows overlooking the avenue. It was a brilliant late-summer day, simply perfect in every way. I sat next to Mayor George Bell Swift in a horse-drawn carriage preceded by two dozen Chicago mounted police officers. Behind us a procession of many hundreds of cyclists and a dozen brass bands followed. The cheering never relented, and I was soon covered in confetti. This road circus ended at City Hall, where a VIP seating area had been arranged, and I was rendered speechless to see many familiar faces smiling happily at me there. Miss Anthony had made a special trip from upstate New York to be there. The Wild West Show was, by coincidence, back in town. Bill Cody and Annie Oakley were there, along with many of the friends I had met during my brief appearance in the show back in San Francisco. Even the great Nellie Bly came, representing the *New York World*, determined to get the first exclusive interview with me after the parade. Thomas Stevens, whose trip around the world was the catalyst for my own, had made the journey from England. Jessie Padman, the woman with whom I had a brief flirtation a year before, came from nearby South Bend. And the Palmers, the wealthy socialites I had met while sailing to France, were there. That evening they hosted an elegant dinner in my honor at their lakefront home. But seeing Mark Johnson, so tall and so handsome, beaming at me was the straw that broke the camel's back. His presence was totally unexpected. I simply broke down and cried, composing myself in time to receive the key to the city from the mayor. At a lavish reception inside City Hall I had the chance to speak again with all of these people whose presence had brought me to tears moments before.

Well, that's how I like to remember it, and that's the story you have heard me tell a hundred times. But that's not what happened. There was no parade. No Miss Anthony, Bill Cody, or Annie Oakley. Nellie Bly, Thomas Stevens, Jessie Padman, and Mark Johnson are also figments of my imagination about that day. The mayor, as far as I know, was working on the city budget in his office.

I like to think that the reason my arrival in Chicago on the twelfth of September 1895, was such a muted affair is that I made little effort to drum up the kind of publicity I'd so eagerly pursued for the previous fifteen months. But, in truth, skepticism about my story had been growing, and I was now widely viewed as something between a celebrity and a charlatan. Interest had waned. Only a modest reception organized for me and my escorts by the Sterling Cycle Works formally marked the journey's end. It was over with a whimper, not a bang, though there would be a colorful second act, which I will come to shortly.

When I signed the guest registry at the Wellington Hotel that evening, I signed it simply "Mrs. Kopchovksy, Boston, Mass." Miss Londonderry had served her purpose. As I lay down my wheel in the hotel lobby, the character I had inhabited for well over a year vanished just like that. Even the Chicago newspapers made little mention that my journey had ended in their city.

Before returning home to Boston, I took the train, alone, to New York City to attend to two pieces of business.

First, I went to visit my sister, Rosa, who, still just a child of seventeen, had married in my absence, and with her husband, Simon Newman, moved to New Brunswick, New Jersey. She was morbidly obese and mentally unstable, and had begged me to come. A local newspaper there got wind of my visit. Though Rosa claimed she had nothing to do with it, her need for attention suggests she did. The reporter proved to be a doubting Thomas and told me that walkers and cyclists claiming to be circling the earth were passing through New Brunswick "on an average of three a day for the past six months." I lost my temper with him and told him the others were fakers, but truly I wasn't in the mood to now have to defend myself to every skeptic. The only skeptics I needed to win over were back in Boston, where I had ten thousand dollars at stake. There were bound to be questions about whether I had vindicated Colonel Pope's faith in me, whether he was entitled through my efforts to collect his winnings, and in turn, whether I was entitled to collect mine. That's all I was focused on at the moment.

And that explains my second piece of business in New York. I went to persuade Morrill Goddard, the Sunday editor at the *World*, to publish a first-person account of my travels, the one I had promised when we'd met in New York more than a year earlier. It was essential to my plan to win the prize money that he do so, and while I had promised him an exclusive, he was under no obligation to publish it. Perhaps he, too, had lost interest in my journey, or had come to regard me as a charlatan.

The *World*, as I said, was a combination of serious news and sensational features that one needed to take with a large grain of salt. They were always on the lookout for dramatic, eye-catching stories that would sell newspapers. Like my lectures, many of those stories were plainly intended to entertain and titillate, not to educate. Even so, publication of my story in the nation's most prominent newspaper, a Pulitzer paper, would bolster the case I expected to have to make to Colonel Pope. It would help establish my bona fides and my fame, and would be a powerful lever if the colonel balked at making good on the prize money. Little did I know when I called on Mr. Goddard in late September that another door, into a future I had neither planned nor predicted, would open wide.

Sixteen

"Miss Londonderry, or should I say Mrs. Kopchovksy now that you have returned?" Mr. Goddard asked with a smile. "It is good to see you again."

He had always known my real name, and it had appeared in one of the early news items about my trip in the *World* a year earlier.

"However you wish, Mr. Goddard," I replied. "I suppose now that the venture is over I am once again Mrs. Kopchovsky."

"Well, you've much to be proud of, Mrs. Kopchovksy. I've followed your progress whenever I could. I suppose you will be glad to get home to Boston."

Truthfully, I was utterly indifferent, even reluctant. I still had no idea how to reenter my old life.

"I suppose so," I answered, "though I am now used to living a life of adventure, and that will be hard to give up."

Mr. Goddard nodded. I could tell from his expression that it was time to get to the point.

"Mr. Goddard, I am here to fulfill my commitment to you to write an exclusive account of my travels. I trust you are still interested." It was more of a question than a statement made with any confidence.

"Tell me, Mrs. Kopchovsky, how do you see putting more than a year's worth of adventure into one page of a broadsheet?"

For ten minutes I gave Mr. Goddard a condensed version of one of my lectures, choosing the most sensational and outlandish anecdotes from among the many—some real, some imagined, some embellished—that I had tried out on the road. In the end it was an easy sell. A woman, alone, around the world on a bicycle, fighting the elements, riding through war zones, often at risk of life and limb, was a natural for the *World*.

"How soon can you have it to me, Mrs. Kopchovksy?" he asked. "We plan the Sunday section a few weeks in advance, and I don't want too much time to pass before we publish. The story needs to be fresh."

"I will be back here at 10 A.M. tomorrow. It will be done by then," I replied.

"Very well, Mrs. Kopchovsky. I make no promise, but let's see what you come up with. I will see you in the morning."

Writing the article that night was a breeze. After all, I had been writing it in my head for fifteen months. Getting it down on paper was the easy part.

The next morning I was back at the *World* in Mr. Goddard's office with a handwritten manuscript of a few thousand words. Little did I know that in addition to delivering the story, I was also auditioning for a job.

Mr. Goddard took his pince-nez, rested them on the bridge of his nose, and began reading silently. I watched his every expression to see if I could discern his reaction. For the most part he was stoic, grinning faintly a few times and grimacing once. I assumed that was when he got to the part about the Japanese soldier who killed a Chinese prisoner before my eyes and "drank his blood while the dead man's muscles were still quivering."

When he was done, he tossed the manuscript onto his desk and removed his pince-nez. For a moment he gazed at me intently, but I could not read him. My heart seemed to skip a beat waiting for his judgment, for with it, I was sure, would rise or fall any chance I had of securing the prize money from Colonel Pope. He seemed to stare at me for a good five minutes, though I am sure it was really just a matter of seconds.

"Brilliant, Mrs. Kopchovksy!" he said at last. "It will be a sensation. You have a real knack for this. We will run it in a few weeks' time."

I was delighted, of course, and smiled broadly and thanked him profusely. But it was what he said next that took me completely by surprise. He told me Nellie Bly had just left the *World* a few weeks earlier—whether she quit or was fired depended on who was doing the telling, I soon learned. The paper, he said, needed a new enterprising woman reporter, and they needed one quick. Bly had an enormous following, especially among women readers, and she sold a lot of papers.

"You have the gumption and the pluck, Mrs. Kopchovsky," said Mr. Goddard. "And this," he continued, picking up my manuscript, "proves you can write. I propose you move to New York and write regular features for the *World*, some of your own devise and others to be assigned. Would that be of interest? Miss Bly left a big hole here, and I think you can fill it if you'd like to take the chance."

Take the chance? Of course I would! I was flattered, overwhelmed, excited, and stunned at the door that was being opened for me. As a teenage girl reading of Bly's adventures, I wanted, as I said at the beginning of this missive, to be like her. Now I was being offered the opportunity to practically *become* her! How could I refuse? As with the bicycle trip, I did not consult with Grandpa. I said yes on the spot. As the expression goes, I wore the pants in the family, literally, based on my riding attire, and figuratively. But now it was time to go home, reunite with Grandpa and the children, explain that we were abruptly moving to New York, and settle my business with Colonel Pope.

As I said, there was more afoot in publishing my story in the *World* than my desire to tell my story and to try to capitalize on the fame I had achieved over the previous fifteen months. The last word I had from Alonzo Peck, the telegram received in Los Angeles, was not encouraging, and I wondered whether Colonel Pope had, given the growing skepticism about my methods, abandoned hope of winning his wager, thus putting in doubt the considerable prize money that would be paid only if I had met the conditions set forth. I had come full circle around the world from Chicago, I had collected the signatures of American diplomats that proved my presence in various cities, and I had, with two weeks to spare, returned within fifteen months. But had I circled the world by bicycle?

I needed leverage, and a full-page story in the country's leading newspaper, one in which I appeared as a true heroine, one in which I was trumpeted as the embodiment of the "New Woman," would provide it. Who would want to publicly renege on a pledge to reward such a deserving woman of her hard-earned prize money? The sum was a modest one for Colonel Pope; a fortune to me. Why would he risk infuriating those who made up the potential market he so coveted? And one thing could not be disputed: I had, as the colonel had hoped, inspired among women great interest in the bicycle. One might quibble about the details, but his purpose had been well served.

Homecoming was a painful affair. Simon and Frieda were so young, they had no memory of me whatsoever. When I walked into the apartment for the first time, with Grandpa and the children gathered to welcome me home, their little bodies went limp when I hugged them. I was a stranger. Mollie simply turned around and walked stoically into her bedroom. Grandpa looked at me balefully as if to say, "What did you expect?" We sat across from each other at the kitchen table. Our conversation was awkward. What could I say? I had abandoned this family well over a year before. I didn't know if I could repair the damage, or if I even had the wherewithal to try.

"It is time to be a family again," said Grandpa simply, in his heavily accented English. I wished he would try harder to sound more like an American than an immigrant. But he never would, right up to the day he died last year.

I nodded, though I wasn't sure how to do that. Become a family, I mean. And I still had to tell Grandpa we were moving to New York. You might wonder how I could be so sure he would agree to such a move, and all I can tell you is that I knew. It was his lot in life to accommodate himself to me.

I was home for a little over a week. Enough time to make amends with Bennett and Baila, though they were, bless them, really quite forgiving. I thanked them profusely for all they had done and acknowledged the burden I had put upon them, which went a long way in putting the past fifteen months behind us. I think they were just relieved that I was back, that they could turn all their attention to their own growing family and no longer face questions from friends and neighbors about the rather odd circumstances into which I had delivered them.

Three days after I arrived home, the children still wary and wondering who the stranger was in their midst, Grandpa took the train to Maine to buy the various goods he sold from his pushcart. My eldest sister Sarah, who lived in Bath, and her husband Isaac had a small department store. It was cheaper for Grandpa to combine his orders with theirs and travel to Maine occasionally to bring them back.

The day after Grandpa left I asked Baila to watch the children—only for a few hours this time, I promised her—so that I could attend to my business with Colonel Pope. Back to the bicycle store on Washington Street I went, the one I had visited so regularly when I was selling adverts for the papers. Alonzo was expecting me—I'd sent him a note two days before—and he knew the purpose of my visit. I brought with me the documentation of where I'd been, the signatures of the various consuls I'd collected along the way, and various souvenirs I'd purchased and shipped home, physical evidence of my presence in far-flung corners of the world.

Alonzo was delighted to see me; I had always liked the man.

"Mrs. Kopchovsky!" he exclaimed. "It has been a long time, and you look no worse for wear." He shook my hand vigorously. Whatever difficulties I might have persuading the colonel that I had met the terms of the wager and was entitled to the prize money, I knew Alonzo would be on my side and do what he could to press my case.

"So tell me, Mrs. Kopchovksy, of your travels!" He never seemed so young as he did in that moment, like a schoolchild about to receive a treat. I gave him more or less the same performance I had given Mr. Goddard a week earlier, holding forth for about ten minutes, just long enough so that when I came to the point, I felt I wasn't being rude.

"Alonzo," I said, "surely you know what is on my mind today. I have made the circuit and done so in the time allotted. Dr. Reeder can attest that I have by my own efforts made the five thousand dollars I was required to earn en route. I am counting on Colonel Pope to make good on the promise of the prize money."

Was I ever! I had told Mr. Goddard we would be moving to New York so I could take up my position with the *World*, and I needed the prize money to do it.

Alonzo looked at me kindly, but it was obvious the colonel had conveyed to Alonzo some doubt as to whether he was obligated.

"Mrs. Kopchovsky," Alonzo said, with more than a note of apology in his voice, "if it were up to me, you know I would give you a draft for the ten thousand dollars today. But the colonel is not convinced you have fulfilled the terms of the contract. As you might imagine, he was distressed when he learned that in Chicago you had changed mounts, for he envisioned your entire venture as a long-running advertisement for the Columbia. But I took the liberty of pointing out to him, at some risk of incurring his wrath, that it was not stipulated that you make the entire journey on a Columbia. To this he grumbled that it was indeed so, an oversight on his part, but still he felt the implication was clear. But more to the point, as you surely know, some of the various cycling periodicals and newspapers have made note that your passage from France to China and Japan was made in remarkable time for a woman who was supposed to be astride a wheel."

He looked at me sheepishly and then at the floor. He was embarrassed to have to confront me with what was unquestionably true. The terms of the wager required that I travel ten thousand miles by bicycle. I was short by at least two thousand miles. My purchase on the prize money was far from certain, to put it generously.

"Alonzo, I will not deny what is perfectly obvious, but I would like to make my case directly to the colonel, if that would be possible,"

I said. "I would tell him that his purpose in sending a woman on such a journey was more than fulfilled. It cannot be measured, but I have piqued the curiosity of many thousands of women in the wheel, maybe tens or hundreds of thousands, and that was the idea, was it not? My name—well, the name Miss Londonderry—is known around the world, and what is it known for? For wheeling around the world, regardless of the fine details."

"The colonel has not made a final decision about this matter yet," Alonzo answered, "and he made it clear that I would be his intermediary in this discussion, one he fully expected. I'm afraid it will fall to me to press your case with him. Remember, for him to collect *his* winnings he must provide the proof to his counterparties that you have complied with the terms of the wager, and he is not holding a strong hand. 'A pair of twos' is how he described it to me."

I did not breathe a word to Alonzo that within a few weeks' time the *World* would be publishing, on the front page of the special Sunday section, an account of my journey, one that would, because I knew their methods, herald me as a heroine, the very embodiment of the "New Woman," a class of women with growing political clout and buying power. "Blackmail" would be too strong a word for it; I prefer to say this was my advantage, my ace in the hole to the pair of twos the colonel was holding. Once the story was published, the colonel would, I was sure, find it more in his self-interest to deliver the prize money than have it become public knowledge that he had withheld it from a woman who was now a national and international sensation. What, after all, would Miss Susan B. Anthony, firmly in my corner, to be sure, have to say about that?! Why didn't I mention the story I'd written for the *World* to Alonzo? A man of Colonel Pope's stature has many friends in high places, and even those he doesn't know could be easily reached. I didn't want him to kill the story.

"Give me a couple of weeks, Mrs. Kopchovsky," Alonzo said. "You know I will put your best foot forward with the colonel, but I can offer no assurance of the outcome."

"I know, Alonzo," I replied sympathetically. "You have been a good friend to me. Let me know when you have some news to share."

And with that I headed home to prepare dinner for the children, wash their clothes, sweep the floor, and scrub the bathroom, chores I had not performed in well over a year and which I had missed not at all.

When I arrived home, there was a telegram waiting for me. It was from Mr. Goddard at the *Sunday World*.

"Dear Mrs. Kopchovksy," it read. "Bicycle feature to appear October 20. In meantime, Boston newspapers reporting of a 'wild man' of the woods near Royalston, Mass., terrorizing local community. Acts of violence targeting a farmer named Richardson. Farm animals killed, stove exploded, heavy objects thrown through windows. Wild Man described as tall, bearded to his waist, and scrawny. Sounds like a good feature. Can you take train to Royalston promptly for possible scoop?"

I hadn't expected to be pressed into service so soon, but the story sounded like more high adventure, and I certainly wanted to please Mr. Goddard, who was intent on making me the next Nellie Bly.

With Grandpa in Maine, I pleaded with Bennett and Baila to watch the children, telling them I had urgent business to attend to in the western part of the state and giving vague answers to their questions as to what it could possibly be about. It will just be a few days, I implored them. They wearily agreed, and the next morning I took the train to Athol, the nearest stop to Royalston, and took a room in the local hotel where I registered as Nellie Bly. A new adventure had begun.

By the time I joined a search party organized by the local sheriff, a man named Doane, to scour the woods for the Wild Man, suspicions had already focused on Charley Richardson, a young man of about twenty, who lived with his mother on the family farm that was the target of the attacks. But I told a different story, published several weeks later in the *Sunday World.* In my telling, as we divided into groups of twos and threes so we could cover more ground, I arranged to be paired with Charley Richardson. And through a careful interrogation in which I gained the young man's confidence, he told me that he was weary of life on the farm and wanted to move to the city but was unable to persuade his mother to sell the place. I questioned him about the various incidents that had so terrorized him, his mother, and the surrounding community, and noted that when he described the mysterious events, he was always conveniently nearby as they happened. Using extraordinary powers of deduction, I confronted young Charley, and he then poured forth his confession. Sherriff Doane lavished praise on me for solving the case. That's supposed to be me in the picture as published in the *Sunday World.*

Oh, what fun I had, Mary! I remember it as if it were yesterday. And the story, which ran in November, delighted Morrill Goddard, for he knew then for sure, he had found his new Nellie Bly.

When Grandpa returned from Maine, he was surprised to find I was not at home, but off in western Massachusetts doing what, he did not know. A letter he had sent me from Maine a few days before had arrived while I was away. In it he expressed the hope that my reunion with the children was going well. I feel badly about it now; his hopes that we would restore the life we had before I pedaled out of Boston had been dashed. And now I had to deliver the news that we were moving to New York so that I could pursue my new career. The look in a man's eyes when he knows he is powerless to resist is a terribly sad one, but my mind was made up, and where I went I knew Grandpa would follow. His sense of duty, his desire to hold the family together, allowed no other choice.

By mid-October I had still heard nothing from Alonzo about the prize money, and I made no effort to press him. I was eagerly waiting for the story of my bicycle journey to appear in the *Sunday World* where it would be read by hundreds of thousands of people. I didn't want the colonel to render his verdict until the story was published. Indeed, I had gone way out on a limb in the story, claiming that I had already collected the prize money!

Then, on October 20, 1895, as Mr. Goddard promised, the entire front page of the special-feature section of the *Sunday World*, perhaps the most widely read newspaper page in America, was given over to the only first-person account of my journey ever published.

THE MOST EXTRAORDINARY JOURNEY EVER UNDERTAKEN BY A WOMAN, cried the headline. Even more remarkable, however, was the byline, a decision about which I was not consulted, but one that thrilled me completely. I was no longer Miss Londonderry, or even Mrs. Kopchovksy, but Nellie Bly, Jr.! This was my debut as the successor to the great Nellie Bly in one of the country's most important and prestigious newspapers. The story of the Wild Man followed just two weeks later. I couldn't have been more excited.

To be compared to the most celebrated woman journalist of the time, and to have my journey compared favorably to the one that made her famous, was more than a great compliment. It was, for my private purposes, great leverage. Annie Londonderry was well enough known that anyone familiar with her journey would have realized that Annie Londonderry and Nellie Bly, Jr., were one and the same person.

Sketch that accompanied my story in the *New York World*, October 20, 1895.

The day after the article appeared, I picked up several copies from the newsstand in Scollay Square. (The *World* usually reached Boston the next day.) The story's publication proved I had a prominent soapbox and the means to make myself heard to a wide audience. I tore the page from one of the copies, autographed it with an inscription designed to flatter ("For Alonzo, who made it possible"), and sealed it in an envelope with a note:

> Dear Alonzo,
>
> Perhaps you have seen this already, but I wanted you to have a keepsake of what we accomplished together. I know the *World* got a little ahead of itself in the introduction where it says, "Her trip also decided a wager made that no woman could accomplish such a feat." But given that it is now public knowledge, I fear that were the colonel to withhold the prize, it would reflect badly on him and the company. I have accepted an offer from the *World* to become a reporter for them and plan to move my family as soon as practical to New York. But to do so depends on my securing the funds promised for making the journey. I do hope you will speak with the colonel as soon as possible. Fondly,
>
> Mrs. Kopchovksy

Three days later I received a note asking me to come to Alonzo's office the next day at noon. I was there promptly. My worst fear, that an enraged Colonel Pope, angered at being boxed into a corner, would be there to confront me did not come to pass.

"I doubt I shall ever meet a woman as clever and, dare I say, as capable of pulling off a scheme as you, Mrs. Kopchovksy, and I mean that as a compliment," Alonzo said. "Men, especially men of industry such as the colonel, are used to such scheming, to probing the weaknesses in their competitors and adversaries, and using whatever leverage they can muster to their advantage. When I met with the colonel and presented him with your article, I expected him to turn purple with rage and reject the pressure that you clearly intended. But he didn't. His respect was grudging, but it was respect nevertheless. He didn't say a word, but I know him well, and what I saw was a man who admired in you traits he knows himself to possess. Without saying a word, he sat down at his desk, opened the top drawer, and wrote out this draft."

Alonzo took an envelope from his pocket and handed it to me. Inside was a check for ten thousand dollars drawn on the Bank of Boston and a note on a small piece of stationery with the colonel's name on top. Written in a neat and stylish cursive, it read, simply: "Well played, Mrs. Kopchovksy. Well played. A. Pope."

Whether Colonel Pope ever collected ten thousand dollars from Mr. Dowe, or Mr. Dowe ever collected twenty thousand dollars from Colonel Pope, I do not know. They could have debated the question of "did she or didn't she" for years without resolution, for I left a long trail of ambiguity, twenty-five-thousand miles long, in fact.

P.S.

I was going to leave it there, Mary dear, but over the past few days I have wrestled with a difficult question: How much should I tell you about what happened to our family, your family, in the years that followed my bicycle trip, for some of it is very painful? But I would be remiss if I went to my grave with this heavy heart about the price others have paid, and may yet pay, for my adventurous spirit and frequent absences, some, like the one of 1894–95, prolonged. You will be an adult when you read this, if my wishes are honored, a woman of thirty, perhaps with a family of your own. You deserve to know the truth. It may help you to understand yourself.

Much of what I am about to tell you has been a weight I have carried for decades now, though I have said nary a word of my burden to anyone. Perhaps this is my confession, for I am not proud of some of the decisions I made. They were selfish, to be sure, but I doubt my life would have been better had I not made them. I probably would have escaped my life in some other way had the opportunity to take up Colonel Pope's wager not presented itself. I did what I felt I needed to do at the time to preserve my own sanity, and believed, perhaps self-servingly, that doing so was important to the well-being of the children, too, especially my daughters. I cannot change it now. I just hope you will not judge me harshly, for we have always been close.

We moved to New York the month after the story of my bicycle ride was published in the *Sunday World*, into a house in the Bronx that I purchased for twenty-five hundred dollars, a handsome sum in those days. For Bennett and Baila it was a mixed blessing. They were sad to see us go, but, I think, relieved, too, for we had leaned heavily on them even as they had their hands full with their own growing family.

I met Susie, now married, for tea the day before we left. Our conversation was awkward and unsatisfying, but important nevertheless to bring some closure to our star-crossed romance. There were no hard feelings, just a shared sense of sadness for what once was and might have been, though Susie seemed reasonably content in her life with Mr. Constable.

Even after the trip ended, I still took a ribbing from some in the press. From as far away as Singapore, a few were still feeling scorched. It bothered me but little, for I had succeeded in my larger purpose. This little item appeared three months after I put my wheel down in Chicago. I get a pleasant tingle down my spine and a smile when I read it now!

> Miss Annie Londonderry, the lady bicyclist, is held up to Exhibition by the writer of Sporting Notes in the *China Mail*, as "a brilliant and

> original fictionalist" in her own account of her travels, the battles she said she saw and the wounds she declared she had received. Reverence for the Eternal Verities compels us to affirm that this sporting damsel has fibbed fluently and incessantly all along the line. Perhaps it would be politer to say that she has displayed a consistent feminine disregard for common, coarse ordinary facts, and has invested her wanderings with the fanciful play of a graceful and inventive imagination. That is much nicer. But we fear thou wilt come no more, Gentle Annie, this way round. You would have too many things to explain.
>
> (*The Singapore Free Press and Mercantile Advertiser*, December 17, 1895)

Over the following months I wrote a couple dozen stories for the *World*, all sensationalized accounts of decidedly more mundane matters. I went to New Jersey to visit a commune established by a self-proclaimed messiah. I went undercover to expose the secrets of a New York matchmaker for lonely hearts. I wrote about a women-only stock exchange near Wall Street and rode the New York mail train, where I became the first woman to sort the mail on the overnight run from upstate New York into the city. I am leaving you with copies of all of them as they may be of interest to you and your own children someday.

But my career at the *World*, such as it was, turned out to be brief, for in the summer of 1896 I started to feel unwell and discovered that I was pregnant with your mother, something I had not intended to happen. I was no longer able to go out on assignments, and by August of that year the doctor told me I needed complete bed rest or I would risk losing the baby. Fortunately, the money I had earned during my journey plus the prize money I received from Colonel Pope allowed us to live comfortably for quite a while, but my stint as Nellie Bly's successor was over.

Your mother was born in early 1897. In late 1899, when she was not quite three years old, I left home yet again. Shortly before the new year I told Grandpa that I had hired a woman to help care for the children, four of them now, and that I would be taking the train to California to try to regain my health. You see, dear, I had become terribly depressed after the birth of your mother and was utterly incapable of attending to the family in any way. Not physically and not emotionally. The modern term is postpartum depression, and it lasted for a long while. I began to wonder if *Le Figaro* had it right when they wrote of me that I had suppressed all love and maternal function.

It was an impulsive decision, and I could not answer Grandpa's questions. No, I did not know how long I would be gone. No, I did not know where exactly I would be, for I planned no further ahead than to take the train across the continent. No, I could not promise that I would return, though I hoped the trip would be restorative and allow me to come back and be a proper mother and wife, much as I thought, naively, that the bicycle trip would.

My memory of the train ride is fuzzy. It took about a week. I spoke to no one except perfunctorily. Mostly I gazed at the passing scenery trying to make sense of my life. I arrived in San Francisco some four years after I had stepped off the *Belgic*, having sailed there from Japan. I took a room by the week near Fisherman's Wharf and from there penned a note to Mark Johnson, the man I had fallen in love with in California and who had proposed to me, and had it delivered to the Olympic Club. His reply came two days later. He was, needless to say, stunned to hear that I was in the city. We had corresponded for a little while after we parted ways in Los Angeles. I had demurred on his marriage proposal but was vague about why, and it had been nearly three years since we'd had any contact. But he was happy to hear I was in town. He met me the following day in the lobby of the Palace Hotel, where we had stayed four years earlier.

The moment I saw him, still so handsome, I knew something had changed. He was warm, eager to hear of all that had transpired since we had last corresponded, but the spark between us had ebbed away. I told him everything, my real name, of Grandpa and the children, all of it. He was shocked, to say the least, but bore me no ill will for having misled him by omission when we rode through California several years before. I think he was actually rather dazzled that I had pulled it all off—keeping my real identity a secret, I mean. And he seemed to understand my reasons, but maybe he was just being polite.

When I finally stopped talking he told me news of his life, which included marriage and a young son, not even a year old. I suppose I was disappointed but not surprised. He was, as they say, quite the catch. I had not traveled west intending to renew our romance, at least not consciously, but it was now clear that the memories of our time together would be the full story of our love affair. We parted with an embrace; no words were needed. We still had the mutual attraction that brought us together four years earlier, but we both knew this was goodbye forever.

I made an excursion to Yosemite Valley, a place of beauty beyond words, and then, simply because a fellow tourist I met hailed from Ukiah, about a hundred miles north of San Francisco, traveled there, rented a room in a boardinghouse, and took a job as a salesclerk in a dry goods store. For a year I lived anonymously and alone in Ukiah, keeping very much to myself and revealing virtually nothing to the curious who wondered who the quiet new woman in town was. I wrote to Grandpa every month, mostly to assure him that I was all right, and his letters back were so typical of him—newsy, matter-of-fact, and always with a single question: When will you be coming home?

By the time I returned to Boston in early 1901, having been gone a little over a year, Grandpa seemed to have aged a decade, and I suppose it's no wonder. He had been, with help from a series of women he had to hire because none stayed on the job more than a couple of months, raising four young children, including a toddler, on his own. Through it all, the bicycle trip, my long absence in California, and my utter unpredictability, he never spoke of divorce. Ours wasn't the marriage of anyone's dreams, and Grandpa was hardly pleased with my repeated comings and goings and lengthy absences. Yet he remained faithful to our marriage and to our family, refusing, quietly, to let it fall apart and carrying the burdens of two with little help from me. In his way, even though he probably felt powerless to stop me, he enabled me to clear a path for myself few women of the day could have walked (or biked). I wish I had told him before he died how much that meant to me. He was a good man, your Grandpa. Not many would have put up with what he did.

Mollie, now twelve, had been attending a public school near the house in the Bronx, as had Libbie and Simon. Your mother was still too young for school. I was, to all of them, still a distant stranger. About a month after my return from California I made a decision that would have profound consequences for the children, for the entire family, consequences that were, in retrospect, completely foreseeable, but which I did not glimpse at all at the time.

Grandpa was weary. I was emotionally unable to nurture the children and provide them with the love every child deserves. Maybe that explains why, of my four children, only your mother had a child: you. She was, after all, not yet born when I first disappeared. Honestly, I am at a loss to this day to explain the decision I made, but I determined that the children should be sent away to school come the fall.

I had heard that there was an excellent French-speaking boarding school for girls in Lewiston, Maine, run by the Dominican Sisters, that the environment was nurturing but strict. It also had the advantage of being not terribly far from my sister Sarah's home in Bath. But, I am sure you are wondering, why on earth would a Jewish family send a child to Catholic boarding school, and to that question I have no good answer. Grandpa of course, was appalled—he was far more devout than I was—but again I had made up my mind. The school had a good reputation, it was affordable, near my sister's, and that was that. Grandpa fretted that his two daughters would be indoctrinated in the theology of the Church, a concern I dismissed as far-fetched.

Early in September we put Mollie and Libbie on the train to Boston with their suitcases and told Mollie to keep a close eye on her sister. Bennett promised he would fetch them at the station, though he was as appalled as Grandpa that his nieces were being dispatched not just to a boarding school, but a Catholic one at that. The girls would spend the weekend with their aunt and uncle and cousins before again boarding a train bound for Portland, where the nuns would meet several girls all heading for the school in Lewiston.

The morning we took them to Grand Central Station, Mollie was subdued, stoic, and slightly bewildered. Libbie, two years younger, seemed to think it was all a big adventure. There were no tears except for Grandpa's, and he did his best to hide them. I told the girls they would be home at Christmastime, to study hard and make friends, and that they would be well cared for at school.

As for your uncle Simon, we sent him off at the tender age of seven to a school for boys in Arthabaska, Quebec, a school recommended by the Dominican Sisters. I confess, Mary, we never visited the children at school and saw them only at Christmastime and in the summer. They wrote letters home, letters filled with news about their studies, complaints about the food, and about the friends they were making. If they ever wrote forlorn letters, or angry letters, or anything likely to arouse our concerns, those were probably confiscated by the nuns and the priests before they were ever sent.

When your mother reached school age, I decided it would be better to keep her closer to home and enrolled all three girls at Mount Saint Mary's, another Catholic school in Newburgh, just a two-hour train ride up the Hudson from the city.

Looking back on it now, it was a harsh decision to dispatch the children this way, a selfish decision. So many of my decisions were. But given how inadequate I was as a mother, perhaps it wasn't such a selfish decision after all. Who can say?

At the beginning of this letter, if you can call such a long account a letter, I told you that you had an aunt Mollie, which I suspect came as a surprise to you, and that she had died when she was twenty-three or, to be more precise, that she was dead to me. Oh, Mary, this is the hardest part and my biggest regret now that I am an old woman.

Why I was surprised to receive the letter I do not know. In retrospect it all seems to have been so predictable, and Grandpa's fears, which I so summarily dismissed more than a decade earlier, had come to pass. The letter was postmarked Saskatoon, Saskatchewan, and dated April 15, 1911. It was direct and to the point.

> Dearest Mother and Father,
>
> More than ten years ago we stood together on a train platform in New York City. It was the day Libbie and I left for school in Maine. For years I felt I had no home, no place where I was accepted and loved without condition.

I say this not to hurt you, and I do forgive you, for I believe you did the best you could. In Maine and later New York, my teachers, the Sisters, became my family. In time I also came to see the Church as my home and to accept Jesus Christ as my savior. I have recently come here, to Saskatchewan, to live in a convent with the Sisters of Sion and to become a nun and a schoolteacher at the academy here. I am most happy here and believe this is where I was meant to be. I have a new name, as well, Sister Thaddea of Sion. It is not my desire to cause you any pain, though I know this will not be welcome news. Nor is it my desire to cut myself off from my family. Please do not try to change my mind. This is the life I have chosen, and you, Mother, should understand as well as anyone that we must each choose our own path and fulfill our own destiny no matter how unusual it may seem to others. Father, I know how hurt you will be by this news, but do know that I have always known that you loved me. I do hope to have a letter from you when you are able.

Your loving daughter,

Sister Thaddea

The line directed to Grandpa, about his love for Mollie, was always, I believed, also directed at me by my omission. And how can I blame her?

I have not seen or spoken to Mollie since she sent that letter nearly forty years ago. Your aunt Libbie has visited with her, but your uncle Simon remains furious with her to this day for the shame she brought upon the family. Your mother, too, has had only occasional contact with her. From the time you were born until this year, your aunt Mollie sent you birthday gifts, which your mother donated to a Jewish charity before you ever saw them.

After we received the letter from Mollie, we sat shiva and recited the kaddish just as we would have had Mollie died, for to us that is precisely what had happened. At first it was a deep sense that she had betrayed not only us but the Jewish people. When she wrote letters to us we burned them unopened and again recited the kaddish. In more recent years the anger and pain has turned into regret, for I had betrayed *her*, a small girl not even six years old whose mother inexplicably disappeared from her life for well over a year to ride a bicycle around the world, disappeared a second time to California, and then disappeared her to boarding schools, seeing her but rarely. I never could bring myself to ask for her forgiveness. Sometimes too much time passes, and we carry the pain as a kind of penance.

Though the anguish of Mollie's conversion remains, and I will carry the burden of our rupture to my grave, I can't help but think that perhaps in some way I freed her by dint of my own example. She even said as much in her letter, written when she was not much younger than I was when I freed myself by escaping on a bicycle. Like me, she created her own path, and I suppose hers was no more outlandish, really, than mine, though living the life of a nun in a Canadian convent is hardly my idea of freedom. But who am I to judge? There is so much I was unable to give my children, but maybe I gave Mollie, at least, the power to choose the life she wanted, to color outside the lines as I like to say.

As long as I am in the mood to confess, there is one more thing I want to get off my chest, and it will, I hope, help you to understand your uncle, who, I am sure you have long noticed by now, is an odd and angry man. It was only after he graduated from high school in Quebec that he confided in your aunt Libbie that he suffered unspeakably at the hands of the priests. I only learned of this when Libbie gave me a copy of a letter he wrote to Mollie the year after her conversion. He had written out a second copy, which he gave to Libbie. He was twenty then, and his wounds were fresh. The letter also describes, quite accurately, I should say, how news of Mollie's conversion was felt by Grandpa and me. He refused to refer to her as Sister Thaddea.

November 14, 1912
Dear Mollie,

Had you pierced my heart with a murderous bullet, or with the glistening blade, I shouldn't have felt the pang any stronger. My life, our lives, will be forever ruined by this curse you have inflicted on the family. We will live a life of degradation carrying this secret to our grave, for we will not breathe a word of what has become of you to anyone. With pain and sorrow I watch my harried young mother strive to keep up a home under impossibly removable obstacles. With a pain of intenseness I see her daily go to work. God! It's terrible; it's frightful. Insanity is a joy compared to this. Can't you realize the extent of your damage, my dear sister? Your father is no longer gray, he is white. Your mother and mine is no longer gray, she is white. You are driving inch by inch a mother to her grave. Do I speak truthfully? Positively. And a father also. Mollie, I predict you will be a murderess in a very short time. Did God command us to kill or did he say, "Thou shalt not kill"? You forget who your mother is; the world famous globe-girdler has no charm for you, has she: a woman who was good enough to interview every living ruler and sovereign in the world. God, how can you remain as you do? Mollie, I spent many years of my life

> amongst these people who claim to be good by closing themselves up, when their leader told them to go out in the world and preach good and virtue. I know their innermost secrets, and someday the world will be startled; both sexes, I make no exceptions. The armies of the world will rise up against them. Do you want to be of them?
>
> Your brother,
>
> Simon

Reading this letter again all these years later, painful as it is, I have to chuckle at one thing. I filled the heads of my children with stories of my bicycle ride that exceeded even those I told at the time, and I was, apparently, very convincing. But, just as the pain of Mollie's conversion is one I have borne to this day, equally painful has been living with the knowledge of Simon's abuse, which made Mollie's choice all the more hurtful to him. Mollie and Simon suffered the most, I think, from my failures as a mother. Your aunt Libbie, despite a tempestuous and short-lived marriage, seemed to come through relatively unscathed, and your mother, too, but maybe I sometimes wear rose-colored glasses.

I will close with one final story because it seems, in many ways, to sum up my life. Young Simon was right about my going to work every day. About a year after returning home from California and reuniting with Grandpa, our bank balance quickly dwindling, I knew it was necessary for me to again make my way in the world financially. I was the family breadwinner, a heavy responsibility I took seriously.

In the spring of 1902, a year or so after I had returned from California, I had a chance encounter that would open another door. I had taken the train into Manhattan just to enjoy the flowers in Central

Park. After walking for nearly two hours, I stopped at a cafeteria on Forty-Second Street for a bite to eat. It was crowded, and I took the only available seat at the counter. Next to me, a man about ten years my senior was thumbing through a catalogue of women's accessories—hats, belts, handbags, that sort of thing. He was gazing at it quite intently. Never at a loss as to how to start a conversation with strangers, I asked him if he was looking for a gift for his wife and offered to provide a feminine opinion on anything he thought would be of interest.

"No, miss, I am a salesman for the company that makes the handbags in this catalogue," he answered. "I'm just familiarizing myself with the new line."

The details are mundane, but over the next hour Morton Feldman and I chatted about his business, about our families, and about the prospects for business now that the country had emerged from the depression of the mid-1890s. Mr. Feldman told me that the company whose handbag line he represented made the basic leather bags but contracted for the straps, for it turned out that the processes for making each are quite different, and it was just more economical to buy the straps from a separate supplier. And, according to Feldman, the supplier was often way behind, because the market was large and they had no competition.

To make a long story short, that was the beginning of Kay & Company (in business I went by Kay, not Kopchovksy), the small manufacturing firm we established in a space adjacent to our home in the Bronx. Grandpa did the books, I oversaw the manufacturing, and Feldman managed the sales. And we did quite well, starting with handbag straps and expanding to straps for dresses, brassieres, nightgowns, and other apparel.

At its peak we employed twenty-five women who did the piecework, mostly immigrant women from Ireland, Eastern Europe, and even Africa, and we treated them well, paying wages above average. Small factories like ours were subject to frequent visits by city inspectors. Ostensibly they came to make sure the place was safe and that we weren't abusing the workers, but really they came for small bribes. But I knew how to handle them. After all, I had handled myself with all kinds of people in all kinds of far-flung parts of the world; I could handle these weak, corrupt pissants. If the inspector was O'Malley, I poured on the Irish brogue. If his name was Martini, I had the accent of a Roman. If his name was Goldberg, I would kibbitz with him in Yiddish. The business did very well.

When the factory building caught fire and burned to the ground in 1924, it took me over a year to settle with the insurance company. They initially deemed the fire "suspicious" and refused to pay. When they finally did, I offered to buy Feldman's half of the company, and he agreed, as he was getting on in years, and I used the rest to start a new company, Grace Strap & Novelty, at the corner of Twenty-Seventh Street and Third Avenue, where, as you know, I still went to work every day until earlier this year.

I suppose, Mary dear, enough years will have passed by the time you read this, so I will tell you. The insurance company was right.

Now, how much of what I have told you in this letter is true? How much of the bedtime stories I told you as a child were true? If you were sitting across from me now, I would wink and say, "My dear, I'm not entirely sure myself. Perhaps one day you will sort it all out."

Author's Note

In 1993, my mother Baila, named for her grandmother, Bennett's wife, received a letter from a stranger who said he was researching the story of the first woman to circle the world on a bicycle, a woman named Annie Cohen Kopchovsky. He was hoping my mother might have information that would help him.

Like Annie, my mother's maiden name was Cohen, but it's a common Jewish name. In addition to copies of a couple of newspaper articles about Annie, the writer laid out some of the genealogical research he had done, research that led him to locate and then write to my mother. The letter writer explained that Annie had a brother Bennett, and that for a time Annie and Bennett shared an address on Spring Street in Boston's West End. Bennett, he wrote, had a son named Harry. My mother's father was Harry Cohen, and her grandfather, who died well before she was born, was Bennett Cohen.

My mother had never heard of Annie, or anything about a bicycle trip. On my mother's behalf I wrote back and explained that while he'd apparently found the right family, we knew nothing about Annie and could not be of help.

Ten years later, the same man wrote me to see if we had learned anything in the interim. We had not. I had kept his letter and the enclosures stashed away in a file. But I was now an avid cyclist, and I wondered why no one in my family—I had made a few querics over the years of family members, all of which came to naught—had heard of this rather remarkable ancestor and her improbable story. I decided to do some research of my own.

The historical record of Annie's life and her bicycle journey is rich in some ways, but frustratingly barren in others. She was a gifted self-promoter and left a trail of newspaper coverage around the world; many hundreds of pieces about her appeared in newspapers from New York to Paris, Singapore to San Francisco, and points in between, in large cities and small towns. I have quoted directly from several of them in this book. But no diary, if she ever kept one, survived, and precious little correspondence of any kind still exists. This left her largely unknowable.

As I was tracking down newspaper accounts from around the world, a painstaking task because few newspaper archives were digitized and searchable online in the early 2000s, I was also trying to locate any distant relatives who might have a closer connection to Annie, biologically, than I did. I hired a professional who specialized in Jewish genealogy. The search was complicated by the fact that Cohen is a common Jewish name, and though Kopchovsky is not, many Jews, and this proved to be the case with Annie, Anglicized their names at some point; Annie's became Kay, at least for business purposes. But after nearly a year of research we finally hit pay dirt when we located Annie's burial place in a Jewish cemetery in Saddle Brook, New Jersey, and cemetery records that listed a contact for the family plot. Annie, Max, and their three youngest children are all buried in that plot; Mollie, Sister Thaddea, for obvious reasons, is not, though at the time I didn't know why she alone among the six family members was not buried with them.

The contact listed for the plot was a woman named Mary Levy Goldiner who, it turns out, is Annie's only direct living biological descendant—her only grandchild. (Mary's two children are adopted.) She is my second cousin once removed. When I wrote to Mary in the fall of 2004 explaining who I was, how we were related, and what I was interested in, I had no idea what her reaction might be, or if she would respond at all. I wasn't even sure she was still alive. But about ten days after I sent my letter, desperately hoping this might help me crack Annie's story wide open, she called me and in her gravelly voice said, "Peter, this is your long-lost cousin Mary." I was excited beyond belief.

A week later I was in her living room in Larchmont, New York, looking at photos of Annie (the first I had ever seen, even after more than a year of research) and other artifacts of her bicycle journey, and the sensational pieces she penned for the *New York World*, all of which Mary had stored in her basement. More than these physical artifacts, Mary also had vivid memories of Annie, for she was a teenager when Annie died in November 1947 and had been very close to her. She was probably the only living person with any direct knowledge of the ghost I'd been chasing around the world for a year.

Mary thought I'd been sent by God, "someone upstairs," she told me. She was in her early seventies then, I was in my early fifties, and ever since Annie had died, she felt she had an obligation to revive Annie's legacy; that Annie would have wanted and expected that. But life had passed and her basement remained the dusty repository of a story completely lost to history. Now I had appeared, not only interested in Annie's story, but a relative to boot. If I were to write Annie's story, Mary could feel, at long last, that she had fulfilled her grandmother's fondest wish.

For three more years I researched Annie's journey, following the many clues left behind in Mary's basement. Many people, including some publishers, urged me to write Annie's story as historical fiction given the gaps in the historical record, gaps that remain to this day. But I felt that to do so would simply obscure the matter; I wanted to write the story as it really happened as best I could.

There came a point in my research when I could not escape the conclusion that while Annie did indeed travel around the world and rode a bicycle thousands of miles in the process, her own story, as she recounted it to reporters along the way, simply didn't add up. For example, no one riding a bicycle, even today, could have traversed India and China in the few weeks between the time she left Marseille and arrived in Japan. And the stories she related along the way are riddled not just with inconsistencies but with outright fabrications. On more than one occasion she claimed she was a student at Harvard Medical School. When I called Harvard to see if I might be able to locate her transcript I was told that Harvard Medical School didn't admit women until 1945. There are countless other examples. She was a serial fabulist with a rich imagination, and she spun improbable tales to keep herself and her audiences entertained. It wasn't just reporters she regaled with these stories, but large audiences who came to hear her speak as she made her way. She was building her fame, and the further 'round the globe she got, the taller the tales became. Sorting fact from fiction became my primary task as I researched and wrote her story in a book called *Around the World on Two Wheels: Annie Londonderry's Extraordinary Ride*, published in 2007.

When I first realized that Annie wasn't exactly what she appeared to be, that her purchase on the title "first woman to cycle around the world" was tenuous at best, I was disappointed. When I began chasing her across the years and around the globe, I saw my task as doing the research that would validate that claim. But in time I came to believe there was an even more interesting story to be discovered, and a much more complicated woman to write about. I found myself charmed by her utter unpredictability, her willingness to tell any story, no matter how far-fetched, to advance her celebrity. There may have been something pathological afoot, but I preferred to see her as my eccentric great-grandaunt (though I was writing about a twenty-three-year-old woman), like the ditzy older women in *Arsenic and Old Lace.* In short, the *true* story of Annie Londonderry would have to include a veritable catalogue of her untruths. Writing historical fiction, as some suggested, about a woman who was an expert in creating her own fictions, about her own life and her own experiences, seemed redundant. After all, she was writing her own historical fiction in real time as she traveled.

In the years since *Around the World on Two Wheels* was published, a short documentary film has been made about Annie (*The New Woman*), and a musical called *SPIN*, inspired by Annie, has toured all across Canada. Another musical, also inspired by Annie, *Ride*, has been produced in London. A street in Bend, Oregon, has been named for her. The book itself has been translated and published in German, Italian, Korean, and Czech. Articles about Annie have appeared in dozens of publications around the world; book chapters and countless blog posts have been written, podcasts created, and a children's book published. Annie was the subject of an episode of the Travel Channel's *Mysteries at the Museum* in 2016. In November 2019, as part of its "Overlooked No More" series of obituaries of notable women and people of color whose deaths went unreported, the *New York Times* ran a full-length obituary of Annie; it took up the better part of a page in the paper, complete with photograph. The same obituary appeared the next day in the *Boston Globe.* The West End Museum, dedicated to keeping alive the memory of Boston's old West End neighborhood, the neighborhood Annie fled in

1894 and which was razed during the "urban renewal" wave of the 1950s, mounted an exhibit about her in 2020. I had an 1890-era Sterling bicycle restored and painted the color of Annie's (cream white), a bicycle now on loan as part of an exhibition on women and cycling that started at the Bloomfield Science Museum in Israel and that has traveled to Germany, Poland, and will make its last stop in Ottawa, Canada. As Annie had hoped, her story has been rescued from the dustheap of history, and it's been gratifying to watch to say the least.

But now, nearly two decades after I first started chasing Annie, seemed a good time to reimagine the story, to take the literary license I was reluctant to take when I was working on *Around the World on Two Wheels*. This retelling is how I imagine Annie's remarkable odyssey may have unfolded, with some flourishes that, true to Annie's spirit, are purely fanciful. It's impossible to know how it all went down. But it's been great fun to put myself in her shoes and tell the story as I imagine she might have told it had she sat down in the days before she died in 1947 and written a long, long letter to her then sixteen-year-old granddaughter, Mary, perhaps Annie's way of atoning for the distant relationships, emotionally and physically, she had with her own children.

For those wondering which parts of the story as told here are true, that I leave to your imagination, as Annie does at the end of her letter to Mary, with two exceptions. First, Annie really did cross paths with the infamous outlaw John Wesley Hardin. He was at her lecture that night in El Paso when he had Martin Mrose murdered. And, second, the letter from Annie's son Simon to her daughter, Mollie, is genuine, though slightly edited and abridged. It was in a slim file about Sister Thaddea that I located in the archives of the Nostra Signora di Sion at the Vatican. Ironically, when I told my mother, who had never even heard of Annie or her bicycle trip, that my research had led to a

Catholic nun in the family, she said simply, "Oh, I knew Grandpa [my grandfather Harry] had a cousin who had become a nun." This was the deep, dark family secret no one spoke of but everyone knew. The bicycle trip was hardly a secret, it was a global sensation in the mid-1890s, but no one in my immediate family knew anything about it!

On that day when we first met in 2004, I asked Mary about Mollie and told her that after visiting the cemetery in New Jersey where Annie, Max, and their three youngest children were buried, I had assumed Mollie predeceased them, the only reason I could think of that would explain why she alone was not buried with the family. Mary teared up as she told me the story of Mollie's conversion and banishment.

Mary never knew she had an aunt Mollie until Mary's thirtieth birthday in 1961. She learned of Mollie not in a letter written by Annie, but from her mother, Annie's youngest child, Frieda. On that day, Frieda told Mary for the first time about her aunt Mollie and arranged for them to speak by telephone for the first and only time. Sister Thaddea was attending a conference in Montreal when they spoke. Mary was stunned to learn of her. "Her voice was my grandmother's voice," Mary told me, "and I started to cry."

When Sister Thaddea died in 1961, just a few months after the phone call with Mary, Mary and Frieda received warm letters from Reverend Mother Edeltrude at St. Mary's Convent in Saskatoon, where Sister Thaddea had lived most of her life.

"You just can't imagine how we miss her," she wrote. "She was so outlandish in her ideas at times . . . She was a great entertainer." From Mother Edeltrude's description, Sister Thaddea sounded a lot like the mother she never really had.

Acknowledgments

In the early 2000s, when I was trying to resurrect Annie from obscurity, many dozens of people helped me in ways large and small. Four years of research led to the publication in 2007 of *Around the World on Two Wheels: Annie Londonderry's Extraordinary Ride* (Citadel Press/Kensington), a non-fiction account of Annie's journey. Because *Spin* stands on the shoulders of that research I thank again everyone mentioned in the acknowledgements in *Around the World on Two Wheels.*

In November 2019, an obituary of Annie appeared in the *New York Times*, some seventy-two years after her death. That obit was part of an ongoing series in the *Times* recognizing the many women and people of color who were overlooked by the *Times* in their day when the obituary pages were dominated by obits of white men. Annie's obituary was written by Bruce Weber, long-time obituarist at the *Times* and a legend in his field. In 2015, Bruce published *Life is a Wheel: Memoirs of a Bike-Riding Obituarist* (Scribner), an account of a cross-country bicycle trip he made several years earlier, in which he mentioned Annie. I didn't know Annie's obit was in the works so it was a delightful surprise and Bruce made good use of *Around the World on Two Wheels* in crafting it. That obituary was the spark for *Spin* so I am very grateful to Bruce for igniting it. I can't resist mentioning, in the small world department, that by and by I learned that Bruce and I went to day camp in New Jersey together six decades ago, though we had no contact since that time and I didn't even know his name. Life is funny that way.

My wife Judy is deeply immersed in the book club world nationally. Among other things she has an online newsletter focusing on food and literature that reaches more than ten thousand avid readers. Knowing that historical fiction is very popular among book clubs, when Bruce's obit appeared in the *Times* she threw down the gantlet. "If you don't write Annie's story as historical fiction," she said to me, "someone else will, and you've already done the research." And so it was that Judy fanned the spark Bruce had lit. Never having written fiction I never thought I'd get very far, but there you have it. So, my thanks to Judy for the kick in the pants. Some people, not many, think I have some good ideas, but when I do they are mostly Judy's.

This is the eighth book I have worked on with my agent Joelle Delbourgo. When I'd written about forty pages or so I sent them to Joelle thinking she'd tell me I'd be well-served to stick to non-fiction (or maybe even find another career) and I'd be done with Annie. But she liked what she read and encouraged me to keep going. So, like Annie, I forged ahead. Thanks to Joelle for that second kick in the pants and guidance along the way.

Prior to *Spin*, my most recent book was *The Dog Went Over the Mountain: Travels with Albie—An American Journey*, published by Pegasus Books in 2019. That was my first book with Pegasus and I am happy that Jessica Case, my publisher and editor, took a fancy to *Spin*, as well. Jessica wears many hats at Pegasus and is a delight to work with. So, many thanks to Jessica and the Pegasus crew that worked on *Spin* and created the beautiful book you hold in your hands: Maria Fernandez who did the interior design, Kathleen Cook for her careful and astute copyediting, and Drew Wheeler for his eagle-eyed proofreading. The striking cover was designed by Molly von Borstel at Faceout Studio in Bend, Oregon where, coincidentally, there is now a street named for Annie.

As I have said in the acknowledgments in previous books, it takes a village.